Love's Cure

A Lilac Lake Book

Judith Keim

Wild Quail Publishing

BOOKS BY JUDITH KEIM

THE HARTWELL WOMEN SERIES:

The Talking Tree – 1

Sweet Talk – 2

Straight Talk – 3

Baby Talk – 4

The Hartwell Women – Boxed Set

THE BEACH HOUSE HOTEL SERIES:

Breakfast at The Beach House Hotel – 1

Lunch at The Beach House Hotel – 2

Dinner at The Beach House Hotel – 3

Christmas at The Beach House Hotel – 4

Margaritas at The Beach House Hotel – 5

Dessert at The Beach House Hotel – 6

Coffee at The Beach House Hotel – 7

High Tea at The Beach House Hotel – 8

Nightcaps at The Beach House Hotel – 9

Bubbles at The Beach House Hotel – 10 (2025)

THE FAT FRIDAYS GROUP:

Fat Fridays – 1

Sassy Saturdays – 2

Secret Sundays – 3

THE SALTY KEY INN SERIES:

Finding Me – 1

Finding My Way – 2

Finding Love – 3

Finding Family – 4

The Salty Key Inn Series – Boxed Set

THE LILAC LAKE INN SERIES

Love by Design – 1
Love Between the Lines – 2
Love Under the Stars – 3

LILAC LAKE BOOKS

Love's Cure
Love's Home Run – (2025)
Love's Bloom – (2025)
Love's Harvest – (2025)
Love's Match – (2025)

OTHER BOOKS:

The ABC's of Living With a Dachshund
Winning BIG – a little love story for all ages
Holiday Hopes
The Winning Tickets

For more information: **www.judithkeim.com**

PRAISE FOR JUDITH KEIM'S NOVELS

THE BEACH HOUSE HOTEL SERIES – Books 1 – 10:
"Love the characters in this series. This series was my first introduction to Judith Keim. She is now one of my favorites. Looking forward to reading more of her books."

BREAKFAST AT THE BEACH HOUSE HOTEL – *"An easy, delightful read that offers romance, family relationships, and strong women learning to be stronger. Real life situations filter through the pages. Enjoy!"*

LUNCH AT THE BEACH HOUSE HOTEL – *"This series is such a joy to read. You feel you are actually living with them. Can't wait to read the latest one."*

DINNER AT THE BEACH HOUSE HOTEL – *"A Terrific Read! As usual, Judith Keim did it again. Enjoyed immensely. Continue writing such pleasantly reading books for all of us readers."*

CHRISTMAS AT THE BEACH HOUSE HOTEL – *"Not Just Another Christmas Novel. This is book number four in the series and my introduction to Judith Keim's writing. I wasn't disappointed. The characters are dimensional and engaging. The plot is well crafted and advances at a pleasing pace.*

MARGARITAS AT THE BEACH HOUSE HOTEL – *"Overall, Margaritas at the Beach House Hotel is another wonderful addition to the series. Judith Keim takes the reader on a journey told through the voices of these amazing characters we have all come to love through the years!*

DESSERT AT THE BEACH HOUSE HOTEL – *"It is a heartwarming and beautiful women's fiction as only Judith Keim can do with her wonderful characters, amazing location. and family and friends whose daily lives circle around Ann and Rhonda and The Beach House Hotel.*

COFFEE AT THE BEACH HOUSE HOTEL – *"Great story*

and characters! A hard to put down book. Lots of things happening, including a kidnapping of a young boy. The beach house hotel is a wonderful hotel run by two women who are best friends. Highly recommend this book.

HIGH TEA AT THE BEACH HOUSE HOTEL – "What a lovely story! The Beach House Hotel series is a always a great read. Each book in the series brings a new aspect to the saga of Ann and Rhonda."

THE HARTWELL WOMEN SERIES – Books 1 – 4:

"This was an EXCELLENT series. When I discovered Judith Keim, I read all of her books back to back. I thoroughly enjoyed the women Keim has written about. They are believable and you want to just jump into their lives and be their friends! I can't wait for any upcoming books!"

"I fell into Judith Keim's Hartwell Women series and have read & enjoyed all of her books in every series. Each centers around a strong & interesting woman character and their family interaction. Good reads that leave you wanting more."

THE FAT FRIDAYS GROUP – Books 1 – 3:

"Excellent story line for each character, and an insightful representation of situations which deal with some of the contemporary issues women are faced with today."

THE SALTY KEY INN SERIES – Books 1 – 4:

FINDING ME – "The characters are endearing with the same struggles we all encounter. The setting makes me feel like I am a guest at The Salty Key Inn...relaxed, happy & light-hearted! The men are yummy and the women strong. You can't get better than that! Happy Reading!"

FINDING MY WAY- "Loved the family dynamics as well as uncertain emotions of dating and falling in love.

Appreciated the morals and strength of parenting throughout. Just couldn't put this book down."

FINDING LOVE – "Judith Keim always puts substance into her books. This book was no different, I learned about PTSD, accepting oneself, there are always going to be problems but stick it out and make it work.

FINDING FAMILY – "Completing this series is like eating the last chip. Love Judith's writing and her female characters are always smart, strong, vulnerable to life and love experiences."

"This was a refreshing book. Bringing the heart and soul of the family to us."

THE CHANDLER HILL INN SERIES – Books 1 – 3:
GOING HOME – "I was completely immersed in this book, with the beautiful descriptive writing, and the author's way of bringing her characters to life. I felt like I was right inside her story."

COMING HOME – "Coming Home was such a wonderful story. The author has such a gift for getting the reader right to the heart of things."

HOME AT LAST – "In this wonderful conclusion, to a heartfelt and emotional trilogy set in Oregon's stunning wine country, Judith Keim has tied up the Chandler Hill series with the perfect bow."

SEASHELL COTTAGE BOOKS:
A CHRISTMAS STAR – "Love, laughter, sadness, great food, and hope for the future, all in one book. It doesn't get any better than this stunning read." CHANGE OF HEART – "CHANGE OF HEART is the summer read we've all been waiting for. Judith Keim is a master at creating fascinating characters that are simply irresistible. Her stories leave you with a big smile on your face and a heart bursting with love."

~Kellie Coates Gilbert, author of the popular Sun Valley Series

A SUMMER OF SURPRISES – "Ms. Keim uses this book as an amazing platform to show that with hard emotional work, belief in yourself, and love, the scars of abuse can be conquered. It in no way preaches, it's a lovely story with a happy ending."

A ROAD TRIP TO REMEMBER – "The characters are so real that they jump off the page. Such a fun, HAPPY book at the perfect time. It will lift your spirits and even remind you of your own grandmother. Spirited and hopeful Aggie gets a second chance at love and she takes the steering wheel and drives straight for it."

THE BEACH BABES – "Another winner at the pen of Judith Keim. I love the characters and the book just flows. It feels as though you are at the beach with them and are a part of you.

THE DESERT SAGE INN SERIES – Books 1 – 4:

THE DESERT FLOWERS – ROSE – "The Desert Flowers - Rose, "In this first of a series, we see each woman come into her own and view new beginnings even as they must take this tearful journey as they slowly lose a dear friend.

THE DESERT FLOWERS – LILY – "The second book in the Desert Flowers series is just as wonderful as the first. Judith Keim is a brilliant storyteller. Her characters are truly lovely and people that you want to be friends with as soon as you start reading. Judith Keim is not afraid to weave real-life conflict and loss into her stories.

THE DESERT FLOWERS – WILLOW – "The feelings of love, joy, happiness, friendship, family, and the pain of loss are deeply felt by Willow Sanchez and her two cohorts Rose and Lily. The Desert Flowers met because of their deep feelings for Alec Thurston, a man who touched their lives in *different ways."*

<u>*MISTLETOE AND HOLLY*</u> – *"As always, the author never ceases to amaze me. She's able to take characters and bring them to life in such a way that you think you're actually among family. It's a great holiday read. You won't be disappointed."*

THE SANDERLING COVE INN SERIES – Books 1 – 3:

<u>*WAVES OF HOPE*</u> – *"Such a wonderful story about several families in a beautiful location in Florida. A grandmother requests her three granddaughters to help her by running the family's inn for the summer. Other grandmothers in the area played a part in this plan to find happiness for their grandsons and granddaughters."*

<u>*SANDY WISHES*</u> – *"Three cousins needing a change and a few of the neighborhood boys from when they were young are back visiting their grandmothers. It is an adventure, a summer of discoveries, and embracing the person they are becoming."*

<u>*SALTY KISSES*</u> – *"I love this story, as well as the entire series because it's about family, friendship, and love. The meddling grandmothers have only the best intentions and want to see their grandchildren find love and happiness. What grandparent wouldn't want that?"*

THE LILAC LAKE INN SERIES – Books 1 – 3:

<u>*LOVE BY DESIGN*</u> –*"Genie Wittner is planning on selling her beloved Lilac Inn B&B, and keeping a cottage for her three granddaughters, Whitney, the movie star, Dani an architect, and Taylor a writer. A little mystery, a possible ghost, and romance all make this a great read and the start of a new series."*

<u>*LOVE BETWEEN THE LINES*</u> – *"Taylor is one of 3 sisters*

who have inherited a cottage in Lilac Lake from their grandmother. She is an accomplished author who is having some issues getting inspired for her next book. Things only get worse when she receives an email from her new editor with a harsh critique of her last book. She's still fuming when Cooper shows up in town, determined to work together on getting the book ready."

Love's Cure

A Lilac Lake Book

Judith Keim

Wild Quail Publishing

Love's Cure is a work of fiction. Names, characters, places, public or private institutions, corporations, towns, and incidents are the product of the author's imagination or are used fictitiously. Any resemblance to actual events, locales, or persons, living or dead, is coincidental.

No part of *Love's Cure* may be reproduced or transmitted in any form or by any electronic or mechanical means, including information storage and retrieval systems, without permission in writing from the author, except by a reviewer who may quote brief passages in a review. This book may not be resold or uploaded for distribution to others. For permissions contact the author directly via electronic mail:

wildquail.pub@gmail.com
www.judithkeim.com

Wild Quail Publishing
PO Box 171332
Boise, ID 83717-1332

ISBN 978-1-962452-05-2

Dedication

To all those who love to visit New England. Enjoy!

CHAPTER ONE

ON THIS SUMMER DAY, Crystal Owen stood in the middle of the Lilac Lake Café in the center of Lilac Lake, a small town in the Lakes District of New Hampshire. At thirty-two, she was the proud owner of a thriving business on Main Street. She brushed back a curly lock of purple hair and let out a sigh of satisfaction. Her success hadn't come easily, but then she'd had a hard life growing up and sometimes felt as if she was hanging onto this dream with bruised fingers.

And now it was time to do something for herself.

Alone, Crystal sat on a bar stool and sipped her cup of coffee. She wanted to settle down in a way she'd been unable to do in the past. She'd married and divorced Nick Woodruff under the best of circumstances. She and Nick would always be friends. They'd married for all the wrong reasons— loneliness and the ease of living in the same town. Besides, Crystal had always known Nick loved Whitney Gilford enough to let her go to Hollywood and become a movie star.

Crystal set down her coffee cup and shook her head. Life sure could get complicated. In the community, she was known as "the poor Owen girl" who'd grown up with an alcoholic, drug-addicted mother and a younger sister to care for. Few people knew that if it hadn't been for Genie Wittner, her best friends' grandmother, "GG," she would never have had the funds to buy the tired old Café several years ago. She'd long since paid the loan back to Mrs. Wittner but she'd never forget her generosity.

After spending summers with GG, Whitney Gilford, her best friend, was now living in Lilac Lake and had married Crystal's ex-husband, Nick Woodruff. Whitney's two sisters, Dani and Taylor, also lived in Lilac Lake. Dani was married to Brad Collister, and Taylor, the youngest of the sisters, was married to Cooper Walker, an editor at a publishing house in New York City. Taylor spent as much time as she could at the cottage the three sisters owned jointly. Someone tapped on the door.

Crystal turned and smiled when she saw Whitney. Any awkwardness about being married to Nick had long since been worked out, made easy because Nick was one of the nicest guys around. He had always been that way.

"Hey, girlfriend," said Crystal opening the door. "What are you doing up at the crack of dawn?"

Whitney gave her a quick hug. "Nick got an early call about a possible robbery at the Beckman Lumber Yard, and I thought this would be a good time to take an early morning walk with Mindy and the baby."

Crystal observed the black-and-tan dachshund, Mindy, and grinned. "Those short legs can't carry you too far, huh?" She bent over and peeked into the baby carriage, smiling at the sleeping little boy named Timothy. "He's adorable," whispered Crystal, feeling a momentary pang of jealousy. Lately, she'd been thinking about children of her own.

Mindy wiggled with excitement when Crystal rubbed her ears. "C'mon, you know where I keep treats for the dogs who visit our patio."

The dog trotted behind Crystal, and Whitney followed, pushing the carriage.

"I've got time for a quick cup of coffee. The sweet rolls are rising, the cookies and pies are cooling off, and I'm pretty much ready for the day." Crystal sighed. "This early morning work can drag you down. I'm glad the Café closes at 4 P.M."

Whitney chuckled softly. "You're so positive all the time. I don't know how you do it."

"Practice, practice, practice," said Crystal.

Whitney sobered. "I admire you, Crystal. What are you doing for fun? Are you doing any summer theater work?"

"Not now. Maybe later. The Ogunquit Theater in Maine keeps me informed about small parts that become available from time to time." She poured Whitney a cup of coffee, sat down on a bar stool again, and faced her. "I'm ready to settle down in a way I wasn't able to do before. My mother is gone, my sister is happy teaching in Florida, and with the Café doing well, I'm freer since I can remember."

"By settling down, do you mean finding the right man for you?" Whitney asked, gazing deeply into her eyes.

"Maybe. I'm thinking of taking some vacation time, getting away for a while, giving myself a break, and letting life happen. See new places, new faces."

"Who would you get to run the Café?" Whitney asked.

"I'm not sure. I'd have to wait until early spring after ski season has ended when the Café is slowest."

"Good for you," said Whitney. "I'd be glad to help you in any way I can, but it's difficult with the baby."

"Thanks. I'm very happy for you and Nick," she said sincerely, though a fresh pang of regret rolled through her. She hadn't wanted children earlier with Nick, but now she was ready.

Crystal rose. "I've been overthinking things. I've got a Café to run. That should be enough for me right now."

Whitney stood and wrapped an arm around her. "It's never wrong to think of finding love and having a family. You're going to make a wonderful partner for the right man. Someone who deserves you."

"Thanks," said Crystal. "You truly are my best friend. You'll never know how much I looked forward to having you and your sisters visit your grandmother and the Lilac Lake Inn each summer."

"It certainly made our summers special while we were growing up. You and the other local kids meant the world to us. You still do." Tears shone in Whitney's eyes, and she fanned the air in front of her face. "Maybe it's my hormones making me teary, but I mean every word. I've always loved my time here."

Crystal faced Whitney. "We loved having you be part of our summers. Those few weeks were magical. Maybe that's what I'm looking for. Something magical. Am I being foolish?"

"No," said Whitney firmly. "We all need a little magic in our lives, something to heal us from the wounds of the world."

Crystal gave Whitney a wry smile. "Are you saying I need love to be my cure?"

Whitney laughed. "I guess you could say that."

A customer knocked on the door.

Crystal became all business and went to open the door. It was time to get back to real life.

That night, Crystal sat with Dani and Brad Collister in Jake's, a favorite spot for locals in Lilac Lake. After working in the Café all day, it was a great place for her to unwind and grab a light dinner.

Melissa Hendrickson, who was a chef at her parents' restaurant, Fins, showed up with a man Crystal hadn't seen before.

"Hey, everybody, I want you to meet, Emmett Chambers. He's visiting from New York and is thinking of going into medical practice here. He came to my parents' restaurant last night. You all know how my mother talks to everyone when she's acting as hostess, and she convinced him to get out and meet some of the people in town."

As Brad stood to shake hands with him, Crystal studied the newcomer. Of average height, he had straight brown hair and unusual eyes, a mix of blue and green. He was dressed in jeans, a green golf shirt, and moccasins. He was attractive, but the look he gave them was reserved, making him seem a little stiff.

Crystal returned his smile and listened as everyone asked him questions about the kind of medical practice he was interested in.

Emmett spoke about attending Cornell, specifically The Weill Medical School in New York, and the agreement he'd made with the school to practice in a rural area for a full year after his residency before opening a practice elsewhere.

"That's why I'm here," he said. "Lilac Lake and the surrounding area was one of the places they'd listed."

There was something about him that didn't ring true. He made it seem as if he was a hard-working guy who'd made it on his own. But his manner suggested otherwise. Gazing around the table, she noticed that she seemed to be the only one who felt that way. Were her disappointments in life making her cynical? She drew a deep breath and told herself to relax and enjoy a new face in the crowd.

"I'm glad you chose Lilac Lake," said Melissa. "Dr. Johnson has been here for years, but he's ready to retire. Portsmouth Regional Hospital is closest to us, and, of course, there are the Dartmouth-Hitchcock Medical Centers here in New Hampshire, and Boston and all the facilities there are not that far away, except for emergencies."

"My sister had her baby in Portsmouth," said Dani. "But as someone who lived and worked in Boston, I would choose to travel to Boston for something more serious."

"I like the idea of Family Medicine," said Emmett. "That's why I chose to enter that field. I want to get to know my patients and their families."

"Well, then, you've come to the right place," said Dani. "Lilac Lake is a true small town where everybody pretty much knows everyone else."

"Where are you staying?" Crystal asked.

"At the Lilac Lake Inn," Emmett said. "It's beautiful."

That nagging feeling of not knowing who Emmett really was traveled through Crystal. As she studied him, his turquoise eyes settled on her. She felt her face burn and drew in a breath as a rush of desire caused her pulse to race. She looked away, wondering why he was bringing out so many different emotions inside her.

"If you chose to work here for a year, where would you live?" asked Melissa. "I've just built a house in The Meadows, a new development of Brad's."

"That's a possibility," said Emmett. "Dr. Johnson wants me to buy his house."

Crystal stood. "Guess I'd better go. You all know how early I must rise."

Her friends said goodnight to her, and she turned and walked away.

In her apartment over the Café, Crystal tried to get comfortable in bed. But her earlier thoughts about wanting to settle down became mixed up with her strong, uncertain reaction to Emmett Chambers.

She stared up at the ceiling and drew deep breaths as she tried to settle herself. Her life was nicely organized. She had many friends who truly cared for her. She'd never been anxious to have a deep relationship with anyone until Nick convinced her that it was safe, that unlike her mother, friends could be loyal, kind, and loving.

Now, honesty was something she demanded of anyone close to her. That's why it bothered her that she had the feeling Emmett wasn't being open with them.

CHAPTER TWO

CRYSTAL WAS BUSY going from cooking in the kitchen to the front of the Café to speak to guests when she noticed Dr. Johnson seated at a table with Emmett Chambers. He saw her and waved her over.

"Hi, Crystal, I want you to meet my replacement, Emmett Chambers. I told him that for the best food in town, he should come here for breakfast or lunch."

"Thank you, Dr. Johnson. I met Emmett last night at Jake's. But I want you to know how much I appreciate your support."

He nodded. "I also told him about the deal I have with you regarding people who need a healthy meal and can't afford to pay."

Crystal could sense Emmett's beautiful eyes on her as she responded, "Yes, that's worked well for us in the past."

Dr. Johnson turned to Emmett. "Crystal is a remarkable woman—someone I truly admire."

She was forced to turn to Emmett. "Good morning. How did you sleep?"

"Great, thanks." He smiled at her. "Like I said, it's a beautiful place. Lilac Lake is lucky to have an inn like that in the area."

"I've warned Emmett that the living quarters assigned to the practice aren't as fancy. He's going to look at it after breakfast," said Dr. Johnson.

"It's a very nice house," said Crystal. "And easy to find, which is important."

Dr. Johnson gave her an approving look. "Yes, I think so too."

A waitress came over to their table with a tray of breakfast dishes for them.

Crystal stepped away. "Nice to see you, Dr. Johnson, Emmett. Now, I've got to get back to work."

At lunchtime, Crystal was pleased to see Whitney's youngest sister, Taylor, and her husband, Cooper, sitting at a table outdoors. She went right over to them. "Glad to see you in town. Are you here for a while?"

Taylor got up to hug her. "I'm going to stay for a couple of weeks to finish my latest novel. I work best at the cottage where it's peaceful."

"As her editor, I've ordered her to do it," said Cooper giving them both a big wink. "It's good for us to get out of New York for a while. I can edit anywhere."

"And I can write anywhere," said Taylor. "I also want to see GG and my sisters."

"Little Timothy is growing fast. Better spend as much time with him as possible," said Crystal.

"I will," said Taylor. "I heard a rumor that Dr. Johnson has found someone to take over his practice. What news do you have?"

"I've met him. His name is Emmett Chambers, and he's from New York City. Do the two of you know him?"

Cooper hesitated. "The name sounds vaguely familiar. I'll ask my sister. You'd think in a city the size of New York that it would be impossible, but people tend to run in the same circles."

"Oh, yes," said Crystal, adding to her suspicion that Emmett was hiding something from them. Cooper's family was a very prominent one in New York City, which meant that

Emmett's family must be as well for the name to be known to him.

Taylor leaned forward. "So, tell me what this new doctor is like. I heard from Dani that he's very handsome and has beautiful eyes."

"He seems nice enough, but I get the feeling he's holding something back," Crystal said. "I don't want to say anything more because I don't know him that well. I've said little beyond hello to him."

"Well, it'll be nice to have a new face in town. I wonder what GG will say about her old friend, Dr. Johnson, leaving town after all these years," said Taylor.

"It'll be a change for a lot of people. I'd better get back to the kitchen," said Crystal. "I'll see you later."

"Yes. We're going to Jake's for dinner," said Cooper.

Smiling, Crystal left them and hurried into the kitchen to help her staff. As usual, the Café was crowded.

After the Café closed, Crystal boxed up some cookies and drove to The Woodlands, the senior-assisted-living complex at the edge of town. Brad and Aaron Collister, with GG's sponsorship, were the general contractors for those buildings, which gave them the qualifications to work on the renovation of the Lilac Lake Inn. GG had owned and operated the inn for as long as Crystal had known her. Over a year ago, she agreed to sell the inn and live at The Woodlands. GG, the dear woman, had always been there for Crystal, making sure she and her sister had everything they needed. She'd even paid for Crystal to go to culinary school and Misty to get her teaching degree. Crystal thought of her as a beloved grandmother.

As she drove up to the Woodlands, Crystal studied the handsome buildings and the inviting landscaping around them. They'd kept to the name, leaving wooded areas open around the edges of the complex.

The receptionist at the front desk knew her and motioned her inside. "Mrs. Wittner is in her room. You can go on in."

Crystal gave her a wave and walked down the hallway to GG's room. As she neared it, she heard voices. The door opened and JoEllen Daniels appeared.

"Fancy seeing you here," said JoEllen.

"Hi, JoEllen," said Crystal, forcing herself to be polite.

JoEllen had a distinct ability to irritate people and had made a nuisance of herself to Brad and Dani. As Brad's former sister-in-law, JoEllen had thought it only right that Brad marry her after her sister's death. Sad as it was to have his wife gone, Brad had no intention of ever marrying JoEllen, and it had made JoEllen a desperate, unhappy woman.

Crystal walked past JoEllen and entered GG's suite. GG was sitting on the couch with a book. Seeing Crystal, GG smiled.

Crystal handed GG the box of cookies and kissed her on the cheek. "Hello. I thought I'd stop by to make sure you knew all about the new doctor in town."

GG laughed. "You're the fourth person to tell me about him. Let's hear your version. But first, will you fix us each a glass of lemonade and then sit for a while?"

"Thanks. I need time to relax. While I get our drinks, what have you heard about him?"

"I've heard his name is Emmett Chambers, that he's handsome, and he has extraordinary eyes. Dr. Johnson stopped by earlier to tell me he might be leaving the area as he's wanted to do for a long time now. He was positively bursting with the happy news about the doctor's qualifications."

Crystal poured lemonade into two glasses and carried them over to the coffee table in front of the couch.

"Thank you, darling," said GG. "Now, what do you have to

say about him?"

"What everyone is saying about him is true," said Crystal.

"But? I hear a 'but' in your voice."

Crystal sighed. "He's very close-mouthed about his family. He loves the classy inn, and I don't think he'll be happy here."

GG gave her a steady look. "What's bothering you?"

"You know how I feel about lying and the need to be honest," Crystal began. "I think he's hiding something."

GG studied her. "People have a right to privacy. Perhaps you're being a little unfair."

Crystal clamped down on the corner of her lips, something she did when she was thinking things over. Then, she said, "You're right. I forget that everyone in town knows my story."

GG gave her an approving look. "We all have secrets—thoughts, wishes, hidden desires. Like you've told me before, it's best just to let life unfold."

"Yes. Lately, I've been thinking about finding love and having a family. Maybe taking a break is what I need."

"What are you thinking?" asked GG.

"Maybe I'll get away in the spring. Or better yet, take a couple of days off to visit my sister in Florida."

"You work very hard. A break might be just what you need. With Taylor here for a couple of weeks, perhaps she could help you out."

The tension left Crystal's shoulders like a bird taking wing. GG always made her feel better. She laughed for the pure pleasure of it. "If I decide to take time off, I'll tell Taylor you said she'd take over for me."

GG laughed. "You'd still have to ask her nicely. But knowing Taylor, I'd say she'd be glad to do it."

"Even if I don't take the time off now, I love knowing I could probably make it happen. Thanks." Crystal finished her drink and leaned back against the couch. "Now, tell me, how are you feeling?"

"Besides old?" GG chuckled. "I'm doing quite well. Living here has been a wise choice for me. I was no longer able to maintain the inn the way I wanted, and heaven knows, operating it was getting way too hard for me."

"I'm glad you're here and healthy. You mean so much to me and many others. I've always been grateful for the help you've given Misty and me."

"How is your darling sister?" GG asked.

Crystal smiled with a mother's pride. "Her second graders love her, and she seems happy. I haven't heard much about her boyfriend, and I suspect that relationship might be over."

"It takes a while for some people to find the right man. I hope you fine one soon."

"Me, too. I've been feeling down lately, and Whitney told me love might be a cure."

GG chuckled. "She's happy with Nick and the baby. She wants everyone to find love."

"At this point, I might be willing to give it a try."

CHAPTER THREE

AFTER CRYSTAL RETURNED TO HER APARTMENT, she decided to go for a run. Or, in her case, a brisk walk. It was one thing to work in the Café all day, standing on her feet. But she needed true exercise, getting her body to move all parts. The Café presented another problem too. Working with delicious food all day meant adding a pound or two that needed to be worked off. Crystal was naturally thin but knew the warning of a few extra pounds.

In running shorts and a tank top, she moved swiftly through town. Though she waved to many people, she kept on walking. In her job, she knew most locals because sooner or later they ended up in the Café.

Curious about Emmett Chambers and wondering if he was going to accept Dr. Johnson's practice, she headed to his office. Situated on the banks of the Pemigewasset River, locally known as "The Pemi," the Cape Cod house and nearby office building were well-known to all. Crystal had never been inside Dr. Johnson's house, but she knew his office well. Working in a kitchen could be dangerous, and she'd had cuts stitched or taken a kitchen staff member there to be checked out.

When she got to Dr. Johnson's office, there were two cars parked in front. Thinking she wouldn't be noticed, she bypassed the office and crossed the grassy lawn to a worn path leading to a dock where a small fishing boat was tied up. A wooden bench sat at the end of the dock, and she headed there. Through the years, she and Dr. Johnson had occasionally sat there talking about everything and nothing.

As she made her way down the path, she realized how much she was going to miss Dr. Johnson. He'd been a stable influence in her life. Growing up with an unpredictable, alcoholic, drug-using mother, she'd needed someone to talk to, and both he and GG had been there for her. Otherwise, she didn't know how she could've raised her sister herself.

Crystal lowered herself onto the bench and stared out at the swirling water of the river that ran along the edge of town. She heard footsteps behind her, and, smiling, turned to face Dr. Johnson and Emmett Chambers.

"I'm glad to see you here, Crystal," said Dr. Johnson. "I've been trying to explain to Emmett how important it is to the practice to be available to patients anytime."

Crystal rose and gave him a hug, realizing how thin age was making him. "You were always there for me, and I'll never forget it."

"You were and still are one of my favorites," he said, smiling at her. He turned to Emmett. "Crystal is a strong woman who had a lot to handle growing up."

Crystal felt Emmett's sympathetic gaze on her. She'd always hated the way people in town had looked at her with pity. She raised her chin. "My mother was an alcoholic druggie who somehow mostly forgot she had two daughters."

Dr. Johnson placed a steadying hand on her shoulder. "It was what it was, and you made the best of it for you and your sister."

Crystal gazed out at the water. Tears blurred her vision, but she refused to let them fall and expose the pain she still felt.

"Why don't we go inside and have some of Martha's famous strawberry lemonade?" said Dr. Johnson. Martha Johnson's lemonade helped many patients to feel better.

"Okay, that would be nice," said Crystal. "I'm going to miss her almost as much as I'm going to miss you."

"Before we go inside, I've already warned Emmett that the house needs refurbishing. Crystal, you might just be the one to help him redecorate. An allowance is being given to update some of the appliances. But it desperately needs a young person's touch. You've done such a beautiful job with the Café and your apartment, that you could be a big help here."

Crystal glanced at Emmett.

"I can use all the help I can get. I'm color blind." He studied her. "But I can tell your hair is not a normal color. Reds and greens are difficult for me. Sometimes, blue."

Crystal patted her curls. "I don't know how much purple you can see, but it's pretty bright."

"Very striking," said Dr. Johnson diplomatically as he led them inside.

Martha Johnson was already taking a pitcher of pinkish lemonade out of the refrigerator when they walked into the kitchen.

"Guess you need some lemonade," she said. "It's nice to see you, Crystal. I'm glad you've met Emmett. We're thrilled he's going to take over for us for one year and hopefully for many years after that. He's bought the house. We're hoping he'll buy the practice."

Emmett glanced at Crystal. "This way, the Johnsons have the money to leave. Later, if I decide not to stay, they can sell the practice."

Crystal was pleased that the settlement seemed very fair to the Johnsons. She studied Martha Johnson and hid a tender smile. She was a picture of an old-fashioned grandmother, completed by the apron she wore over her blouse and skirt. Her gray hair was tied back behind her head, and she wore no makeup.

She gazed at Dr. Johnson. Though he seemed more

modern with his apparel, he had the stooped appearance of someone who spent a lot of time examining patients. His white hair, blue eyes, and jovial manner had some younger patients wondering if he was Santa Claus. Something he encouraged as he dressed wounds or placed a comforting hand on an overheated brow.

"Please sit down," said Martha, setting four glasses of lemonade on the table as they took seats. "When I saw you outside talking to Emmett, I had the idea that you might be the perfect choice to help him with the upgrades to this house."

"I already mentioned that, Martha," said Dr. Johnson. "Great minds think alike."

"More like old minds that have lived together for so long," said Martha smiling at him. She turned to Crystal. "Do you think you could help Emmett out? I feel terrible leaving the house to him in such poor condition. We kept meaning to do some upgrades but then we knew we were selling."

Emmett turned to Crystal. "If you're willing, I could use your help."

"Sure," said Crystal. "I can also ask my friend, Whitney, to help. She just furnished the renovated cottage she and her sisters now own at the Lilac Lake Inn site."

"Oh, I think I've seen it," said Emmett. "I wandered around a bit at the Inn."

"It's a bit like this house, with its history. Now, it's very contemporary inside and like this house, focuses on water."

"That sounds lovely, Crystal," said Martha. "I knew I was right to ask you to help." She turned to face Emmett. "Of course, the choice is yours. We just want to make this transfer as pleasant and as easy as possible."

"With a satisfactory outcome," added Dr. Johnson.

"I appreciate it," said Emmett.

Crystal rose. "I'm sorry, but I'm going to have to leave. I must make sure my afternoon staff has prepared for tomorrow. Work at the Café never ends."

Dr. Johnson stood. "Nice to see you, my dear. I'll set up an appointment with you before we leave, which will be soon."

"Good luck to everyone," she said, and walked outside, her mind spinning.

Back at the Café, Crystal made sure each table was set for the morning rush, and supplies were set aside for a busy day with daily specials. After she was satisfied, she called Whitney to tell her about her visit with Emmett and the Johnsons.

"Can you help me?" she asked after she'd told Whitney what was needed. "I didn't get a chance to talk to Emmett about what work he'd want done to the house. I figure we could do that together if you're willing."

"Willing? I'm thrilled. I've been feeling very house-bound lately and would love to help with a project like this. Together, we can do a good job for him. Does he have a budget? You said he was buying it. Even though it's old, I remember that the house has good bones and has a gorgeous setting right on the river."

"Yes, it has all of that. The doctor's office is close to the road while the house is set back. Growing up, I used to go there often."

"I remember. That's why you have a better sense than most about what we're trying to achieve. The first thing we need to do is to arrange a meeting with Emmett. Please call him and let me know what time is best. Timothy goes down for both mid-morning and afternoon naps."

"If necessary, you can bring him to do a walkthrough of the place," said Crystal.

"Thanks," said Whitney.

Crystal ended the call, pleased that Whitney would help her. She had excellent taste.

The next afternoon, after the Café closed, Crystal headed to Dr. Johnson's with Whitney, who was delighted to be on her own while Taylor babysat Timothy.

Emmett met them as they pulled their car into the driveway. "Glad to see you. Martha has left the house, so we can talk freely."

"Oh, that was thoughtful of her," said Crystal. "Emmett, have you met my best friend, Whitney? She's married to Nick Woodruff, our chief of police."

Whitney and Emmett smiled at one another. Before Emmett could ask, Crystal said, "Yes, she's that television star."

He laughed. "Sorry. I didn't mean to stare."

Whitney shrugged. "No problem."

Crystal studied her friend. Tall and thin, Whitney was a natural beauty with blonde hair, green eyes, and refined features. Television didn't do her justice.

Whitney held up a pad of paper. "I'm here to take notes for Crystal. Before we came here, we talked about some ideas."

"Come on inside. I've got some ideas of my own." Emmett waved them forward and they followed.

The Cape Cod house was similar in design to Brad's old house. A kitchen, dining room, living room, and master suite sat on the first floor. Three bedrooms and two baths were on the second floor.

"Before we get started, we need to know what your budget is. Do you want to make some structural changes? Do you just want new furniture? What?" asked Whitney,

"Let's assume that the budget is accommodating and we'll pare down from there. Fair?"

"Sure," said Crystal and Whitney together.

"Okay," said Emmett. First of all, I want to open the kitchen, maybe add on a year-round porch open to the river setting."

"Stop," said Crystal. "Let me make a call to Dani, Whitney's sister. She's an architect and, I'm sure, can help you with that end of things. Whitney and I have ideas too and can help with decorating the interior."

She stepped aside and called Dani to explain the situation to her. A few moments later, she told Emmett. "She's at The Meadows but will be here in about twenty minutes."

Whitney said, "I'm glad you're thinking of making some big changes to the house, Emmett. This property is spectacular."

"Whitney and I had already talked about putting a skylight in the kitchen, maybe more. But if you're going to rip out part of the wall, which will give you much more light, you might not need it. Let's take a look at the living room."

A red brick fireplace sat in the middle of an outside wall in the living room. Bookcases lined the wall on either side.

"How about brightening up the space, maybe painting the fireplace white as well as the bookshelves," said Crystal.

"I love that idea," said Whitney, and Emmett nodded his agreement.

"What would you say to opening the dining room to the living room, making it one large space?" asked Whitney.

By the time Dani arrived, Crystal and Whitney had several notes on the downstairs rooms.

Dani greeted them eagerly. "You know how much I love doing this kind of work. Thanks, Emmett. It's nice to see you again."

"I'm told you're the expert for any architectural changes," he said.

"I left a decent job in Boston to be here. I wouldn't change that for anything, and I do like projects like this," said Dani. "I'm glad you decided to stay right here instead of buying elsewhere. People in this town are used to making a mad dash to Dr. Johnson when they're in trouble."

"Yes, he explained that to me." He waved his arm toward the water. "And you can't beat a location like this."

"Okay, let's talk about this." She turned to Crystal. "What have you come up with?"

"First floor only. We haven't looked farther than that," said Crystal. "The kitchen is the area where we need your input. Adding a porch and perhaps removing dining room walls. Maybe a skylight in the kitchen and master bedroom."

"Okay, let's start in the kitchen," Dani said. She opened her leather-bound notebook and began taking notes as Emmett explained what he had in mind. She tapped on walls and took measurements. Then she went to the dining room and checked the walls.

"I can tell you from similar work we did at the cottage, that the flooring will need to be replaced, and that by replacing the appliances and using space from the back hallway and laundry, we can add a half bath and put in a mud room, which I think will be important."

Crystal waited for Emmett to flinch at the cost of doing that work, but he didn't seem upset at all. "Whitney and I are suggesting he use the space of the dining room for creating an open kitchen."

"Yes, like we've done at the cottage," said Whitney.

"The master suite needs upgrading. Perhaps adding a skylight in that back wing and upgrading the bathroom with new cabinetry and fixtures," Crystal said. "The rest of what we've listed is cosmetic, like painting."

"Having recently completed the cottage and working with my husband at The Meadows, I can come up with a quick ballpark figure of $150,000 for the first-floor improvements," said Dani. "Should we proceed?"

"Yes. If this is done the way I want, I know I'd get that value back and more if I ever decided to sell. Again, because of the location and the fact that the house is solid. I've taken a full tour of the property with Dr. Johnson, who is, as we all know, very honest."

"Let's look at the upstairs, and then, if you wish, I'll draw up a proposal for you. You'll want the work done before winter. It'll be a push, but we can do it because we're crewed up for the summer," said Dani. "We can maybe do double time to keep everyone busy."

"So, you've committed to living in Lilac Lake for at least a year?" Whitney said to Emmett.

"That's my plan."

"I'm glad," said Whitney. "It's always nice to have a new face in town. Right?" She gave Crystal a self-satisfied smile for drawing attention to her.

Fighting the urge to give Whitney a little shove, Crystal nodded, hoping Emmett didn't notice how flushed she was. Though she was attracted to him, she had a long way to go before wanting a relationship beyond friendship. There was still the matter of trust.

CHAPTER FOUR

THAT EVENING, Crystal sat in Jake's with Dani and Brad, Melissa, Aaron Collister, Ross Roberts, and his friend, Ben Gooding. It was a congenial group. Aaron, Brad's brother, had an interesting background. Part native-American, he was left at the Collister household by his mother who was dying of cancer. Though his coloring was different, there was no mistaking they were brothers. They owned Collister Construction together.

Ross Roberts was as famous a baseball player as Whitney had been as a television star. Forced to leave baseball because of knee injuries, Ross was one of the trio of people who now owned the Lilac Lake Inn. With sandy hair, blue eyes, and a well-known boyish smile, he could still be seen in sports ads on television. He was one of the first to build a house in The Meadows by Collister Construction and set many female hearts aflutter in town. Crystal liked him a lot as a friend. His friend, Ben, had grown up in New Jersey with Ross and was a former catcher who'd played ball with Ross in high school and college. He looked the part with his broad, heavy-set body.

Crystal liked the easy companionship between all of them.

"I asked Emmett to join us," said Dani, "but he said he had to go to New York for a few days. He'll stay at Dr. Johnson's house after they move out."

"Dr. Johnson called to say that he and Martha will be gone by the beginning of next week," said Crystal. "They'd already bought a place in Florida at the beginning of the year and won't be taking much with them. After the move, if necessary, he'll be back for a couple of weeks to help Emmett get settled in the practice."

"That's nice. It'll give his patients time to get used to a new doctor. I imagine a few women in town will be delighted to see his replacement," said Whitney. "Emmett is awfully cute." She glanced at Nick and grinned. "Not as cute as Nick, though."

Talk turned to the annual Summer Faire, which was held in August. Though it was still early to discuss the finer details, Crystal was glad to hear that Estelle Bookbinder, owner of Pages Bookstore, was in charge of it, as she had been for several years. The Summer Faire consisted of three days of shopping, food, music, and games, including canoe races on the lake. This year, the Lilac Lake Inn was offering special rates to visitors who came for the entire event.

As more and more young families returned to the area, these events grew their success. Crystal served on the committee in charge of publicity and offered specials at the Café during Summer Faire. This year, she hoped to hold a baking contest for residents, young and old.

Brooks and Bethany Beckman, whose family owned Beckman Lumber, arrived. After they greeted everyone and ordered some food, talk turned to children. Their first child had just started to walk, and it was big news joyously shared.

After a while, Crystal made her escape. As much as she loved these gatherings, duty called. Besides, she had mixed feelings about all the talk of babies.

Later, lying in bed, she thought of her life and realized her restlessness wasn't a fleeting thing. She had no idea if it was hormones talking, but she wanted a family.

The next few days were typical of summer in Lilac Lake with visitors roaming Main Street and stopping inside the Café for breakfast or lunch. Crystal loved greeting and chatting with people, happy her Café was a success. To her, it was about more than the food; the Café was a welcoming place to all. Having grown up in a town where she sometimes felt like an outsider, it was important to her.

One morning, she was surprised by a visit from Emmett. "Good morning. Back in town to stay?"

He grinned. "I think so. I brought just enough of my things to get by while the renovation of the house took place. I'll be staying at the house in one of the bedrooms upstairs while work is being done on the first floor. It's helpful that the medical offices remain set up and separate from the construction because I still have to learn my way around it."

"I'm sure you'll be fine," she said, pleased to see him.

He took a seat at the counter, and Crystal went outside to the patio to see how things were going. Satisfied, she returned to the kitchen to check on their progress. It had taken a lot of work to train her crew well enough so she wouldn't be confined to the kitchen.

Before Emmett left, he approached her. "Do you do any catering?"

"Not usually. What do you need?"

He gave her a sheepish grin. "I'm not very handy in the kitchen."

"I'll tell you what. If you order off the menu, I'd be happy to bring an order to you from time to time for these first couple of weeks."

"That's a deal. I'll make it up to you by treating you to dinner."

"That's a sweet idea but not necessary," said Crystal.

His turquoise eyes studied her. "Thanks, but I'd feel better by showing my appreciation."

After he left, she still felt the heat of his smile.

###

After a few days had gone by, Crystal almost forgot their deal. Then one day, after eating breakfast at the Café, Emmett said, "If your offer stands, I'd love to have a sandwich delivered to the office today, and I'll take you to dinner."

Surprised but pleased, she grinned. "Deal. What would you like?"

He placed an order and said, "How about Fins, seven o'clock?"

"That would be a real treat," she said. "I look forward to it."

When the time came, she could've had someone else make the lunchtime delivery, but with things running smoothly at the Café, she decided to do it herself.

She packaged up Emmett's lunch and took it to his office.

When she stepped inside, Lucille Young, the nurse/receptionist smiled at her. "That's for Emmett? He's outside, down at the dock taking a break. He said you'd be stopping by." Lucille, a pretty woman with graying brown hair, was in her 50s and had raised four boys. She was a calming influence in the office and had been with Dr. Johnson for years. "Dr. Chambers certainly is handsome. He'll be glad to see you."

"It's just a deal we have for meals," explained Crystal. Though she was intrigued by him, she decided she wasn't going to do more than try to be friends with Emmett. GG's thoughts about allowing people their privacy made her rethink the situation. If their friendship grew, he might be willing to talk about his family and his life.

"You go on then. Dr. Chambers doesn't have an appointment for an hour," said Lucille. "Enjoy the sunshine. It's a beautiful day in the neighborhood, as I tell the kids who come in for a visit."

Crystal smiled at her. "Mr. Rogers, huh?"

"Yes," said Lucille grinning. "I've always thought he was a

sweet man with his television programs, books, and all. The movie was great."

Crystal left the office and headed to the dock. Even from a distance, she could see the outline of Emmett sitting on the bench. There was something about the way he hunched his shoulders that touched her.

She waited until she was closer to call out to him. But before she could, he turned around and waved at her, getting to his feet to greet her.

"Ah, personal delivery. I like it," he teased.

"I figure it's well worth a dinner," she joked.

"I hope you brought enough for the two of us. It's a nice day for a picnic." He led her to the bench.

She set down the bags she'd been carrying. "I brought lemonade for both of us and your sandwich." She took out a paper plate, unwrapped it, and handed it to him with a sandwich, chips, and a pickle. Then she removed two large paper cups with lemonade and set one down beside him.

Lowering herself onto the dock, she stared out at the moving water and listened to the soothing sound of it swirling around the pilings holding up the dock. "This is very peaceful," she murmured closing her eyes and looking up at the sun.

"Hold it right there," said Emmett softly. "You're so beautiful."

At the sound of his phone camera clicking, Crystal opened her eyes and turned to him with a silent question.

"I mean it," said Emmett. "I can't see the exact color of your hair but whatever it is, I like it. And your face ..."

Crystal held up her hand. "Stop. You're embarrassing me. I never think of myself that way."

Emmett's gaze met hers. "Maybe it's time you did. That's all I'm saying."

"Well, thank you." She turned away and gazed out over the lazy river not in a rush to go anywhere, just moving along at a steady pace. She was startled by Emmet's words. Her mother had thought she was ugly and had told her so when she was drunk or high and Crystal was trying to get her to come home to sleep it off. Later, attending Al-Anon meetings, Crystal understood her mother's words had been spoken as part of her defensive stance. Her mother had apologized to Crystal before she died, but the damage had already been done. Even Nick, sweet Nick, hadn't been able to convince Crystal that she was better in every way than she'd always believed.

Emmett placed a hand on her shoulder. "Hey. I'm here anytime you want to talk."

She turned and stared up at him. "Thanks. It's old baggage. I thought I'd dealt with that issue, but I guess I'll have to rethink it."

"We all have stuff we need to deal with," he said. "I'm glad to help you with yours. That's why I like the idea of a family practice. It's a chance to help entire families because when one is in trouble, they all are. Of course, I'm talking mostly about health problems."

"And mostly about other people. Right?"

He shrugged. "I guess." He took a last bite of his sandwich. "I met with Dani, Brad, and Aaron at Collister Construction. I gave them the go-ahead to start with the renovation. Dr. Johnson has been delayed in getting back here, but I told him we can do most of the training online, and since Lucille is the one who handles all the office procedures, I'm covered there."

"I'm happy that he and Martha can retire. He's wanted to for a long time but felt he couldn't leave until he was replaced. He's that kind of person."

"I hope I can be as well-respected as he is," said Emmett honestly.

Crystal studied him. "I think you will be. Thanks for the break. I must get back to the Café."

He stood as she got to her feet. "Thanks for the sandwich and the special delivery. I'll see you tonight at seven. I'll pick you up at your place, and we can walk down the street to the restaurant."

"It sounds wonderful. After cooking most days, it's a treat not to have to worry about it." She left him and hurried back to her car aware his gaze was on her.

CHAPTER FIVE

THAT EVENING, Crystal looked at herself critically in the mirror. Emmett thought she was beautiful. Was it a line he used on all women he wanted to get to know? An image of her younger self appeared, and she closed her eyes at the sight of the scrawny, unkempt child she once was. She colored her hair purple to remind herself that she was different now—a successful young woman with a business of her own. And talented too. Not as good an actress as Whitney, of course, but she could perform some lesser singing roles with ease, a total break from her normal routine.

Life is complicated, she thought, putting a last swipe of mascara on her long lashes. Their darkness highlighted the unusual color of her eyes, slightly more purple than dark blue in certain sunlight. Funny, that both she and Emmett had unusual eyes. She wondered if he was able to see hers clearly. She'd read that in addition to difficulty with red and green hues, a person who is colorblind might have trouble with the color blue.

Her doorbell rang, and as she went to answer it, a shiver went through her. Behind the offer of dinner and her acceptance was a chance for her to move forward, if not to love, to a meaningful friendship. He, unlike others in town, wouldn't remember her as she was growing up. He'd only see her for what she'd become.

She opened the door and noticed his hair was still a little damp from a recent shower. He'd put on a fresh golf shirt and now wore khaki pants instead of the jeans he'd worn earlier.

"Wow!" He grinned at her. "You look nice."

"Thanks." She couldn't help blushing as she nervously brushed a speck of dust from the skirt of her sundress. She was used to wearing jeans or shorts and a T-shirt at work. The way he was looking at her made her realize it was worth it occasionally to dress up in something a little more feminine. She'd even worn dressy drop earrings instead of her usual silver hoops.

"It's nice that we can simply walk to the restaurant," he said as they emerged onto the street. He took her arm. "It's a little bit like New York, where neighborhoods have all kinds of conveniences close by."

"Did you always live in New York City?" she asked.

"Most of the time," he answered. "Right now, I don't even want to think about anything but getting comfortable here in town. I've met a lot of nice people."

"Like every other small town, there are some easier to like than others, but Lilac Lake is full of great people. We tend to attract people who want to enjoy a simple life. You must admit, the town and surrounding areas are gorgeous."

"Oh, yes. When I was searching for a place to fulfill my obligation for my residency, it was something I noticed right away in my research."

They arrived at Fins, and Emmett held the door while Crystal stepped inside. Melissa's mother greeted them with wide smiles. "Nice to see you here, Crystal, and a big welcome to our new doctor."

Crystal returned Susan Hendrickson's smile, well aware that Susan never missed a bit of gossip in town. Still, it was nice to be greeted warmly.

Susan led them to a lovely table in the corner. There, they'd not only have privacy, but Crystal had an easy view of who else was in the restaurant.

"I'm hungry," said Emmett. "How about you?"

"Me, too. I purposely kept myself from snacking or even taste-testing certain recipes. Dinner here is always a treat."

"How about my ordering a bottle of wine? White or red? I'm leaning toward a white or a light red because of the seafood."

"I'm happy with only a glass of red wine," said Crystal. She didn't want Emmett to spend a lot of money on the wine when she drank so little. Growing up with an alcoholic mother, she had no intention of getting into that kind of trouble and limited her drinks to two on occasional celebrations. Not that she was going to explain that to Emmett.

After perusing the menu, Emmett decided on clam pie and Crystal, the grilled salmon.

"Okay, let's order a bottle of a nice pinot," said Emmett.

Crystal was silent as Emmett discussed vintages with the wine steward before they placed their orders. Observing the quiet but confident way he'd handled the order, Crystal couldn't help but wonder about his background. He'd given out little information about himself or his family. But surely, he'd had some experience with wine, especially when he ordered a Chandler Hill Inn pinot, a special one she'd read about.

Later, after approving it, Emmett waited while the wine steward poured some into her glass and then his. The man left, and Emmett lifted his glass. "Here's to getting to know you and Lilac Lake a lot better."

"I'll applaud that," she said. "It's wonderful to have you here."

They chatted about various things to do in the area and then ordered their meal.

Crystal enjoyed the idea of not rushing their meal. Eating at the Café rarely happened that way. Now, she listened as

Emmett told her about the plans that he'd agreed on to renovate the house.

"You're lucky," he said, "to have friends like Dani, Brad, and Aaron who are willing to go overboard to help. They certainly are being cooperative about moving fast on the project."

"They're good people. Dani and her sisters used to come to Lilac Lake every summer growing up. They, Brad, Aaron, Nick, and a whole bunch of us have remained close since childhood. It's great that we're all coming together again."

"I can understand why," said Emmett. Crystal had the feeling he didn't have many friends. Her heart ached for him. Her friends had "saved" her over and over again.

As they were eating, one of the customers in the restaurant came over to their table. "I'm sorry to interrupt but I have to ask, aren't you Rory Chamberlain?"

"The movie star? No, ma'am, I'm not." Emmett's expression hardened. "He's a distant relative."

"I noticed your eyes in addition to your features and couldn't let it go. I'm very sorry." The woman returned to her table, but Crystal could tell Emmett was uncomfortable.

"Does that happen often?" she asked him.

"Every once in a while. I don't know why it bothers me except I find it annoying. I don't know how Whitney graciously acknowledges the people who recognize her. Not that I'm famous or wish to be."

"It's a bit of an intrusion, but I suppose someone like Whitney gets used to it." Crystal leaned forward. "You never talk about your family. Now I know that Rory Chamberlain is a distant relative."

Emmett shrugged. "I don't like to talk about my family. They like their privacy as much as I do." He settled his gaze on her. "You've kept pretty quiet about your background."

"As anyone in town knows, I was married to Whitney's husband, Nick, for a brief time. But we both knew we'd married for the wrong reasons. I'm pleased to see them happy together because I consider them to be my best friends. I grew up in a difficult situation with an alcoholic, drug-addicted mother who left me to care for my younger sister from an early age. Not your typical Lilac Lake family.

"I asked Dr. Johnson about you, and that's all he'd tell me. Just so you know, like him, I'd never divulge medical or other private information about any of my patients."

"One thing about growing up with a parent you never want to emulate is that neither my sister nor I have ever been into drugs or abuse of alcohol," said Crystal. "I'm enjoying a glass of wine tonight, but I have no need or desire to have more."

"That's good. Because addiction is a disease that runs in families."

"So, no problems like mine in your family?" Crystal asked, unable to hold back the question. He'd been reticent about them.

He shook his head. "Not drug addiction, but they have problems of their own. And because my father is in the public eye, they're all on display."

Crystal wanted to ask for more information but could see from the grim expression on his face that Emmett was finished talking about them.

They finished their main course and then were handed dessert menus.

Emmett perused his and regarded her with a sparkle in his eye. "What do you think? Ready for something? I'm opting for the Apple Pie a la Mode. Can't resist that."

"Well, I was thinking about the lemon tart," admitted Crystal.

"Let's go for it." Emmett grinned at the waitress. "The lady will have the tart and I'll take the apple pie."

After she left, Crystal said, "I didn't know you had a sweet tooth. I'll have to remember that going forward with any of your orders."

He laughed. "I try not to have sweets too often. But on a night like this, with food like this and a beautiful woman with me, I couldn't resist."

Warmth weaved through Crystal. She was having a wonderful time.

As they left, Crystal noticed how some of the other people in the restaurant stared at them and realized they were checking out the new doctor.

Outside, Emmett turned to her. "Do you want to meet up with your friends at Jake's?"

"No, I'd rather take a walk with you and then go up to my apartment for coffee or a cup of tea."

"That sounds nice. I've enjoyed this evening and I'm not ready for it to end." Emmett took her hand, and they headed down the quiet end of the street.

Crystal had dated and married, but as Emmett's fingers wrapped around her hand, she felt a sense of connection that she knew was special. She hardly knew Emmett, but she was attracted to him. To some people, he might seem pleasant but ordinary, except for his eyes. But she'd understood he was a decent man. If only she could get rid of the thought he was hiding something about his background. But then, she told herself, she was someone who should never judge a person by his family.

They walked down one side of Main Street, turned around, and walked back on the other side, and, like tourists, stopped and gazed into the windows of the cute shops. Crystal had viewed them before but seeing them through his eyes helped her to be charmed all over again. Lilac Lake was a darling small town.

"I'm glad I chose to come here. The downtown is a real slice of Americana. Very cool. So far, the people I've met have been great. Dr. Johnson says he'll be sad to leave his patients. I believe him."

"We're here at my place. Do you want to come up?" Crystal asked him.

Emmett gazed at her and smiled. "I'd like that very much."

For all the fun she had in town with friends, she didn't often invite them to come into her apartment. The Café was as much social as business, and she liked keeping her apartment to herself.

She climbed the stairs in back of the Café and unlocked the door to her apartment, experiencing a rush of heat. Coffee or tea wasn't the only thing either one of them had been thinking about. Suddenly shy, Crystal wished it wasn't too late to change her mind. But then, she scolded herself. She'd be all right. At the threshold of the door, she snapped on the light and the living area glowed with light, accenting her tasteful décor. In addition to a couch and comfortable chairs atop a large Oriental rug, tables were scattered at the right places and showcased her interest in Native American art.

"This is nice," said Emmett. He walked over to one of the tables and lifted a ceramic bowl.

"I love reading about various east coast tribes in the New York region—the Mohawks, Iroquois, Senecas, Onondagas, and others, and the tribes of New Hampshire—the Abenaki and Wampanoag tribes. But the tribes of the Southwest –the Navaho, Apache, Hopi, and Zuni, among others, are known for their arts and crafts. After a visit to Arizona, I became interested in them. Once in a while, I add pieces to my collection."

"I've always admired their crafts," said Emmett carefully setting the bowl down. "My aunt has a home in Tucson."

"Do you mean Rory's mother?" Crystal asked, eager to learn more.

"No," Emmett said and left it at that.

"I have a selection of teas, coffee—both decaf and regular, water, and cold beer. What would you like?"

"A cold beer sounds delicious," Emmett replied, following her to the kitchen.

Crystal reached into her refrigerator and handed a bottle of beer to him before pouring herself a glass of cold water.

"Let's sit on the front deck and watch the activity in town," said Crystal. "In the morning, before the town awakes, I sit and watch the fog rise from the lake. It's pretty and peaceful then."

"Don't you ever get tired of being such a part of Main Street life?" he asked.

"Sometimes," she admitted, "but I love this town. It's not a house but the town itself that has always been home to me. Maybe because the people here are very kind. Without the help of Whitney's grandmother, Genie Wittner, I might never have been able to buy the Café."

"I've met her," said Emmett. "She's very nice, though I had the feeling she was interviewing me for the job of local physician."

Crystal laughed. "It sounds just like GG. She's helped many of us in town and elsewhere. Especially before she lost a lot of her money in a financial scam from what once was a well-respected firm in Boston."

"Sort of like a Bernie Madoff scandal?" he asked.

"Yes. It's quite awful to lose your money that way. And for GG, it meant she had to sell the inn and move into The Woodlands, where she lives."

"I've been asked to do a presentation there, to introduce myself and to ensure that the residents know they can rely on me, that I come with Dr. Johnson's recommendation."

"While you're there, you might meet JoEllen Daniels, Brad's ex-sister-in-law, who works as an aide at the facility. JoEllen has a lot of problems. But then, *she* is a problem." Crystal spoke quietly so people below them wouldn't hear. She might know a lot of people in town, but she wasn't a gossip.

"Thanks for the 'heads up.' Even though the town is small, it'll take time to learn about all the residents," said Emmett. "It's important to me. As I've mentioned before, that's why I chose family medicine and a small town."

"So, family is important to you?" She studied him.

"Mine is complicated but, yes, it's something I look forward to—having a family of my own."

"I grew up raising my sister, so I've never been eager to have children of my own. Until recently. Now, I've begun to think of it. Who knows if it will happen."

"I like your honesty. It's something I admire." He reached over and clasped her hand.

Her lips curved then she grew serious. "Honesty is very important to me."

Emmett looked away and then turned to her. "It's getting late. I think I'd better go."

When he stood, Crystal got to her feet puzzled by his abruptness. But when he bent down and kissed her on the lips, a sweet gentle one, she felt a spark that took her by surprise.

He grinned as if he knew her feelings and said, "Would you be willing to show me around the area a bit? I have Wednesday afternoons and Sundays off."

"I'd be happy to do that. Do you want to aim for Wednesday afternoon? We could drive over to Portsmouth and look around there and the southern coast of Maine."

"That would be a nice start. Thanks. I have a meeting with the Collister Construction people in the morning, but the afternoon will be fine."

"My brunch rush will be over by one. And I can leave things in the hands of my staff." Crystal walked him to the door. They stood gazing at one another. Emmett's turquoise eyes seemed to reach deep inside her. Then he lowered his lips to hers.

A warmth enveloped Crystal. Her response was as much spiritual as sexual. And when they stepped apart, his cheeks were as flushed as hers.

"Goodnight," Emmett said softly and turned and went down the stairway.

Crystal hugged herself to stop the chills that still ran through her with his absence.

She closed the door behind her and leaned against it. "Wow!"

Holding onto that thought, she turned off the lights and went to bed.

There, she hugged her pillow and relived that kiss over and over again.

CHAPTER SIX

THE NEXT MORNING, Dani came into the Café with Brad and Aaron Collister. Crystal walked over to their table. "Are you having a full breakfast or just a coffee break?"

"I want the works," said Aaron, smiling at her with those deep, brown eyes that always seemed to know what people were feeling.

"Okay, then. What'll you have?" Crystal said, quickly jotting down their orders and delivering them to the kitchen window opening before returning to the table to talk.

"What's going on with you besides having dinner with our new doctor?" asked Dani, giving her an impish grin.

Crystal shook her head. Lilac Lake did have a drawback or two, one of which was having no secrets. "Emmett and I have a deal. Every time I deliver a luncheon order, he'll take me out to dinner. Fins was special. It will be a little more low-key than that in the future. It's just a friend thing while he gets acquainted with the townspeople."

"He told us earlier that you were helping him," said Aaron. "We're doing the work on the house, and our day starts early, hoping to complete the work on schedule. He's got an outstanding piece of property."

"Yes, I think so too."

"You should see the design for the house renovations," said Dani. "It's going to be fantastic."

"A lot more open," said Brad.

"That'll be lovely," said Crystal, waving to an older couple who'd just arrived. "Gotta go. Nice to see you."

She left them and walked over to Edie and Bob Bullard, who owned the hardware store in town. "Good morning! How can I help you?"

They smiled as they greeted her. "You look especially nice today," said Edie. "But then, you're always beautiful."

"Thanks," Crystal said, leaning over and kissing her cheek. Edie had been one of the women in town who'd helped her with makeup and outfits for many of the high school dances. Her daughter, Sarah, now widowed and living out of town, always sought her out when she returned to Lilac Lake for a visit.

"Still keeping that hair purple, huh?" asked Bob, and both Edie and Crystal chuckled. Bob was a conservative guy who never got the reasoning behind Crystal's choice and Edie's love of it.

"We've met the new doctor in town," said Edie. "Bob had to see him about a cut on his hand."

Bob held up his left hand which was bandaged nicely. "He did a superb job of stitching me up. Seems like a great guy."

"He's very nice. Dr. Johnson is happy with him."

"He told me he's renovating the house, and Collister Construction is doing the job for him," said Bob.

"It's nice that all of you young folks are together again. It adds something wonderful to the town." Edie teased her with a knowing smile. "And Dr. Chambers is really cute. And available."

Crystal tried to stem the flow of red to her cheeks, but she could feel how hot they'd become. She seated them at a booth inside. "Here's your waitress now." She turned and hurried to the kitchen. Darned if the whole town wasn't trying to put her together with Emmett.

Later, when he called to place an order, Crystal hesitated and decided she wouldn't let gossip or her friends' eagerness for her to find someone stop her. She'd just keep working and living as she normally would.

At the appointed time. Crystal placed Emmett's BLT sandwich in a bag, along with carrot sticks and a single chocolate chip cookie, and carried it out to her car. She wouldn't stay long but wanted to see the work Dani and the Collister brothers were doing on the house.

Emmett met her at the front door to his medical offices. "Thanks. I haven't got much time today, so I appreciate the service. The kitchen in the house is about to be torn apart, so I won't be able to function there."

"I came to see what they were doing to it. I met Dani and the men at the Café. They're excited about doing the work."

Emmett accepted the bag from her. "Let's go take a look. They've knocked out the back wall of the house and are taking down some of the inner walls."

As they walked to his house, Emmett took out his sandwich and took a big bite. "M-m-m-m."

When they arrived at the house, Crystal could hardly believe the change. "Wow! The kitchen is a total mess. But I can already see what it will look like with the space extended in the back and becoming part of a sunroom. What are you going to do about keeping any wildlife out while the place is opened up?"

"Aaron and Brad are putting up heavy-duty plastic sheets and tacking them in place to protect the rest of the house. But I'm concerned about wildlife and the weather. Aaron says we have time to enclose the space before rainy weather lingers." Emmett shook his head. "Aaron says he has a sense about these things, and I'm going to believe him. I've got too much on my mind to worry about it. The practice is busy."

"I saw Bob Bullard earlier. He says you did a superb job

with his hand."

"Thanks for telling me."

"You're going to do just fine," Crystal said.

"By the way, your warning came in handy. JoEllen Daniels came to see me. She told me she wanted to introduce herself and offer her services to help me to become comfortable in town. She was quite weird about it. I thanked her and told her I knew she worked at The Woodlands and would no doubt see her there."

"I bet she didn't like that," Crystal said.

"No, she said she had more in mind than that." He shrugged. "I don't have time to get involved with anyone. I've got to get my practice running smoothly. There's stuff I still don't know about some people's medical care requirements."

Rather than be disappointed by his comment about not wanting to get involved with anyone, Crystal was relieved. Now they truly could just be friends.

"I've got to get back to work," she said. "Thanks for letting me see the start of your reconstruction. It's going to be beautiful."

"I agree. I'm glad you and Whitney will help with the interior décor. That's out of my league," said Emmett walking with her back to the medical office building.

"It's going to be fun. I loved renovating the Café, and Whitney did a superb job with the Lilac Lake Cottage, as she and her sisters are calling it. I keep telling her, it could become a real business if she wanted to do it."

"What about her doing more television or movies?" asked Emmett.

"She told me it's something she'll decide on when and if the opportunity arises."

They arrived at the office, and Crystal left with her head spinning. There was a lot for her to think about. The kiss they'd shared was much more than friendship.

On Wednesday, Emmett showed up early at the Café and took a seat at the breakfast bar.

"I know we said we'd meet up a little later, but I've had a meeting with Collister Construction already and need a hot breakfast before we take off on our trip to Portsmouth and Maine."

"No problem," said Crystal. "It's a beautiful day for a drive around the area. I've arranged to have the whole day off, and I'm ready any time after you eat. What'll you have?"

"Large O.J., scrambled eggs on wheat toast, bacon, and hash browns," he said. "And coffee."

Crystal poured him a cup of coffee and placed the order with the kitchen. "Be right back. I see Nick and want to say hi."

As she approached his table out on the patio, her ex-husband, Nick, glimpsed her and grinned. "Hi, Crystal. How are you doing? Whitney says you and the new doctor might be becoming friends. I hope it's working out for you."

Crystal drew a deep breath and took a seat opposite him. Though they'd ended their marriage, their friendship remained intact with Whitney's blessing. It was Crystal who'd pushed Nick and Whitney to get together after sharing a teen romance. Strange as it might seem, the three of them had a solid friendship.

"Nick, you and Whitney know me better than anyone else. Do you think I'm foolish to leave myself open to getting to know Emmett Chambers better? There's not much I know about him except he went to medical school in New York. I don't find much about him on the internet but he's ... interesting ... kind ... and has a good reputation."

Nick gave her a thoughtful look. "Sounds like you're

already into him. Why don't you see where it leads? You can end it whenever you feel it isn't right."

Crystal looked away. That's pretty much what they'd said to one another when she and Nick realized their marriage was more about one friend taking care of another. He'd always been protective of her.

"Okay, thanks. I knew you'd be honest with me." She hesitated. "I still wonder why he doesn't talk about his family, but then again, I never like to talk about mine."

"Just enjoy getting to know him. You don't have to decide anything beyond that."

"Thanks." Crystal rose and headed inside, pleased by Nick's encouragement. She and Emmett weren't even dating yet. They were just two people getting to know one another as she helped him get acquainted with the area. Maybe that's where it would end.

CHAPTER SEVEN

AFTER EMMETT FINISHED HIS BREAKFAST, Crystal pulled her car around to the front. Typical of her, she'd made sure they had plenty of refreshments packed in her red Toyota RAV4. A cooler sitting in the back seat held bottled water, apples, and cookies. Emmett loved her chocolate chip cookies.

"You don't mind me driving?" she asked him as he buckled himself into the passenger's seat.

"I figure you know your way around, and it'll be easier for you to have the wheel."

As they took off, she liked that he wasn't a man who would feel his manhood threatened by giving control to her.

It took less than an hour to reach Portsmouth on the coast of New Hampshire. She pulled into a parking garage and turned to him. "This is a very walkable city. Besides the restaurants and shops in and around Market Square, there are many other things to see."

"Okay. Let's pretend we're both tourists. Where should we start?"

"I think we should take a guided tour to get the lay of the land this morning, and then we have a choice of visiting historic homes of famous Navy captains, merchants, explorers, and governors, or we could visit Strawbery Banke, the oldest neighborhood here, which has 32 historic buildings. We can meet people there dressed in costume. Or we could take a scenic drive to Portsmouth Harbor Lighthouse in New Castle. Or visit Wentworth by the Sea Hotel & Resort. There are lots of things to see."

"Wow! All of this in a relatively small area. I say we start with a guided tour and go from there, just as you suggested."

"Let me call to see if we can have a private tour." Crystal phoned the number she'd written down earlier, and after arranging a tour to begin in a half-hour, she ended the call and turned to Emmett. "We have time for a cup of coffee before the tour. Let's go to Market Square. We'll meet our guide there in thirty minutes."

In Market Square, they found a Dunkin' coffee shop and took seats inside. After ordering a decaf café mocha for her, Emmett ordered a plain coffee for himself.

"I like what I've seen so far," said Emmett, sipping his coffee and staring out at the people strolling the brick sidewalks in the square.

"It's charming," said Crystal. "And in some parts of town, it's like taking a step back in history. I'm glad you like it. It's an easy place to come to when needing a break from Lilac Lake."

"I understand how you might need that. I suppose I'll reach that point too." Emmett got to his feet as an older woman called out to Crystal and walked toward them.

Crystal stood and smiled at her. "I told the receptionist I'd be hard to miss with my hair."

The woman laughed. "I'm your guide. Helena Tribble."

Crystal shook her hand. "Crystal Owen. And this is Dr. Emmett Chambers, the new physician in Lilac Lake. He wanted to learn more about the area."

"Lilac Lake is such a pretty place, but I think you'll find lots to admire in Portsmouth," Helena said to him. "The tour will take about an hour. Ready?"

Crystal followed Emmett and Helena out of the coffee shop.

Helena stood and told them about some of the shops and

restaurants around Market Square and then told them about English settlers being drawn to the commercial potential of the region's fish and timber, along with the deep-water Piscataqua River.

"The community's original name was Strawbery Banke because of the strawberry-strewn waterfront banks, but the name was changed in 1653 to Portsmouth."

"You know a lot about the area. Do you live here?"

Helena shook her head. "My husband is a professor of history at the University of New Hampshire in Durham, and we live not far from here in New Castle. I feel as if I'm a native of Portsmouth because I've learned so much about it."

"You're trained to be a guide?" Crystal asked.

"Oh, yes. And believe me, there's a lot to learn." Helena beamed at her and brushed a lock of gray hair behind her ear. "Let's continue."

After an hour of learning about the city, its early settlers, artifacts at St. John's Episcopal Church, where President Washington once worshipped, and tugboats on the river, Crystal was ready to sit down at one of the places back at Market Square.

"Thank you for letting me show you around," said Helena, ending their tour. "You're a lovely couple."

Crystal glanced at Emmett, but he looked away.

Uncomfortable by that, Crystal tipped Helena and thanked her for an interesting tour, then turned to Emmett. "What would you like to do next?"

"I want to try one of the restaurants here for chowder and lobster rolls like Helena suggested and then continue the drive up along the southern coast of Maine. I already know I want to return to Portsmouth to see more of it."

"Perfect. I'm hungry and ready to eat. Then we'll just do a

quick overview of the southern coast of Maine. Along Route One, Kittery has several discount malls, but I'm sure you'll be more interested in the Portsmouth Naval Shipyard on Seavey's Island."

"All right. We don't need to hurry. I already know I want to spend another day with you poking around the area." He put an arm around her. "Let's go eat."

They chose one of the restaurants Helena had suggested right on the waterfront. The saltwater smells from the river were pleasing though not as fresh as ocean air farther up the coast. Helena had told them that the Piscataqua River was the second fastest flowing river in the U.S. and wasn't safe for swimming, so Crystal wasn't surprised to see, instead, a busy harbor full of boats, some moored right off the dockside entrance to the restaurant.

Though the summer day was warm, a breeze cooled them at their table under an umbrella on the deck.

Emmett leaned back in his chair and lifted her hand in his. "This has been a wonderful morning. I've enjoyed being with you. I haven't found someone I could be comfortable with in a long time." He squeezed her hand, sending electric shock waves up her arm and into her body.

She gazed at his smiling face and let out a long sigh, wishing she could look into his eyes, but they were covered by sunglasses. "I've enjoyed it too. I like you, Emmett. I really do."

"Thanks. That means a lot to me." He gazed out at the water deep in thought.

A waitress appeared at their table and the contemplative look on his face was replaced with a wide smile. "We hear this is the place to come for seafood chowder and a lobster roll."

The waitress lifted her order pad. "I take it that's what you're ordering for lunch?"

"Yes, ma'am. But, Crystal, what are you having?"

"I'll have the same. I'm told they're both delicious."

"We sell a lot of them," said the waitress. "They're among my favorites."

After placing the orders, the waitress brought them the Cokes they wanted.

Crystal took a deep, satisfying sip and watched as a young couple pulled their motorboat up to the dock, tied it to a bollard, and started to walk along the rocking dock to the restaurant.

The young woman, obviously a novice, was wearing high heels, and as a wave moved the dock under her feet, she teetered for a moment and then fell on her knees.

When she stood, blood was running down her legs. The man with her observed the accident helplessly and then gazed around for help.

Emmett was out of his chair in a flash. Carrying his clean white linen napkin, he hurried to them.

"Hey, let me give you a hand," Crystal heard him say. "You took a hard tumble. Looks like you've got a couple of nasty scrapes."

"Thanks," the man said. "I'm not handy with these kinds of things. Here's some water to help clean it up. I really appreciate your help."

"No worries. I'm used to dealing with scrapes like this." In a matter of minutes, Emmett cleaned around the wounds and then told the manager who'd come to check on them that they needed some bandages and first aid ointment.

"Thank you," the young woman told Emmett as he quickly dabbed on the ointment and bandaged the deepest cuts.

"You're welcome. It could've been worse. You could have broken a hand or an arm with the way you fell. These cuts should heal quickly. Next time, you might not want to wear heels to go boating," said Emmett kindly.

After accepting their thanks, Emmett returned to their table.

"Sorry to leave you," Emmett said. "I could see that accident just waiting to happen."

"I know you love your profession. You did an excellent job very quickly," Crystal said with approval.

He gave her a shy smile. "I like being able to help in a situation like that."

Their meal came shortly after he returned from washing his hands, and they both sat back and tasted the hot chowder.

"M-m-m. Helena was right. It's some of the best chowder I've ever had," said Emmett. "This is turning into a day to remember for many reasons. I'm glad we decided to do this trip."

"Me, too," said Crystal. She was finding it a convenient way to get to know Emmett better, and she liked what she saw.

When it came time to leave, Emmett asked for the check. The waitress said, "I'll be right back."

A moment later, she returned with the manager of the restaurant, who introduced himself as Kevin Archer. "Your lunch is on us. I appreciate your quick response to the young woman in distress after falling on our dock. Having the dock available to boaters is important to us, and we want to be able to keep our water access to the restaurant without complaints. Some think it's too dangerous."

"Thanks," said Emmett. "I was happy to be of assistance."

After the manager walked away, Crystal said, "Nice job, doctor."

He grinned. "Hey, we got a free meal out of it. We should've ordered the ice cream pie."

Crystal laughed and got to her feet. "Let's check out Kittery and the Portsmouth Naval Shipyard. I'll have you know that

Kittery is the oldest incorporated town in Maine, and I read that the shipyard was the first federal navy yard."

"Ah, you've been reading up on information for this trip," teased Emmett.

"You caught me. But once I started, I couldn't stop. This area is full of interesting history."

They left the restaurant and returned to the parking garage.

"Where do we go from here?" Emmett asked.

"We cross Memorial Bridge and presto, we're in Maine. Beyond that, we can get on Route One which is where all the outlet stores are. Kittery is famous for them. I couldn't even count them. Do you need to get anything for your house? They have kitchen supply and furniture stores there."

Emmett hesitated and then said, "Tell you what, I need to do that. While I was gone from Lilac Lake after accepting the job and purchasing the house, Martha had movers come in and pack up almost all of the kitchen. And I kept some furniture, but the rest was given away."

"Whitney and I will help you with the furnishings after the renovation is done. But you can get new kitchen supplies anytime and set them aside until the kitchen is completed. Why don't we take advantage of being here and just look around for them?"

"Okay. Let's do that right now so we can get back to Lilac Lake at a decent time. No emergencies yet, but I'll feel better if I'm available to patients this evening."

She studied him for a moment and returned her gaze to the road. "You take your job seriously."

"Yes, I do." Emmett's eyes rounded when he realized she wasn't kidding about outlets. Different groupings of stores lined the road. "You were telling the truth when you said there were a lot of discount stores. Where do we begin?"

"How about here?" Crystal pulled into an area on her left. The Kitchen Collection and Villeroy & Boch stores were there. "I've got a paper and pencil in my purse. We can make notes on what you might need, or you can purchase whatever you want."

"Are you always this organized?" he teased.

She chuckled at the grin on his face. "Running a Café takes a whole lot of organization. So, yes. I carry a small notebook and a pen with me in my purse at all times in case I need to jot something down."

"Okay, then. Let's go. You know your way around a kitchen far better than I do. Let's get some essentials and look around for other stuff. Pretend I don't have anything in the kitchen. If it means upgrading the few things I do have, that'll be good."

Crystal rubbed her hands together playfully with exaggerated eagerness. "Okay, let's go."

The first place she took him was to the Le Creuset Outlet Store. "You certainly will want to pick up a few pieces here. They have some color collections. Tell me what you like and what pots, pans, casseroles, and other items you might like, and I'll make a note of it."

After looking at several items and marking them down, they decided to try the Crate & Barrel Outlet.

Crystal pulled out of the parking lot onto Route One and headed north to reach the location of the store, which was on the opposite side of the road.

She put on her right blinker and slowed to make the turn when a small truck traveling much too fast came barreling toward them. She held onto the wheel, braced herself, and called a warning to Emmett.

CHAPTER EIGHT

THE IMPACT OF THE COLLISION sent the car flying before coming to a stop on the verge.

Crystal heard the sound of glass breaking. Dazed, she groaned and rubbed the

back of her neck, feeling disoriented. She glanced at Emmett and held in a scream.

Still strapped in, his body hung forward. When he lifted his head and turned to look at her, blood dripped down his face.

"Oh, my God! You're hurt!" She stretched and reached out to him, then unbuckled herself.

"I think my nose is broken and I've got a gash in my forehead," he said more calmly than she would have. "I need a cloth to stop the flow."

Crystal found her purse on the floor and took out a cloth handkerchief she'd bought at the Summer Faire one year. She'd chided herself in the past for carrying too much in her purse but now she was glad she did.

She handed it to him. "Stay there. I'm getting out and will come around to your side of the car to see what I can do to help. It looks like you may have shards of glass in your face. Be careful."

She climbed out and stood a moment, weaving back and forth on unsteady legs. She heard a siren, and a police car drove toward her.

The driver of the truck was standing by the smashed front of it, looking scared. She guessed he wasn't more than eighteen.

A policeman pulled up next to her and got out, talking on his mic.

"My passenger has been injured. He needs help," she said.

"Okay. What happened," he said, walking toward the passenger side of Crystal's car.

"That teenager hit the side of my car as I was turning. He was driving too fast to stop," she said, her voice quaking.

"Okay. Let's see about your passenger."

She watched helplessly as the policeman struggled to open the battered passenger door. The window was mostly gone, with bits of glass everywhere, including some in Emmett's face. She realized he must have turned to see what was happening, making his face vulnerable, even with his air bag.

"I think we'd better get you to the hospital," the policeman told Emmett. "The closest one is Portsmouth Regional Hospital."

"I'm a doctor," said Emmett. "I'm going to need some help with my face and my nose." He turned to Crystal. "How are you?"

"I'm sore from the jolt, but I think I'm fine," Crystal said. "My seat belt and the air bag saved me."

"Can someone take us to the hospital?" said Emmett.

"I need to take a report, and that's going to take time. Can you wait?"

"Yes. I'll stay seated in the car." He turned to her." I think you'd better sit down for the interview. I'm concerned you may have suffered whiplash."

"I'm going to call AAA. Hopefully, they can tow the car to the closest Toyota dealership where an insurance adjuster can look at it," said Crystal.

The teen approached. "I've got my insurance information here. Can you give me yours?" He looked from Crystal to Emmett and sighed. "I'm sorry. I really am. But you turned awfully fast."

"I wasn't the one going too fast," said Crystal firmly, and the young man gazed down and shuffled his feet.

Crystal glanced at his truck. It had suffered a lot of damage too.

"My Dad is going to kill me," said the young man, and for a moment, Crystal felt sorry for him.

Then her anger flared. "You were driving too fast on a road where cars constantly enter and leave. What were you thinking?"

He studied her, and Crystal realized his eyes were glassy. Holding back her fury, she decided to leave him to the policeman, who was inspecting his driver's license.

Crystal patiently went over the report with the policeman. Another officer was writing up a report with the teenager.

A firetruck pulled up beside them, behind the truck.

"What are they doing here?" asked Crystal.

"Just making sure there's not going to be anything explosive happening with his motor," the policeman answered. "The front of his truck got smashed. Your car is not in danger of that."

Traffic had quickly backed up as the road narrowed down to one lane. A policewoman who'd arrived in the second car was directing traffic.

Another police car drove up, along with an EMT truck.

An EMT walked over to them as Emmett stood, holding the handkerchief to his forehead. Chips of glass fell to the ground around him.

"I'm a doctor," said Emmett. "I think my nose is broken, and I've got cuts on my face. The gash on my forehead isn't deep, just bloody."

The EMT ran back to the truck and returned with a white cloth to stem the flow of blood and a bag of equipment. "I'm going to take your blood pressure and check for other injuries. Let's move around to the other side of the car. You can sit in the back."

"My date was driving and says she's fine, but I suspect she might have a bit of a whiplash because she's complained of a sore neck," Emmett explained.

The EMT glanced at Crystal. "We'll check her out. I think it's best to get you, sir, to a hospital to have your face and nose checked. The nearest hospital is in Portsmouth. We can take you there."

"No sirens or fuss," Emmett said.

The EMT studied Crystal. "How are you doing?"

"I'm shook up, but okay," she answered honestly. "It's Emmett I'm worried about."

"That's an unusual name," the EMT said to him. "Are you Emmett Chambers, the new doctor at Lilac Lake?"

Emmett appeared surprised. "Yes."

"I've heard excellent things about you. C'mon, let's take a careful look at you, and then, when you guys are ready, we'll drive you to Portsmouth Regional. They've got a good ER team there."

A tow truck with the AAA logo on it pulled onto the verge across the road. He got out and made his way through stopped traffic to her.

Crystal explained that she wanted her car towed to the car dealership in Portsmouth. After taking care of the paperwork, she called her insurance agent, who was able to confirm that they'd pay a portion of renting a replacement car until hers was either repaired or declared a total loss.

She got permission from a policeman to leave the scene with Emmett, and she joined him as he conversed with the two EMTs.

"I'm ready," she told Emmett. "I want to ride with you to

the hospital to make sure you're all right."

"I'll drive," said one of the EMTs.

"I'll get in the back of the ambulance with the two of you," said the other. "We have to keep an eye on you both until we deliver you to the ER at Portsmouth Regional Hospital."

"Of course," said Emmett. "A required policy." He stood, and Crystal watched as more broken glass rolled off his clothing and fell to the ground.

One of the EMTs tried to make sure Emmett's clothing was free of the glass and then assisted him to the ambulance. As Crystal took Emmett's other arm, she noticed a television crew filming the scene.

"Guess you made the news," said one of the EMTs. He helped them into the back of the ambulance and took a seat in a chair opposite Emmett and Crystal sitting on a bench-shaped container that held supplies.

The ambulance pulled away from the accident scene.

At the memory of the truck hurtling toward them, a tremor shook Crystal's body. She couldn't control the shivering as she thought of what could have happened to them.

Beside her, Emmett was aware that she was trying to hold it together and clasped her hand for support.

"I'm sorry," she told him. "I saw the truck coming but wasn't able to do anything but warn you to hang on as it hit us."

Emmett squeezed her fingers. "It was an accident. That kid shouldn't have been driving so fast. We were stuck with nowhere to go. Don't blame yourself."

"But your face, your nose... Thank God, you didn't get glass in your eyes."

"I have a feeling I'm going to have a couple of black eyes because of the injury to my nose. If that's the worst of it, I consider myself lucky." He studied her. "How are you?"

"Okay. I'm starting to get a little stiff but nothing serious. It was a big jolt."

"Yes, you might have to take it easy for the next couple of days," he said.

She didn't respond. She knew she'd be needed in the Café, just as Emmett would be required to be in his medical office.

The EMTs delivered them to the emergency room at the hospital and bid them goodbye.

A doctor checked her over, quickly concluding with her that she was okay, but that she might get a headache, and if it got bad, she'd need to be seen by a doctor again for possible medication.

She left Emmett in his cubicle and went outside to make some calls. After informing her insurance company where the car was being towed and requesting the insurance adjuster to inspect it there, she got more details on the procedure for renting a car. Then she called the dealership and spoke to the manager. He agreed to handle the insurance company on a rental for her and said he'd have one ready to go.

Sighing with relief, shaking her head at what had happened, she made her way inside to check on Emmett.

He was sitting up on a gurney, talking to the doctor. He turned and smiled crookedly at Crystal. His nose had been taped into place. His facial cuts had been treated. Most were left as they were, but a couple were covered by small pads taped to the skin.

"This ENT specialist says my nose is going to be fine. He barely had to realign it and taped it just to help keep the position secure for the next couple of days. It looks worse than it is."

"You'll be a prime example of quality care for your patients," said Crystal, standing by as the ENT doctor helped

Emmett off the gurney.

She took hold of his arm. "I've got everything arranged. We'll take an Uber to the dealership and pick up a rental car there. I'm anxious to get you home to give you time to rest. I know how busy you are." She caught the edge of her lip between her teeth and fought tears. "I'm sorry this happened."

"That stretch of road by the outlets can get very busy," said the doctor.

"It's not your fault, Crystal," said Emmett. He shook hands with the ENT doctor. "Thanks for seeing me so quickly."

"I'm glad I was in the hospital and able to help." He bobbed his head at Crystal and left.

In the reception area, Crystal called an Uber driver and shortly after, a driver pulled up to the ER entrance.

As they made their way to the dealership, Crystal and Emmett were quiet. Crystal didn't know what he was thinking, but she was reflecting on how lucky they were that it hadn't been worse. Still, she'd never forget her helplessness at the sight of that truck coming at them.

CHAPTER NINE

AFTER TAKING CARE of all the necessary paperwork at the dealership, Crystal climbed behind the wheel of her rented RAV4 and waited for Emmett to get comfortable in the passenger seat.

"Are you sure you don't mind me driving?" Crystal asked.

"Not at all." He waved away her concern. "You know where we're going, and I don't think it would be wise for me to drive. I was given some pain medication. Besides, you need to do it, sort of like getting back on a horse after you've fallen off."

"I'm glad you feel that way."

They headed back home in a much different spirit from when they'd started. Crystal had removed all her personal belongings from her car and noticed the cooler in the back seat. "How about a cookie?" she asked him.

"That sounds delicious." Emmett got them out of the cooler, and they enjoyed them as they headed back to Lilac Lake.

At one point, a truck followed behind them. Though she told herself it was no problem, she gripped the steering wheel hard. And when the truck gunned its engine and pulled up beside her to pass, she felt a trickle of sweat roll down her cheek.

"It's okay," said Emmett with a soothing voice. "It may take a while for you to forget it."

"I just felt so helpless," she said. "And I didn't want you, or me, to get hurt."

"We're lucky," he said. "And you're doing fine driving."

Crystal let out a long sigh and told herself to be strong.

As she pulled into town, she turned to Emmett. "Are you going to be okay? If you think you shouldn't be alone, you're welcome to stay in my guest room tonight," said Crystal.

"I'll be fine. Besides, everyone will find out we were together in the accident. No need to let them think it's more than being friends."

"You're right," Crystal said. "They'll gossip about us anyway until we put an end to it."

She continued driving to his house.

Crystal pulled into his driveway and turned to Emmett. Much to her embarrassment, her eyes filled with threatening tears. "I was having a wonderful time until the accident happened."

He cupped her cheek with his hand. "I like you, Crystal, and want to get to know you better. I appreciate the day we've had together and don't want it to end this way. Right now, I've got a lot of work to do to get both the house and the practice under control. But when the time is right, I hope we can go back to our lunch and dinner arrangement."

Crystal gazed into those beautiful eyes of his, too emotional to speak. She watched as he climbed out of the car and entered his house.

After he'd waved and gone inside, she drove to her apartment reminding herself that she and Emmett were just friends who'd had a tough, but lucky day.

The next morning, she was busy working when Whitney came into the Café with the baby. "Are you alright?" She studied her. "I came to check on you. You and Emmett made the news."

"What on earth are you talking about?"

"Your fender bender made the area news. It showed a video

of your car and you and Emmett talking to EMTs. It was all part of an ongoing discussion about how to slow down the traffic on Route 1."

Crystal sighed and shook her head. "It was an accident I'm still trying to forget. A truck was coming too fast as I was turning. It was awful. Emmett has cuts on his face and a broken nose from the impact. I feel very bad about it."

"And you?" Whitney studied her.

"My back and neck are sore, and I have a headache but nothing beyond that. It could've been much worse. Glass could have gotten into Emmett's eyes. As it is, he's probably going to have black eyes, and his nose is taped in place for a couple of days."

"Poor guy. I hope he's better soon."

"Me, too. But, Whitney, everyone is going to make more of it than it is."

"They probably will, but you can't let that rattle you. Only the two of you know what's happening. If you want to talk to me about it, you know I'm here for you."

"Thanks." Crystal didn't want Whitney to know how confused she felt. Emmett's goodbye had seemed like a brush-off. But she didn't want a real love relationship with him, did she? Isn't that idea what made her feel safe with him? The thought that he wanted nothing more than friendship from her.

As the Café filled with customers, the locals asked her about the accident. Through the front window, she could see Bob Bullard crossing the street to her.

"How are you, Crystal?" he asked, stepping inside the Café. "I had to see the doctor about that cut on my hand, and Doc Chambers looked in bad shape. He said it was all minor stuff, but I had to be sure you were all right. You and our Sarah have always been good friends."

Tears sprang to Crystal's eyes. It was this kind of caring that had helped her sister and her through their childhood and adolescent years. "I'm fine. Just a bit shaken."

"Glad to hear it. I was surprised to see the accident on the news. It must've been a slow news day. But I'm glad I did. If you need any help with anything, you know I'm here."

"Thanks. I appreciate it." Crystal gave Bob a quick hug and then turned to business as Bob sat on a stool at the kitchen bar. "What can I get you?"

He ordered breakfast, and the day continued to be busy with visitors and locals alike. Crystal hid her impatience with everyone's questions and comments about the accident and the fact that she was with Emmett. All this caring and curiosity was part of living in a small town, and she was as determined as they to stay abreast of town news.

By the time four o'clock arrived, the headache that had kept her company all day flared. Asking her staff to follow through on the closing procedures, she went up to her apartment to lie down. She'd sleep for a while and then make sure everything was done for the day, and they were ready to begin all over again.

She was resting on her couch when her cell rang. She decided to let it ring unanswered and then thought better of it. When she lifted her phone, she was happy to see it was Emmett.

"Hello," she said sleepily. "How are you managing today?"

"Okay, though the office has been packed. Some with real problems. Others with curiosity. I feel like a celebrity. I'll have to get hints on how to handle it from Whitney. But I called to check on you. Any unusual soreness to your head, neck, and back?"

"I'm sore but nothing unexpected," she said. "Like you, though, I've had to cope with more than just doing my job.

Everyone has apparently seen the report on the news or has heard about it. I'm just taking a rest before making sure we're set for tomorrow. It's a good thing I have a well-trained staff. They've been wonderful."

"I feel the same about Lucille. She's terrific. While names are just that on paper, she gives me all the details about the people themselves. It's very helpful when you're trying to get to know them and build rapport. She must know every little thing about anyone in town."

Crystal laughed. "That doesn't surprise me."

"I'm glad you feel better," said Emmett. "Maybe after all this excitement dies down, you'll allow me to take you to dinner. Somewhere casual. I hear *Fresh* has excellent food. How about tomorrow night?"

"Yes, they have delicious farm-to-table meals. I'm looking forward to it."

"Great. I'll pick you up at seven." He hung up and she couldn't help smiling. Even if neither one of them wanted anything beyond friendship, she enjoyed being with him.

Feeling better, she got up and went downstairs to the Café. The crew had done a nice job of cleaning up and refreshing the tables for tomorrow morning. As usual, she prepared the daily financials and deposited the day's receipts at the bank.

The evening was pleasantly cool, and she decided to go to Jake's to see who, if anyone, in her crowd was there. She and her friends had a tacit understanding that if anyone showed up for drinks and supper, they'd sit at their special table and save places for the others.

When she entered Jake's, she stopped for a moment to get accustomed to the darkened interior. She glanced at two middle-aged women sitting at a table at the far end of the room and turned to see David Graham, who owned Graham

Landscaping with his father.

Smiling, she waved and walked over to him.

A good-looking man with deep-blue eyes and reddish-brown hair that had natural streaks of blond from the sun, David was a quiet man who loved a good joke. Fun company for a night like this. He stood, like the gentleman he was.

She sat down at the table with him. Soon after she ordered a pilsner ale and a grilled chicken sandwich, Aaron Collister joined them. With a Native American mother, Aaron's coloring was a warm brown, and his features were strong. Crystal had always thought he was handsome and admired his love of the outdoors. He and David greeted each other warmly. They were close friends and enjoyed hunting together.

She was laughing at a joke David had just told when one of the women who'd been sitting at the other end of the room walked over to her.

"Aren't you the person who was in the recent accident with Emmett Chamberlain?" The woman was tall and imposing with a domineering air about her. Maybe it was her expensive clothes, her jewels, and the look of disdain on her face, but Crystal felt herself shrinking.

"Do you mean Emmett Chambers?" was the only response Crystal thought to say.

"No. I mean Emmett Chamberlain, son of Senator Everett Chamberlain," the woman snapped.

As Crystal gasped, Aaron got to his feet. "Do you have a problem?"

"I just want to tell this woman with the godawful purple hair she has no business being with my son. I'll make that very clear to him, as well."

Everett Chamberlain? The Senator? Crystal was still trying to process the information that sweet, kind Emmett was the son of such a rich, controlling man when Emmett walked into the restaurant.

His face fell when he saw them. He hurried over and turned to his mother. "What are you doing here?" He shot Crystal a look of concern.

His mother glared at him. "After watching the news on television, I had to come see you, to warn you against a gold digger like this woman. You know we must be careful about that. Just look at you. Your face is a disaster."

Crystal gazed at Emmett, unable to hide her hurt and dismay. "No wonder you never wanted to talk about your family."

"Look, Crystal, don't let this meeting come between ... us ... our friendship."

The other woman Crystal had seen earlier joined them. She put an arm around Emmett. "I told Natalie not to come. That's why I'm here with her."

"Hi, Aunt Margaret," said Emmett. "We need to leave now. We can talk elsewhere." He turned to Crystal. "I'm sorry. I really am."

After Emmett hustled his mother and aunt out, Crystal took deep breaths.

"What a bitch!" said David, rising and putting an arm around her.

"No wonder Emmett changed his name," said Aaron in a firm voice that held disgust. "Being the son of Everett Chamberlain would be difficult at best. He's not considered a decent man by many. Too self-centered, too manipulative."

"Some people say he bought his senate seat. God knows he can afford it," said David.

Crystal studied them. "Emmett should have told us. I would never have spent a day with him if I'd known who he is."

"And that would be fair to Emmett?" asked Aaron, giving

her a steady gaze.

Crystal looked away, knowing Aaron was right. She'd been judged by many for her background and the way she appeared with purple hair. Why should he be judged because of his parents?

She turned back to Aaron. "No, it wouldn't be fair. Especially from me. He's a great guy who's already becoming a member of Lilac Lake. I don't want to ruin that for him."

Crystal neglected her sandwich and stood. "It's been a long day. I think I'll go home."

"Are you sure?" David asked, giving her a worried look.

Crystal nodded, and before her emotions could take over, she quickly left Jake's.

Crystal entered her apartment and went to the bathroom to get a cold, wet washcloth for her face. Her cheeks were still aflame from the humiliation of Natalie Chamberlain's words.

In the past, she'd struggled to be accepted for who she was as a person, not as the daughter of the town drunk. Though she sympathized with Emmett's situation, she knew any hope of being more than friends with him was gone forever.

She started to cry and blindly reached for the cooling cloth. Maybe it was time to get rid of the purple hair. She'd dyed it shortly after her mother died, to remind herself and everyone else that though she might look like her mother, she was not like her at all. She'd always thought changing her hair color to something fun was a sign she'd moved on from the past and had started a new chapter in her life where she'd be safe from the likes of men who'd been with her mother. Her friends understood.

A knock on the door awakened Crystal. She sat up on the

living room couch and gazed around sleepily. She checked her watch. It was ten o'clock.

The knock sounded again. "Crystal, it's Emmett. Open up. I need to talk to you."

Crystal hesitated and then told herself not to be a coward. It was best to settle the situation between them.

She went over to the door and cracked it open.

Emmett stood there looking silly with the tape across his nose. But his eyes seemed haunted.

She pulled back, opened the door, and stood aside.

He stepped inside, took both of her shoulders in his hands, and gave her a steady look through eyes circled with black. "I'm sorry, Crystal. I didn't know she was coming to town."

"But the news would still be the same." She studied him. "You didn't trust me with the truth? It normally doesn't matter to me who your family is. Now, From the beginning, I had this weird feeling you were hiding something. Now, I know."

"You know nothing. I'm not even Everett Chamberlain's real son. He adopted me when he married my mother when I was four. It was a heart-warming piece, making positive news for him, nothing more than a PR move."

"There are advantages to that name if you want them. But when I turned eighteen, I decided to change my name to Chambers. Close enough to Chamberlain to appease my mother, though she was furious with me. I wanted to be my own person, attend college and medical school with my new name independently."

"And how has that worked for you?" she asked.

"Pretty well. I stay away from political discussions and out of the news."

"Until our accident. Even then, you didn't tell me the truth about you and your family," said Crystal, trying to hide her hurt.

"I was hoping I could tell you in my own way, in my own time. Having my mother here, acting like that, is the worst way I can think of. Crystal, I like you a lot. I hope we can still be friends because, like you, I need them."

Crystal let out a long sigh, acknowledging the truth. They both needed friendship until the right person came along for something deeper. "I won't let this stop us from being friends. But that's as far as it goes. I'm sorry you felt you couldn't tell me the truth. Someday I'd like to hear it. All of it."

"Deal," Emmett said. He held out his hand and Crystal took it, telling herself the shot of electricity his clasp gave her was nothing more than her overactive imagination.

"Where's your mother now?" Crystal asked.

"She's staying at the Lilac Lake Inn, then she and Aunt Margaret are heading back to Mt. Desert tomorrow."

Crystal knew Mt. Desert was an island off the coast of Maine that was, for the most part, an enclave for privileged families of wealth.

"No need to worry. I don't think she'll be spending more time in Lilac Lake. I told her that if she bothered you again, she'd be sorry, that I knew a few newspeople to contact should it become necessary." Emmett shook his head. "It would be bad press for her, and she and my father won't tolerate that."

"I'm sorry I made the accident worse for you by bringing in family issues. You're embarrassed by them for different reasons than I had with my mother. Still, I know it hurts."

Emmett cupped her cheek in his hand. "Thank you. You're such a treasure, Crystal."

She looked away from him, suddenly shy.

"And don't change your hair color. It suits you," he said before lowering his hand. "So, I'll see you tomorrow?"

"Of course. You know where to find me."

"I'll come for coffee before the office opens. I want to make sure everyone understands that my mother's visit changes nothing."

"Okay," she said, walking him to the door, and stepping back.

He gave her a wave and left.

Still not hungry, Crystal switched off the lights and headed to her bedroom.

CHAPTER TEN

THE NEXT MORNING, true to his word, Emmett showed up in the Café as Crystal was chatting with Rich Robinson, a local dentist. His nephew, Dirk McArthur, was arriving in the next day or two to help him with the practice after graduating from dental school.

Crystal introduced Emmett to him and while they chatted, she welcomed a gathering of customers to the Café. It was easy to tell who the new people in town were by the way they paused at the entryway or stared at her hair. After the last couple in the group was seated, Crystal returned to the kitchen to help with the sudden rush.

Crystal had hired a hard-working, reliable kitchen staff by offering flexible hours, and an opportunity for mothers who had to see their children off to school before handling prep work for the lunch shift. Now, in summer, it took a little more juggling, but everyone on the staff cooperated knowing how hard it was for some to handle mom duties as well as work. Still, there were plenty of times she was needed in the kitchen.

When she was finally able to take a break, Emmett was gone. It was just as well she told herself. After tossing and turning in bed all night, she'd decided to spend as little time with him as possible.

During the quieter, mid-morning time, Whitney appeared in the Café alone.

"Where's the baby?" Crystal asked.

Whitney did a little happy dance, then became serious. "I'm out on my own, taking a break. I wanted to talk to you privately. I heard the story about Emmett's mother making a scene at Jake's. I wanted to be sure you're alright."

Crystal grimaced. "I'm trying to put everything in perspective. Having seen his mother just briefly, I can understand why Emmett wanted to change his name to save his identity. His mother was very unpleasant, and we've all heard tales about his father. He's among the worst of the notorious politicians for various reasons."

"Yes, his reputation is awful," agreed Whitney. "I know someone who lives on Mt. Desert and is acquainted with the family. She feels sorry for Emmett's mother for the way her husband treats her but says that Natalie has become impossibly overbearing and rude. Especially after having a few drinks."

"Yes, I can attest to that," said Crystal. "She certainly didn't like me or my purple hair."

"She doesn't know you or she'd know why such a thing as your hair doesn't matter to friends. I know why you color it and believe it's your right to wear it any way you like. Really, making your hair an issue is ridiculous."

"Ah, but people everywhere are judged for things they can't change. That's why I've decided not to change it." She patted her soft curls. By keeping her hair colored, she'd always felt known in a different way from her childhood.

"I love you," said Whitney, throwing her arms around her. "You're so strong."

"Not as strong as you think, but I'm trying," said Crystal, hugging her back.

"Okay, meet Nick and me for dinner at Jake's, our treat," said Whitney. "I think it's important that everyone knows you're not going to let that scene prevent you from enjoying yourself."

Crystal held up her hand for a high-five and Whitney

clapped it.

"Thatta girl," said Whitney, "now how about a cup of coffee before I head back home."

Crystal signaled a waitress who came right over to them with a coffee pot. "This one's on me."

Whitney laughed. "I'll take it."

As the time drew near, Crystal wondered if Emmett would place a lunch order. When he didn't, she figured that particular part of their friendship was over. No lunches. No dinners.

She got through the rest of the afternoon by concentrating on the business at hand, though she was trying to come to terms with the end of a friendship that she'd thought was special.

When the time came for her to go to Jake's, she was more than ready for a break and a chance to be with long-time friends.

As soon as she stepped into the bar, someone called her name. She turned to find Nick and Whitney sitting with Brooks Beckman, one of the owners of Beckman Lumber, with a red-haired man and a blonde she didn't recognize.

She walked over to them, and the three men stood as Nick made introductions. The redhead was Dirk McArthur, who'd arrived in town to help with his uncle's dental practice. The regal-looking woman with him was his younger sister, Diana. Both greeted her with ready smiles.

Crystal sat next to Dirk. "I'm happy that you're here to help your uncle. Dr. Robinson is busier than ever as our little town grows."

"He encouraged me to go into dental studies, and I figure I owe him for that. I'm here on a trial basis. After a year, if I choose not to stay, there'll be no hard feelings."

"I hope you're able to enjoy the area in both our summer and winter weather. There's a lot to do," she said.

"Oh, I know. I used to come to Uncle Bob's cabin during Christmas vacations to ski."

"That's why he was never part of our summer groups," said Nick.

"I went to summer camp in Maine and then did some traveling abroad," Dirk explained.

"Our mother and stepfather have a part-time home in Italy," said Diana. "Dirk and I have spent summers there for the last several years."

"That sounds lovely," said Crystal. "All that food, wine, and cheese ... well, you know what I'm talking about."

"You'd love that," said Whitney. "You ought to take a vacation there, Crystal."

"I'd have to find someone to run the Café," said Crystal. "But maybe someday ..."

Emmett entered the bar and waved to them.

Diana jumped out of her chair and ran to him with open arms. She stared at his face and then wrapped her arms around him.

Crystal watched as they hugged one another and then walked arm-in-arm toward them.

They stood before them smiling.

"I went to prep school with Emmett's cousin, Elise Chamberlain. When I heard he was living in Lilac Lake, I begged Dirk to let me ride along with him." She turned to Emmett. "You know I've always had a crush on you."

Emmett's ears turned red. "You were just a kid when I knew you."

"And now I'm not," she said.

He gazed at her and said, "Guess not."

"How are you doing, Doc?" said Nick, staring at his black

eyes and taped nose. "I was sorry to learn about the accident with Crystal. I'm glad it wasn't more serious. That stretch of road in Maine has had more fender benders than most."

Emmett glanced at her. "It wasn't Crystal's fault. It was just a stupid accident."

"Your nose is looking better," said Whitney. "Emmett, I don't think you've met Brooks Beckham yet. He and his brother Garth, along with their parents, own Beckman Lumber."

"I've heard of you," said Emmett. "Dani and Brad Collister are using your lumber for the renovation of my house."

While they shook hands, Diana said, "His house must be beautiful. Like all the family homes." Her eyes glistened with approval.

Crystal knew now why Emmett's mother had been furious with him for being with someone like her. Seeing Diana and hearing a bit about his family Crystal knew she and Emmett were a very unsuitable match.

"So, you're the owner of the Café in town?" Dirk said to her now.

"I am," said Crystal. "Have you been there? I don't recall seeing you."

"Not yet, but I will. Uncle Bob says it's the best in town."

Crystal laughed. "It's the only one in town, but I'll take it."

As they waited for a waitress to take their orders, Crystal tried to relax as Emmett and Diana chatted about mutual friends. On the other side of her, Whitney squeezed her arm. "Maybe we can catch up with a spa evening event. 'Body Bliss' is running evening specials, and I'd like to try it with you. My treat."

"That sounds lovely," said Crystal. There was a time when she would've fought someone wanting to pay for her, but she'd learned to graciously accept offers from close friends. She more than paid them back at the Café with service and food.

"I'd like to go too," said Diana overhearing them. "I'm starting to get a couple of lines around my eyes." She faced Emmett sitting next to her and lifted her face close to him.

Crystal didn't say anything, but Whitney couldn't hold back. "Those are laugh lines, silly. At your young age, that's about all you get. But I'd love to have you join us. The spa is new in town, and we're all loving it, especially in the summer when we don't have to fight the ski crowd to get in."

"Thanks," Diana said. "Sign me up."

"Maybe I should go into the spa business," teased Brooks.

Crystal chuckled. She knew how well Beckman Lumber was doing with no sign of stoppage ahead, in part because of all the media work Brooks was doing.

"How's the gift shop doing?" Whitney asked. "I bought several things there when my sisters and I were renovating Lilac Lake Cottage. Beth does a remarkable job deciding on her inventory. Everything is irresistible."

"The shop is doing well," Brooks replied. "Beth is talented. A great mom, too."

Deanna, their waitress came over to their table. "Is everyone ready to order?"

Whitney gave the newcomers her menu and Nick's and placed an order for a chicken Caesar salad and white wine. The others soon followed with their requests, leaving Crystal to place the last order. After working with food all day, she was picky about her choices. She chose a veggie pizza and a coke.

"Drinks are coming right up," said Deanna, who fluttered her eyelashes at Dirk.

After Deanna left, Brooks teased Dirk. "Deanna is available, in case you hadn't noticed."

Dirk grinned. "I got that impression." He glanced at Crystal. "How about you? Are you dating anyone special?"

Crystal didn't dare look at Emmett as she shook her head.

"With your hair, you two would look colorful together," said Diana to her brother.

As the others at the table chuckled, Crystal told herself maybe it was time to change her hair. First, she wanted to visit GG.

The rest of the evening passed pleasantly for Crystal, even though observing Diana and Emmett chat quietly together cut her with regret. But then, she realized Diana was someone Emmett's mother would approve of, not someone like her.

After eating and chatting for a while, Crystal rose. "I have to get up early. See you all tomorrow."

"I'll set something up at the spa. Maybe tomorrow," said Whitney getting a nod from Nick. Even though he had time off from work, his job entailed other obligations such as town meetings and community outreach. That meant working out time commitments together.

"Sounds doable," said Crystal, waving goodbye.

Back at her apartment, she studied herself in the mirror and realized it was time to take a giant step forward. She'd always had a voluptuous figure, and that, combined with blond hair, made her appear too much like her mother. She needed to present to the world the successful woman she was, and not be judged by something as superficial as hair color.

The next morning after the early rush, Crystal plated some of the molasses cookies GG loved and headed out to The Woodlands to see her. Diminutive in size, GG's spirit more than made up for it. Those light-blue eyes of hers missed nothing, and where there was a monetary need, GG was all too happy to step in. Few families in Lilac Lake hadn't received such kindness. Crystal and her sister would always be grateful to her.

When she pulled in front of the one-story, brown wooden structure, Crystal thought of GG's help in making sure that Aaron and Brad Collister's construction company received a chance to bid on the project. They'd won, getting their fledging business off to a successful start. They'd worked on the renovation of the Lilac Lake Inn and were now busy developing housing at the end of Lilac Lake.

When she went inside, she saw JoEllen Daniels, and though she said hello, she quickly moved by her and down the hallway to GG's room. Conversations with JoEllen were always unsettling because of the way the woman loved to put others down.

Crystal knocked on the door and opened it a crack.

GG was sitting on the couch reading. She looked up. "Crystal, dear, it's lovely to see you. And I see you brought treats."

"One of your favorites—molasses cookies," she said, carrying the plate of them over to her.

Giving her a broad smile, GG removed the foil and took one cookie, then two. "Thank you."

"Can I bring you something to drink with them?" Crystal asked.

"Be a dear and pour me some lemonade. There's a pitcher of it in the refrigerator. Help yourself to some."

Crystal went to the kitchen.

"I've got something I want to talk over with you," GG called to her.

Crystal reacted to the warmth in GG's voice. "Me, too. That's why I'm here. And to say hello."

She carried the lemonade over to GG, handed her a glass, and held onto the other as she took a seat on a nearby chair and faced her.

"You go first," said GG, before taking another bite of

cookie.

"It's about me and my hair. It's time for a change. Last night, Dirk McArthur and his sister, Diana, joined our group at Jake's. He's going to be Dr. Robinson's partner in the dental office, and Diana is here because of Emmett. She went to prep school with his cousin and has always had a crush on him."

GG focused her gaze on Crystal. "Go on."

"At one point, Diana said Dirk and I would be good together because of our hair colors. Hearing that comment was the final straw about being judged because of my hair. That got me thinking about changing to my natural blond to be better judged for who I am. Between Emmett's mother judging me for my purple and then Diana, I've decided it's time for me to learn to be comfortable with who I am. You alone know why I changed my hair color to begin with."

"Yes, I do," said GG solemnly. "Your mother's boyfriend almost got away with raping you. If you hadn't been strong, and he hadn't had too much to drink, it might've happened. That's when you chose to look different from her. At the time, it was important to do so. And then it became your signature look. But I like the idea of your being ready to make the change. You're a beautiful woman, Crystal."

"You know how much I hated my mother growing up. With help, I've learned to forgive her and to understand I'm not like her at all."

"Perhaps it's time to prove you've moved on. Is that what you came to hear?" said GG. "If it is, I can't tell you how proud I am of you. Your childhood wasn't easy. You raised your sister and fought to keep her safe, away from a lot of the turmoil." GG raised a hand to stop her. "I know a lot more about it than you might suspect."

Crystal drew a shaky breath and blinked back tears. She didn't allow herself too much time to think about those years, which is why being able to talk to GG was important. "So, you think I'm right?"

"Indeed, I do," said GG. "Now come give me that hug we both want."

Laughing and crying at the same time, Crystal went over to the couch and allowed GG to wrap her in a perfumed embrace.

When she sat up, Crystal said, "What did you want to talk to me about?"

"I heard about the incident with Emmett's mother at Jake's. You must have been humiliated. She's such an unhappy person. But that doesn't make it okay to be unkind to others."

"What do you mean?" Crystal asked, intrigued.

"Natalie Chamberlain comes from a modest background. She married Everett for prestige as much as his money. Instead of being grateful and using her resources for good, she's hurt a lot of people along the way by not following through on commitments she's made. Her husband has cheated on her so many times, it's not news anymore. She has every reason to be unhappy because of it, but she has no excuse for treating others badly."

"And you wanted me to know this because?" Crystal asked.

"Because no one should ever speak to you in such an awful way when they don't even know you. The real you," said GG with a tone of anger Crystal seldom had heard. "I was horrified to hear it. If she were here, I'd tell Natalie myself. I knew her back when she'd just married Everett. I know what she could've made of her life with him by serving others."

"Poor Emmett. No wonder he wanted to change his name. Everett isn't his birth father," said Crystal. "I wonder where he is."

"My understanding is that his father was killed in service to his country. Desert Storm, I believe. At least that's what I heard."

"Now that I've heard this story, I like Emmett even more," said Crystal. "Just as a friend," she quickly added.

"Oh, yes," said GG. "He's a man to admire."

Later, Crystal left The Woodlands, full of conviction that she was doing the right thing.

CHAPTER ELEVEN

THE NEXT DAY, Crystal waited until the Café was ready for the breakfast crowd and then left it to the care of her staff so she could be off on her secret mission to Boston. *High Styles* was the "in" hair salon in the Back Bay area. Missy Howell, a friend of hers from summer theater jobs in Maine, worked there and was squeezing her in for an appointment. She was as excited about the task as Crystal was nervous.

But when Crystal arrived at the upscale salon and saw some of the women with attractive hairdos, she relaxed. She knew she was doing the right thing, the healthy thing for her.

Missy emerged from one of the back rooms to greet her. "Crystal, I'm excited to see you. It's been almost a year since we worked together in Ogunquit at the summer theater. You look gorgeous as usual, but I'm going to make you look even better. The purple was cute but now it's time for a new you, like you said."

Crystal gave her a quick hug. "Thanks for doing this. As long as I was changing color, I wanted to change style too, and you're the best."

"Let's get you in a robe and we'll take care of the rest. I'm sorry we don't have time to fit in a mani-pedi."

"No worries," said Crystal. "I'm going to the spa with friends later this week. It was supposed to be tonight, but we had to change it. This will be perfect."

Almost three hours later, Crystal took a last look in the mirror, startled to see how the changes had given her an entirely different look. Gone was the funky, fun color and style of her tousled hair. In its place was a sleek blond look that made her appear much more sophisticated. It was something she'd get used to over time.

After paying, she gave Missy another hug. "Thanks. Let me know when you're in Ogunquit and I'll come see you. In the meantime, you know you always have a place to stay in Lilac Lake."

"Love you, girl," said Missy. "You look hot, hot, hot."

"Thanks," said Crystal, but she knew it would be a while before she was comfortable with such comments. Still, she'd done the right thing.

Driving home, Crystal tried not to look into the mirror, but she caught herself glancing at it more than she wanted. She resembled her mother when she'd been young before drugs and alcohol destroyed her beauty. But as GG had mentioned to Crystal many times, she and her mother were very different people. She wondered what her sister, Misty, would have to say about the new look.

Thinking of her sister, she realized it had been too long since they'd chatted. Crystal called Misty and left a message asking her to call back.

When she was driving through town, she easily passed by people who didn't recognize her new silver car or the blonde driving it. She liked the idea of starting fresh.

And then, when she walked into the Café's kitchen, she laughed when it took her staff a few seconds to recognize her.

"I love the new color," said a staff member.

"It suits you," another told her.

"Thanks," she said, wrapping an apron around her waist. "Now, let's get busy. The afternoon crowd will be showing up." Having sweets and something hot or cold had become a popular thing for both tourists and locals to do before the Café shut down for the day.

Whitney strolled inside the Café pushing a stroller and grinned when she saw Crystal. "Oh, my gosh! I talked to GG this morning and she mentioned you might have a surprise for us. I love it. This is how I remember you as a teenager before you had that big fight with your mother."

"GG and I discussed my hair issue and she encouraged me to change it. That and all the bad talk about my purple hair. As shallow as it was, that talk made me think about making some changes. Last night, I left a message for my sister to call me. It's been too long since I've heard from her."

"Is Misty still living in Florida?" Whitney asked, motioning for Crystal to turn around. Nodding with approval, she said, "You are beautiful. Much prettier than Diana."

At the knowing look Whitney gave her, Crystal laughed. "Okay, one of the reasons for changing was that I wanted to be seen as the person I've become. Not the one in high school."

Whitney gave her a hug. "No matter what, you're my best friend and always will be. Meet me at Jake's tonight for an early supper. I can't stay long but I want to see everyone's reaction to the new you. Especially from a couple of the guys we know."

"That's another change. I don't give a flying 'eff' what anyone else thinks. I'm me. Period."

"Good for you." Whitney turned as the baby began to cry. She picked him up and hugged him. "Tim is a little fussy today. That's why we're out for a walk."

"He's the cutest," said Crystal. "Let Auntie Crys hold him."

Whitney handed her the baby and a pang went through Crystal as he snuggled against her. Maybe she could do the parenting thing, after all. She was not her mother.

Customers came into the Café in three groups.

Crystal handed the baby back to Whitney. "Better go. See

you later."

"Is that a promise?" Whitney asked.

Crystal laughed. "Okay. I promise."

That night, Crystal waited as long as she could before going to Jake's. She'd made a promise and she intended to keep it, though she hated the idea of being judged.

Stepping inside the bar, she made her way to the large table in the corner, pleased to see Whitney, Nick, Dani, and Brad. Though friends might come and go, these meetings were important to her. Friends were family to her.

Nick gave her a thumbs up. "It's been years since I've seen you with this natural color and it looks great, Crystal."

"Thank you." She patted her hair self-consciously.

"Beautiful as always," said Dani. "But I liked the purple too. Why did you change it?"

Crystal sighed. This group of friends had always been honest with one another. "I realized I didn't have to make a statement anymore; I could just be myself."

Dani gave her a steady look. "I get it. Good for you. I think we've all made changes as we've grown."

"Speaking of changes," said Whitney. "I talked to Taylor earlier. Our baby sister has decided to spend some time in Lilac Lake to work on her latest book. She said she needs to have freedom from New York City to let her ideas flow."

"It'll be nice to see her, and I'm glad the cottage will be put to use," said Dani. "We've got to keep to our promise to use it at least six months of the year."

"Right," said Whitney. "Nick and I talked about moving there for the summer but with him being chief of police, we felt we should stay in town during the busiest time of year."

"Maybe you can move to the cottage in the fall," Dani said. "I'm willing to help out by staying there as needed, but you know how happy I am with our new home."

"It's a beautiful house," said Crystal. "And a perfect showcase for The Meadows."

"Yes, it's helped us sell a few homesites," said Brad with a note of well-deserved pride. The housing development he and his brother owned was becoming a very special place for those who could afford it.

"Speaking of sisters," said Whitney. "Did you hear back from Misty?"

Crystal shook her head. "It's not like her not to call."

Before the conversation could go further, Dirk, Diana, and Emmett arrived.

"Thought we'd find you here," said Emmett, his gaze sweeping the table. "I promised I'd help Dirk get to know the community."

"Emmett's house is going to be beautiful when it's completed," said Diana.

"Dani and Brad are part of the team," said Emmett and then made the introductions.

"Are you going to stay in town, Diana?" asked Dani. "You said you're here to see Emmett."

Diana shot Emmett a coy look. "I'm leaving in a couple of days, but I'm hoping to be asked back."

Emmett appeared surprised and then he smiled. "I'm sure Dirk would like to have his sister visit from time to time."

Diana playfully slapped at Emmett's arm. "That's not what I'm talking about, and you know it." Her gaze landed on Crystal. "Oh, my God! Crystal, is that you? I didn't recognize you. You look different ... very pretty."

"Crystal has always been beautiful," Emmett said in a quiet but firm way that sent a rush of heat through her. Though she was attractive, Crystal knew she wasn't beautiful. Still, his words meant so much to her she felt a sting of tears and quickly blinked them away.

Diana's gaze kept swinging back to Crystal throughout the evening. Determined not to show how uneasy that made her feel, Crystal tried to ignore her. She was well aware that Emmett's complimentary remark about her had caused Diana to be unhappy.

Nick and Whitney were the first to leave, just as Melissa Hendrickson, who worked for her parents' restaurant, arrived.

"Crystal, I love your hair. Very pretty," said Melissa.

"The chef is done cheffing?" teased Brad.

"Yes, it's an early crowd and I slipped out. I thought Ross and some of his friends were supposed to be back by now." She noticed Dirk and Diana. "Who are you? And, Crystal, I love your new do. Very pretty."

Dani introduced Dirk and his sister and commented, "You wouldn't know to look at her thin figure, but Melissa is a fantastic chef."

"Just one of the chefs at Fins, but thanks for the compliment, Dani. How are plans coming for the Summer Faire? I wasn't able to attend the last planning meeting."

"Neither was I. But we have time. The Faire won't happen for three more weeks," said Crystal. "This year, I'm in charge of the baking contest, and I'm adding a prize for school kids. We have some aspiring young chefs. I hope you'll be a judge, Melissa."

"Sure," said Melissa, taking a sip of the beer she'd ordered at the bar when she'd arrived.

"What is this Summer Faire?" asked Diana. "I want to come back for that."

"It's fun," said Dani. "There are games, contests, and celebrations. The stores go all out with souvenirs and specials."

"A great way to see this town," Brad told Dirk and Emmett.

"I can help you judge, Crystal," said Emmett.

"Excellent," said Crystal, both surprised and pleased.

"As a kid, I used to do some baking with our cook. To me, it's just like a chemistry test, but with delicious results," said Emmett. "But I know the difference between good and bad."

"Okay, deal," said Crystal. Emmett was full of surprises. She felt prickles on her skin remembering the look on his face when he'd announced she'd always been beautiful.

CHAPTER TWELVE

CRYSTAL WAS SLEEPING COMFORTABLY when she was awakened by pounding on the door. Startled, she sat up in bed.

"Open up," came a voice she recognized.

She hurried out of bed and to the door. Cracking it open, she peered out to make sure all was safe. "Misty! What are you doing here?" She stepped back. "Come on in, honey. Are you alright?"

"No, I need to hide," said Misty. "There was only one place I could think of where I knew I'd be safe." She squinted at Crystal. "What did you do to your hair?"

Crystal turned on the living room lights, glanced at her sister, and let out a gasp. "Oh, my darling! What happened to you?" She had a black eye and a bruise on her cheek.

"A bad boyfriend," said Misty, crying as Crystal wrapped her arms around her. "Can you believe it? I'm going to end up like our mother who was beaten up regularly."

"No, you're not," Crystal said, quietly, firmly. "Have a seat and let me get a careful look at you."

Wearing jeans and a T-shirt, Misty lowered herself on the couch and covered her face in her hands. "I should've ended it after the first time he hit me. But, Crystal, he seemed nice, and he came from a wealthy background. I thought I would be safe with him, that he'd take care of me."

"You're a strong woman, Misty. You don't need someone to take care of you. That's something that Mom thought she needed. You're much more courageous than that."

Misty lifted her face and Crystal caught her breath as she assessed the black eye and bruises marring Misty's pretty brown face. With one finger, she lightly traced Misty's cheek. "Where else did the bastard hit you?"

Misty caught her swollen lip. "I've got a few other bruises ..."

Crystal checked her clock. It was almost six. Emmett would be up or close to it. "I'm calling a friend. The new doctor in town. While it's quiet, I'll take you to see him without causing any embarrassment to you."

"I don't need ..." Misty began.

Crystal gave her a withering stare. "I'm not going to let this go. Can I get you a glass of water? Anything?"

Misty shook her head and began to cry. "I love you," she managed to get out.

"I love you, too, sis." She went into her bedroom and grabbed her cell, then quickly returned to the living room where she could keep an eye on Misty.

Emmett answered the phone sleepily. "Hi, Crystal. What's wrong?"

Crystal explained that she needed to bring her abused sister to him to be checked over.

Alert now, Emmett asked, "Is a hospital needed?"

"Not that I know of, but I want you to examine her. I'll take photos for any necessary legal records. I want to give Misty some privacy by coming to your practice early."

"Understood," said Emmett. "Come now. I'll meet you at the office."

"Thanks," said Crystal, holding in her emotions as memories of her mother in similar circumstances swirled around her. She thought of the times she'd protected her sister from being abused and now, here she was.

Crystal handed her sister a bottle of water and a couple of

cookies. "When did you last eat?"

Misty shrugged. "I got a couple of snacks on the road, though I didn't want to waste any time getting here."

"After we meet with the doctor, I'll fix you a nice hot meal at the Café," said Crystal leading Misty outside to her SUV.

On the drive through town to Emmett's practice, Crystal felt as if she was reliving her painful past. But determined not to show the horror she felt, she patted Misty's shoulder gently. "We'll sort this out. You know you're welcome to stay as long as you want."

"I brought my belongings from the apartment I share with my friend Maddie. She's out of town, but I trust her to pack anything I've left behind."

Crystal pulled up to the medical building and went around the back of the car to help Misty. She'd seen a few bruises on her arms but wanted to know the full extent of her injuries.

A light snapped on inside the building, and Emmett came to the door.

The concerned look that crossed his face seeing Misty brought a sting of tears to Crystal's eyes. He was such a decent man, a sympathetic doctor.

"Emmett, this is my sister, Misty. Misty, Dr. Chambers."

Emmett shook Misty's hand. "Hello, Misty. I'm here to help you in whatever way I can. Please come inside."

Misty stared at his bruised face but remained quiet.

"He and I were in an auto accident," explained Crystal. "I'll tell you about it later."

Emmett led them through the reception area and into an examination room. "I'll check your pulse and temperature and then get a look at those bruises. Want to tell me what happened?"

"My boyfriend got mad," mumbled Misty. She studied the floor.

"Does this happen often? His hitting you?" asked Emmett as he began taking her vitals.

Misty shook her head. "It just started a couple of weeks ago. He said he couldn't help it. But I know better. Two days ago, he hit me again. After he stormed off, I packed my things as quickly as I could and drove here."

"I believe I heard you live in Florida --

Misty lifted her face and cut him off. "Lived in Florida. No more. I won't go back."

Emmett and Crystal exchanged glances.

Crystal gave her a nod of approval. "Good for you, Misty. You know you have a home here with me for as long as you want."

"I know," Misty said softly. "You've always taken care of me."

"Heart, pulse, and temperature fine. Now, let's get that look at you," said Emmett. "Please strip down to your underwear and put on a robe. I'll leave the room and come back when you're ready."

He returned moments later. He studied Misty's face and gingerly touched the areas around the blackened eye and then the rest of her face. Her tan skin had grown darker from the sun in Florida, but even standing away from her, Crystal could see spots of bruising. Her stomach filled with acid.

Emmett softly spoke to Misty as he examined her torso. "Did he ever hurt you sexually?"

Misty shook her head and glanced at Crystal. "It's just like Mom all over again, huh."

"My mother used to get beaten by boyfriends," Crystal explained to Emmet and turned to Misty. "You're not the same. You were smart enough to get away, and you're not addicted to drugs and alcohol."

"My boyfriend never hit me sober. He always got angry

after he'd been drinking."

"Your mother was unable to get help for her addictions?" Emmett asked.

"She wouldn't accept it," said Crystal. "Believe me, I tried. She'd go on a binge and wake up not remembering anything. That's why Misty and I have two different unknown fathers. I was eight when Misty was born."

"And who took care of her?" Emmett asked, his expression neutral, though Crystal could tell from the tightening of his jaw he already knew the answer.

"Crystal has been like my mother," said Misty, her dark eyes shiny with tears.

"She was my baby in many respects. I loved Misty and cared for her. I didn't want her to be taken away from us by social workers," said Crystal. "I've always been her big sister watching out for her."

"That's very admirable of you," said Emmett as he checked the last of Misty's limbs. "Nothing is broken but it will take a while for your bruises to go away," he said to Misty. "Most are on your torso, and in checking you out, you don't appear to have any excessive pain in that area. Are you having any trouble with your teeth?"

Misty shook her head. "No, but if I'd stayed, I know things would've gotten worse. Like I said, it only happened twice before I took off. I knew enough to get away."

"I want to take photographs of your face and torso," Crystal said to Misty. She snapped a few from her cell phone while Emmett began typing information into his computer.

"What are you going to do from here?" Emmett asked, turning from his computer to Misty with a sympathetic expression.

"I'm staying with Crystal. I think I might want to live here for a while. It was great to leave Lilac Lake and be on my own, but maybe it's time for me to come home. I'm a very good teacher. I know schools are always looking for them."

"It sounds like a good plan." He stood. "There's nothing more to be done for you. You probably already know you'll be sore and stiff for a while. Take a light painkiller if necessary and get some rest. I know you'll have some excellent food from the Café."

"Thank you, Dr. Chambers. I appreciate your seeing me," said Misty, standing before him.

"Yes, Emmett, thank you. I wanted Misty to have some privacy before facing old friends. It was good of you to see her before your day has officially started. Want to come to the Café for breakfast? It's on me, of course."

Emmett grinned and checked his watch. "You know what? I've got time. I'll be right there."

Crystal and Misty got into her car and headed back to the Café.

"What is Emmett to you, anyway?" Misty asked her.

"He's a friend. Someone new in town," Crystal answered, trying not to give away her feelings for him.

Misty studied her. "Uh, huh. Just a friend? I saw the way you two were looking at one another."

"No matter what I think about him, it will come to nothing. His father is Senator Chamberlain, and his mother hated me before she even met me."

"Wow! I'll do anything to help you. I owe you big time. And I don't mean just for this," said Misty.

"We're sisters. We take care of one another. Like always." Crystal reached over and squeezed Misty's hand.

Misty nodded and gave her a shaky smile. "Like always."

CHAPTER THIRTEEN

CRYSTAL PULLED INTO HER PARKING SPOT behind the Café and indicated the outside door to her apartment. "If you need some time to yourself, feel free to go upstairs and get settled in my guest room, which is always reserved for you anytime you want ."

"Thanks. I think I will," said Misty. "I don't feel like facing anyone right now."

"I'll bring up a nice hot breakfast for you whenever you call," said Crystal. "But it's important for you to get some rest after two hard days of driving and everything else that's happened."

"Yes, I think I'll grab some orange juice and take a nap. I'm too upset to eat."

Crystal waited until her sister had climbed the stairs and walked inside her apartment before she went downstairs and entered the chaos of a busy kitchen. As soon as she could, she went into the dining room and sat at a small table opposite Emmett.

He was eating scrambled eggs and toast and regarded her with a smile. "How's Misty?"

"She's going to try to sleep for a while. Again, I thank you for seeing us and being very sensitive and kind to her. I had no idea that her new boyfriend was abusive."

"She was in Florida, and you were here," said Emmett, giving her a sympathetic look. "You can't keep her safe from everything. She's smart. She proved it by coming home to you. Some women would have tried to hide it. But Misty knew enough to end a bad situation right away."

"Growing up, we certainly had a good example of what not to do," said Crystal, making a face.

"I imagine you had to protect your sister from prejudice too."

"At times," said Crystal. "But Misty was as accepted as I, probably because living in a small town like this where everyone knows your business, means more acceptance. At least, that's been my experience. That doesn't mean I wasn't embarrassed by my mother and her problems. Sometimes, the kindness of strangers can make it seem even worse."

"How old were you when your mother died?" Emmett studied her.

"I was eighteen, thank God. That meant I was an adult who could take care of my sister. She was ten."

"And you got her through those rough teen years by yourself?" Emmett's eyes rounded with surprise.

"Not really. As I mentioned, others in town helped. GG, Whitney, Dani, and Taylor's grandmother, made sure we could go to college with financial help and scholarships. Others, like Edie Bullard, who owns the hardware store, and her daughter, Sarah, helped with nice hand-me-down clothing, along with the Gilford girls. A little help here, and a little there from people in town made it possible. It's one reason I never want to leave Lilac Lake. It, not my mother, made it home for us."

"That's unusual, but very nice," said Emmett.

"You've met a lot of my friends, but you'll meet more. Then you'll see for yourself," said Crystal. "Whitney and Dani's sister, Taylor, is a well-known author. She and her husband are coming here for the rest of the summer."

"I've heard stories about the Gilford girls," said Emmett. "It seems they were a nice part of past summers as you were all growing up. They're remarkable women."

"Yes, very special friends," said Crystal. "And whenever you visit The Woodlands, I hope you'll make it a point to stop in and see their grandmother GG, Eugenia Wittner as often as you can."

"Definitely," said Emmett. He checked his watch and rose. "Are you sure I can't pay for breakfast?"

"Positive," Crystal replied, standing, holding back a sudden urge to kiss him for all he'd done for Misty and her.

His gaze remained on her face, and she observed a tenderness enter the way he was looking at her before he turned away.

The usual morning crowd entered the Café, along with some tourists, and Crystal's attention was drawn to them. When she turned to give Emmett a wave, he was gone.

Later, during a brief lull, Crystal climbed the stairs to her apartment to check on Misty.

She went to the guest room and peered inside. Misty's full suitcases were open on the floor. Misty was asleep on the bed, wrapped in her favorite pink blanket atop the queen bed.

Crystal stared at her, her heart filling with love for the sister who was more like a daughter to her. Misty's long, straight, black hair fanned out across her white pillow. Though her eyes were puffy, it didn't take away from her short straight nose and the full lips that covered her white teeth.

As if sensing Crystal's presence, Misty stirred.

Crystal left the room and quietly closed the door behind her. Sleep would do Misty good.

That afternoon, Crystal held her first cooking class for middle schoolers who wanted to enter the Summer Faire baking contest. She was going to spend the next three days teaching them some basic lessons about baking as they made cookies, brownies, and finally, a cake. Twelve kids—nine girls and three boys—had signed up for the classes.

Misty entered the kitchen, which had closed for the day as Crystal was getting set up for the class.

"Need help?" Misty asked.

"Thanks. That would be nice." Crystal explained what she was doing, and Misty easily stepped in to assist her.

"Feels a little bit like old times," said Misty. "Remember how you used to teach me how to cook?"

"Yes, I wanted to be sure you could provide a healthy meal for yourself," Crystal said, giving her a tender hug.

"Maybe I can help you in the kitchen while I'm here," said Misty. "I can't just sit around and scrounge food and a place to stay without repaying you in some way."

Crystal studied her. "I've been thinking of hiring an assistant manager for the summer. Interested?"

"Yes. I'm thinking of staying here and applying for a teaching job in the area. Maybe even in Boston. I just want to be closer to you."

"Okay, then, I'm going to call the Ogunquit theater and tell them I'll take a supporting role in the traveling production of *Seven Brides for Seven Brothers*. It's going to play in Maine for eight nights in August."

"That'll work. I can take over for you while you're gone. Helping you will still give me time to prepare for a teaching job. It makes me happy to be able to help you." Misty smiled at her. "I remember how you loved the theater. A way for you to escape."

"Yes, it still is. Nothing like becoming someone else for a while." Crystal turned to the doorway as her cooking students arrived.

When all the kids had their special Café aprons on and stood in their assigned spaces at the long wooden table in the kitchen, Crystal introduced Misty and herself. She explained about the basic tools and supplies used in baking. She was especially glad to see Elise Sawyer in the group of children. She'd played the mouse in Whitney's first community play, and her mother, Pam, and father, Tyrone, were both schoolteachers. Maybe they could help Misty.

"Today, we'll make Chocolate Chip cookies. It's a basic recipe that you can change by adding more than chocolate chips or changing up the chips for something else. Not only is it important to follow the recipe with the right ingredients, it's important to bake them at the proper temperature. Fortunately, we have two large ovens to handle the cooking."

The recipe had been enlarged and posted on a blackboard hanging on the nearby wall.

As Misty read aloud the recipe, Crystal watched each child. Most were nodding their heads, comfortable with it. One girl and a boy seemed a little uncertain.

"Okay, let's get started. If at any time you've got questions, Misty and I will assist you. Don't be afraid to ask for help. We who work in the Café kitchen do it all the time."

She'd set the ingredients at each place. She was pleased to see how quickly the kids got to measuring and mixing. As she observed them, she was surprised by a sharp longing for a family of her own.

The cooking class became a real success when the bakers could taste their products. Watching them enjoy the fruits of their labors, Crystal couldn't hold back a little chuckle. Cookies warm from the oven were always special.

When parents came to the Café to pick up their children, Crystal sought out Pam. "I was hoping to see you. My sister is home and looking for a teaching position. I thought you might be able to point her in the right direction."

"Sure. We need teachers."

Before Crystal could answer, Misty approached them.

Crystal made the introductions and left them talking while she saw that all the children were being met.

As soon as she could, she went back to where Pam and Misty were still talking.

Pam smiled at Crystal. "I'm confident we can find a spot for Misty. I'll talk to my principal about it. We can always use more teachers in our system."

"Excellent," said Crystal, putting an arm around Misty. "Now that she's back home, I want to be sure she can stay."

"See?" Misty said to Pam.

They both laughed and then Pam said, "Once a big sister, always a big sister. I know because I am one myself."

"Oh, I don't mean to be pushy ..." Crystal began.

"What you're doing helping me is sweet," said Misty. "And I appreciate it."

"Nice to meet you, Misty," said Pam. "I'll message you with all the information you'll need to apply. One of my favorite lower-grade teachers has unexpectedly moved away for her husband's job."

"Perfect," said Misty.

Pam left and Misty turned to her. "Now, let's go have a taste of the cookies I made."

Crystal grinned. "They did look tempting." Though she worked with food all day, Crystal was careful about what she ate. She had no intention of giving in to all the tempting choices around her.

"Do you still meet the gang at Jake's a lot of evenings?" Misty asked her.

"Yes. At least to say hello. Why?"

"Because I want to join you tonight. Everyone might as well know why I'm back and that I intend to stay. It'll be easier that way."

"Okay. That's what we'll do," said Crystal, proud of the fact that Misty wasn't choosing to hide.

Walking into Jake's with her sister felt special to Crystal. Misty had always been someone who added to a group with her humor and kindness.

She glanced over at the regulars' table. Tonight, Dani and Brad were sitting with Dani's sister, Taylor, Ross Roberts, the retired baseball player, his friend, Mike Dawson, a former pro who taught tennis at his clinic in Florida, Dirk McArthur, and his sister, Diana.

"Lots of new people, I see," murmured Misty as they made their way to the table.

Taylor jumped to her feet and moved to hug Crystal. "Whitney told me you were going back to your natural blond. You look fantastic." She turned to Misty, studied the bruises on her face, and then hugged her. "I'm glad you're back in town."

"Thanks. Hi, everyone! For those of you who are new, I'm Misty Owen, Crystal's baby sister."

Ross introduced himself and Mike to her. Dirk stood, gave his name, offered her his chair, and went to get another one. Diana told Misty her name as she moved her chair over to accommodate room for one more.

Conversation was lively as Crystal and her sister sipped their sodas and then ordered dinner. Crystal was wondering what Emmett was doing when he showed up and took a seat in a chair beside her.

"How was the rest of your day?" she asked him quietly.

"Busy, but good. I'm getting to know more people. I had time to stop in at The Woodlands and was able to spend a few minutes with GG. I'll tell you about it later."

Though she was curious about it, she tuned into the

conversation between Mike and Misty. It turned out that they'd lived close to each other in Florida but had never met. She listened to Dirk talk about the rental property he'd found at one of the older lakeside estates. Once a carriage house, it was now a vacation rental that would become his residence until he found something more permanent.

"I like the property a lot, but, for now, it's just a rental. We'll see how I do in the dental practice with Uncle Bob and then I'll decide what I want to do," Dirk explained.

"It's nice that you're here. Everyone needs dental care at one time or another," said Taylor.

"Thanks. I'm hoping it works out," Dirk said.

Ross announced that he was going to start a sports program with Mike. "Mike will handle the tennis and I'll take care of the baseball program. We're talking about building an indoor tennis facility for year-round use."

"We can use it for high school programs, individual classes, and as an exercise facility," said Mike. "The people in this area are sports-minded, and this will give them the opportunity for a year-round facility."

"What about your training center in Florida?" asked Brad.

"I like the idea of having four seasons and living here," Mike said. "We were thinking of talking to Collister Construction to build what we want."

Brad grinned. "Aaron and I would like that."

"Speaking of Aaron ... where is he?" asked Taylor. "I was hoping to see him."

"He'll be along. We sold another house, and he wants to celebrate with us," said Dani. "Here he is now."

All eyes turned to the tall, dark-haired, handsome man strolling toward them. "Looks like a big group tonight. Glad to see it." Aaron's gaze rested on Misty. "You're back for a while?"

Misty nodded at him. "Back to stay."

"Good," he said, returning Misty's smile and then facing Diana with a questioning look.

Her eyelashes fluttering, Diana introduced herself to Aaron.

He nodded politely and spoke to Dirk and then Emmett before taking a seat next to Diana. "It's great to see more people here."

"I may stay here all summer," said Diana smiling at him.

"Nice," he said in a noncommittal way.

Sensing Diana's frustration with Aaron's lack of interest, Crystal couldn't help but be amused. True to the teachings of his mother, appearances meant little to him.

Taylor caught Crystal's eye and gave her a knowing wink.

As she and Misty were about to leave, Emmett said, "I'll walk you out. I've got an early day tomorrow."

Outside, Misty said, "If you don't mind, I'll go ahead. Thanks again, Dr. Chambers, er, Emmett, for taking care of me this morning."

"I'm here to help anytime, Misty."

After Misty walked away, Emmett turned to Crystal. "I'm happy to see Misty out and about. She's very courageous."

"I was pleased to see she wanted to face the world and not hide the abuse she's suffered. It's a very positive sign toward healing. In the past, we've talked to a psychologist about our family, and if I see a need for more visits, I'll remind Misty of that option."

Emmett studied her and then his expression softened and those unusual eyes of his, outlined with less bruising, seemed to flare with an even brighter turquoise. "I like you, Crystal. A lot."

"I feel the same way about you but realistically, we both know I'm not what you're looking for."

Emmett's back stiffened. "I don't know why you're saying that. I'll decide for myself."

Crystal laid a hand on his arm. "That's sweet of you, Emmett. But I don't want either of us to get hurt."

"I want to see you again. Can I give you a call? Spend another free day with you?"

Crystal sighed. "I want to do the right thing ..."

"Then say yes. You owe it to both of us to see where our friendship may take us." Before she could protest, he swept her in his arms and kissed her.

With his warm lips on hers, Crystal's pulse raced so hard she collapsed against him.

His hand caressed her back in loving circles as he kept kissing her.

Crystal felt her whole body go weak. She'd never been kissed like that before.

When they finally pulled apart, she gazed at him, speechless.

"That's the right thing," he said with satisfaction. "Shall I call you tomorrow and order lunch?"

"Okay," she said, still reeling from the sensations going through her like a freight train out of control.

When Crystal entered her apartment, Misty gave her an impish grin. "How's the doctor? Did he give your heart a checkup? The two of you were staring at one another each time I looked. It was very hot."

"I'm attracted to Emmett. More than I'd like, because there are many problems with our even dating. His family is just the start. You know as well as I that our backgrounds sometimes work against us. This is one of those times with a capital T."

"Okay, big sister, listen to me. You have no reason to be ashamed of yourself. You're an outstanding person who proves her success each day. You're beautiful and well-mannered. No fancy family can rightfully attack that. Maybe Emmett's family isn't up to our standards. Right?"

At the image of Emmett's mother being told she wasn't good enough, Crystal burst out laughing. Maybe Misty was right.

CHAPTER FOURTEEN

CRYSTAL LAY IN BED STARING at the ceiling both sad and happy. She couldn't deny her attraction to Emmett and loved that he was taking a stand and forcing her to face it. But what if they both ended up getting hurt? They had commitments to remain in this small town together. She recalled when she and Nick decided to divorce, they did so amicably and were comfortable staying in Lilac Lake regardless of their history. But still ...

By morning, Crystal decided to see where a friendship with Emmett would go. They were two independent people who had the right to choose their own destinies.

She let Misty sleep in and got ready for the day. Her summer business was what carried her through leaner times when weather and other factors affected her financial security.

Downstairs, she checked the Café's dining room to make sure all was in order, saw that the kitchen staff was prepping for the day, her inventory was up to date, and the wait staff was coming in.

She'd just opened the door for the 7 AM crowd when she saw Whitney pushing a stroller and waving at her.

Smiling, she waited for her to approach. "'Morning! You're bright and early."

"Timothy is up bright and early. Is it possible he might be starting to teethe already?"

Crystal laughed and shrugged. "You're asking the wrong person. What brings you here?"

"I wanted a cup of hot coffee and one of your blueberry scones. Anything to keep me going. I'm exhausted."

"Well, dear friend. Come inside. I'll see that you get them."

"That isn't the only reason I'm here," Whitney confessed. "Both Dani and Taylor called to tell me Misty is back in town. I'm so glad. What's the story?"

"Come in, have a seat, and the first moment I get, I'll sit with you for a few minutes."

Crystal loved this time of morning when customers came in seeking a tasty breakfast and a pleasant day to follow. People were either cheerful or quiet. Her staff had been trained to react to both.

After customers were seated and orders were placed, Crystal took a few minutes to spend with Whitney, who'd taken a quiet corner table in the back where they could have some privacy.

A waitress stopped by. "Would either of you care for anything?"

"I'll have coffee," said Crystal. "What would you like, Whitney?"

"I'd like another scone, but I'll have only a second cup of coffee." The waitress left and Whitney told Crystal, "I still have to watch what I eat. I never know when or if I'll be called upon to read for a part."

"I understand," Crystal said. Whitney had left acting for a while to enjoy her husband and baby and to get their marriage off to a solid start. But both she and Nick understood that if a very special role came along, Whitney would seriously consider it.

Whitney leaned forward. "Tell me why Misty is back and what's going on with her. Both of my sisters said she had bruises on her face. Is she okay?"

Crystal told Whitney the story of Misty leaving after being

abused for the second time. "Unfortunately, Misty knows from our mother's experiences that once a man begins to beat you, he won't stop. She was missing Lilac Lake and now wants to stay here. Pam Sawyer is going to help her find a teaching position."

"How nice of her," said Whitney. "Is Misty going to stay with you?"

The waitress came with their coffee and Crystal took a satisfying sip.

"Misty will stay with me for the time being. If she finds work here, I'm hoping she'll want to live on her own to give us both our privacy."

"Yes, especially now with you dating Emmett," said Whitney, giving her a knowing look.

"What? How do you know that?"

Whitney laughed. "Both Dani and Taylor said the two of you couldn't keep your eyes off one another. I like Emmett, and I'd like to see you happy with a family of your own. I know you're ready."

Crystal sighed. "I can't look at babies or kids and not want one. I don't know if it's hormones speaking or the fear that it might never happen. But I can't stop thinking about it, which is the reason dating Emmett is dangerous. Stupid, really. I want to find a husband, and his family would never approve of a marriage between us." Crystal peered up at Whitney with a sadness that ate at her. "You know I'm telling the truth."

Whitney shook her head firmly. "It doesn't have to be that way. Take it one step at a time and see where it leads. Love can overcome a lot of obstacles."

Crystal let out a snort. "You know what his mother is like. Everyone in town either saw or heard about her attack on me."

"And what did Emmett do? Stand by and let her carry on?" taunted Whitney.

Crystal shook her head. "No, he got her out of there. But what about his father? I heard he might be running for the Senate again. That would be the end of it for Emmett and me."

"Seems to me like you're projecting a whole lot of negative thoughts into what is otherwise a sweet scene. Two people simply wanting to date."

Crystal gazed at her friend's earnest expression. "You're right. I'm letting it get out of control in my mind. One step, one day at a time. Thanks for helping me put it in perspective." She rose, hugged Whitney, and left to check on the people sitting on the outside patio.

Late morning, Crystal received a call from Lucille Young in Emmett's office requesting a ham and cheese sandwich for Emmett.

Smiling and humming to herself, Crystal prepared the sandwich and fixings for him. Packing it into a bag with the Café's logo, she told the kitchen crew she'd be gone for a short time.

A few minutes later, she pulled into the parking area of the medical practice building and as instructed, drove around to the back and down the long driveway to Emmett's house. As she pulled to a stop beside two trucks from Collister Construction, she could see Emmett sitting on the bench on the dock staring out at the river.

She got out of her car and walked to the dock to meet him.

He seemed to sense her arrival and turned as she approached him.

"Hey, there. I'm glad to see you," he said, rising and kissing her cheek. "Because our time is limited, I figure this is the best way to see each other during the day."

She held up the bags she'd brought. "This way, I can make sure you have a decent lunch."

He laughed. "Okay. The best of both worlds." He accepted a bag from her and sat down to open it. "I've got about twenty minutes."

"Speaking of two worlds, I need to ask you one more time. Are we being foolish to begin dating seriously?" She hesitated, let out a long breath, and blurted, "What if we want more than friendship?"

He set down his sandwich and studied her. "Are you prepared for that? I've been hurt in the past and don't intend to rush into anything."

"That's just it. I don't want either of us to get hurt," she said.

"Well, then, let's go slowly, be honest with one another, and give each other a chance to see how we're both feeling. That's how I like to behave anyway."

Crystal studied Emmett. She admired him.

She sat down beside him, handed him a lemonade, and took one for herself. A cardinal trilled and she saw a flash of red as it flew among the trees lining the river. "The birdlife here is spectacular."

"Yes, as soon as the workmen leave, I'm going to put out some birdfeeders," Emmett commented. "Would you like to go to dinner at Stan's tonight? A patient was telling me about the delicious seafood there, and I'd like to try it out."

"Stan's is great. They have a fried lobster special among other things."

"Okay, then. How about I pick you up at seven? If Misty would like to join us, she can also be my guest."

"Thanks. I'll mention it to her," said Crystal, but she was disappointed he didn't want to spend time alone.

He took hold of her hand. "Slowly. Remember?" His gaze never left her face as he seemed to take in all of her. Then, just when she thought he might kiss her, he cleared his throat and stood. "Guess I'd better get back to work."

"Me, too," she said, rising to stand beside him.

He studied her and this time, he pulled her into his arms and kissed her in a lingering fashion.

Crystal let out a little moan as desire rose within her.

"M-m-m. Guess we both needed that," he murmured.

She laughed with him and then sat down as he trotted toward the office. Still filled with conflicting emotions, she stared out at the water. There was no point in telling herself that common sense would prevail. She couldn't pretend she wasn't falling for Emmett. And though she knew it wouldn't be easy with his family, she wasn't ready to step away from those growing feelings.

"Hey, there!"

Crystal turned and saw Dani approaching.

Dani sat beside her. "I was working over a problem with the large window in the master bedroom and couldn't help seeing you and Emmett. I don't mean to pry, but I'm hoping the two of you aren't going to let his mother or anyone else interfere. You're great together."

"Thanks. I was just thinking about the risks involved in that relationship, and I decided to follow my heart."

"I hope it works out for you," said Dani. "Are we going to see you at Jake's tonight?"

Crystal shook her head. "Emmett and I are going to Stan's. A patient told him about it, and he's anxious to go."

"Okay, well Brad and I will see you another time. Tell Misty we'll be there and she can join us."

"Thanks," Crystal said, grateful for how that summer gang had remained close.

That night, Emmett drove down a long dirt road into the woods to Stan's. The ramshackle wooden building appeared uninviting from the outside, but she knew that the atmosphere inside with red-and-white-checked tablecloths and a small stage for musicians would be welcoming. Best of all, the food was delicious.

A carved sign above the front door read: *Stan's*. A colorful metal sign by the door read: *craft beers and seafood.*

Emmett's look of doubt changed to one of surprise when they stepped inside and inhaled the aroma of delicious food. First-timers usually became steadfast patrons after a pleasant evening experience.

Onstage, a guitar player was singing jazzy blues songs.

"Very cool," said Emmett taking a seat at one of the four-top tables.

A waitress appeared wearing a denim skirt and a red T-shirt with Stan's logo. "What'll you have?"

Crystal ordered a strawberry lemonade and fried lobster and waited while Emmett decided on a draft beer and fish and chips. It was early enough that there were a few seats left, but Crystal knew the place would fill up shortly and would stay busy until closing.

"There's a nice path through the woods along the creek. We can work off dinner there," said Crystal.

Emmett accepted the beer brought to him and tested it. "Delicious craft beer."

Crystal sipped her lemonade and let out a sigh of contentment. It was nice to be here away from town for a change. "Thanks again for asking Misty to join us. I'm sure you understand that she's content to stay home for a while."

"I was happy to see her at Jake's, but I understand she might need time to adjust to a new life, a safe one," he answered with concern. "I've been thinking about abuse. It isn't always physical. It can be emotional and with a lot of cruelty. In a way, my household was like that. Emotional mistreatment. Belittling comments." He shook his head. "I've done quite a bit of studying on the topic."

Crystal remained quiet, aware he wasn't through talking.

"I suppose every family has some difficulties, but when you have a well-known stepfather who doesn't have the best character, it makes it hard to be true to yourself and not get sucked into thinking his behavior is okay. That's always been a struggle with both my parents. That's why I got out, changed my name, and have made it on my own with an inheritance from my birth grandmother."

"I admire your choices," said Crystal. "But they're still your parents."

"Yes, that's the hard part. I still want my family."

Crystal reached over and wrapped her fingers around his. "You're lucky you still have one."

"I know," he said, lifting her hand and kissing it.

"There you are," said a voice.

Crystal whipped around and hid her dismay as JoEllen Daniels headed their way.

"I was hoping you took my suggestion. That's why I'm here. I thought it would be fun to introduce you to my favorite beer, and I already told you about their fish and chips."

"Hi, Crystal. I didn't recognize you without your purple hair. May I join you?"

Emmett looked surprised and glanced at Crystal for approval.

Sighing softly, Crystal said, "I guess."

JoEllen ignored the lack of enthusiasm and sat between them. "It's such a pleasure getting to know you, Dr. Chambers. I was happy to meet you at The Woodlands and again this morning when you helped me out with a prescription."

"I hope to meet almost everyone in Lilac Lake," said Emmett. "That's one of the pleasures of working in a small town."

"Oh, yes. And Lilac Lake is very pleasant." She turned to Crystal. "Wouldn't you say so?"

"Yes. It will always be my home. At least in my heart."

"I know you're busy with the Café, so I'm offering my services in helping Dr. Chambers, I mean Emmett, get settled." She turned to Crystal once more. "I heard about the incident at Jake's."

"Do you mean with his mother?" Crystal asked, doing her best to remain polite even as she glanced at Emmett for help.

"A total misunderstanding," said Emmett, winking at Crystal. "Here's our food now. We have other plans for this evening, private ones. We won't be staying late."

"Oh! I didn't realize ..." JoEllen's eyes widened, and her gaze pinged back and forth between Emmett and Crystal. A look of frustration crossed her features. She huffed out a sigh and gazed around the room, then gave a little wave. "No problem. I see someone I know from work." She got up and left.

"Thank you," said Crystal. "I've mentioned her before."

"Yes." He dug into his dinner.

Crystal took a bit of the fried lobster, allowing the taste of it to rest a moment in her mouth, and groaned. "This is delicious."

"Mine, too." Emmett moved aside the French fries and took another bit of cod.

Toward the end of the meal, Crystal said, "So, what are these private plans for the rest of the evening?"

Emmett grinned. "I'm not sure. I thought it was something we could work out together."

Crystal laughed. "I thought so."

CHAPTER FIFTEEN

AFTER THEY FINISHED EATING, Crystal and Emmett took a walk along the creek, stopping when they found an empty bench with a pleasant view of the burbling water.

Emmett had been staring at her during dinner, and Crystal could tell he was as anxious as she to see where their attraction might lead them.

"Maybe we could go to my house. You haven't seen some of the work on it, and we could have some privacy there," suggested Emmett.

"Okay. I can't promise any time alone as long as Misty is staying with me."

They walked hand-in-hand back to his car, each step adding to the anticipation Crystal felt growing inside her.

On the ride to his house, she and Emmett exchanged small talk, but nothing of consequence was said. Instead, he glanced and smiled at her whenever he could. And as they drew closer to his house, he gave her hand a squeeze.

Emmett pulled into his driveway and slammed on his brakes. "Damn!"

Crystal stared at the black Cadillac Escalade. "Who is it?"

"If I'm not mistaken, it's my father. I wonder what he wants." Emmett got out of the car, went around to her side, and waited for her to emerge.

A tall, well-built man with short but thick gray hair and strong, classic features left the dock and crossed the lawn to them.

"Hi, son," Everett Chamberlain said, walking briskly.

Crystal felt Emmett tense beside her and took his hand.

"Who is this pretty little woman?" the senator said, giving her a wide, practiced smile.

It was Crystal's turn to freeze.

"Hi, Dad. This is Crystal Owen."

"Miss Owen." He dipped his chin.

What are you doing here?" Emmett asked him. "Did Mom ask you to drop by?"

"As a matter of fact, she did. I left Mt. Desert this morning for a meeting in Portsmouth. She wanted me to check on you, see how you're doing with your new job and such." His gaze settled on Crystal.

Crystal decided she wasn't about to be intimidated by Emmett's father and straightened her back, staring back at him steadily.

"You can tell my mother that I'm fine, the practice is fine, and I'm making nice friends," said Emmett firmly. He put his arm around Crystal.

"Look, I don't want to judge you. I'm pleased that you're doing well on your own. I've always been impressed by the way you stood up to me. That won't change. But I think you ought to know I'm considering a run for president of the United States in the next election, and I want to keep things in order. That means I'll need your support. I hope you can give that to me."

"Is that why you and Mom are suddenly getting together more often?" Emmett asked. He eyed his father with suspicion.

"That's only part of it. I'm through being less than an ideal family man. I want you to know that."

Hearing the silky voice that she'd often heard in the news, Crystal realized how that smooth talk could easily sway some people. She waited to see what Emmett had to say.

"I've heard this before," said Emmett.

"Well, your mother doesn't make it easy. We both know that," said the senator.

"Yes, but I won't give up my independence because you're thinking of running for president. I'll hold back any negative stuff, but that's it. So, don't go holding me up as a perfect son because it'll blow up in your face."

"I know, I know. I couldn't talk to you and change your mind back when you decided to change your name. I just don't want any dirty fights in the press."

"Neither do I," said Emmett. "Now, my girlfriend and I are going to enjoy some time together."

"What happened to the one with the purple hair?" his father asked, giving Crystal an admiring glance.

Emmett shook his head. "I won't bother to answer such a crass question."

"Well, I guess I'll go. But I'll be back. Next time, I'll call before I come." He stepped forward and gave Emmett a pat on the back. "See you, son."

Crystal noted a look of pain on Emmett's face, but he said, "Goodbye, Dad."

She stood beside Emmett as they watched his father get into the SUV and drive away.

As soon as the senator was out of sight, Emmett let out a long sigh. "I'm sorry you had to be part of that. You see how superficial my relationship is with my stepdad. I never had the chance to know my real father, but from the start with the senator, I never felt as if we belonged together. It's sad, but true. I sometimes wonder why he ever married my mother. They certainly haven't been the happiest of couples."

"It seems like a very difficult situation. I can tell it hurts you, and I'm sorry. How old were you when your mother married him?"

"Four. My father died when I was two."

"So, Everett raised you," Crystal said.

"Not really. He was gone most of the time with or without my mother, with or without other women. I give credit to my birth grandmother for helping me through some difficult times. And it's her money that allowed me to make an independent break from the family. I'll always be grateful to her."

"GG, the Gilford girls' grandmother, is that person for me. Guess we're both lucky that way."

Emmett took her hand. "Let's walk down to the dock. The moon has risen and it's a special sight to see it reflected on the river."

"Okay," said Crystal, understanding the turmoil with his father had erased some of the earlier passion rising between them.

They walked across the well-maintained grass and onto the dock. The moon, a glowing yellow ball in the dark sky above them, shed a silvery light on the moving river. They sat together on the bench staring out at the sight that was as mesmerizing as flames in a fire.

Emmett put his arm around her and drew her close.

With her head against his chest, Crystal heard the strong beat of his heart and realized Emmett was a survivor, like her. She lifted her face. "I want you to know I'll always be here for you whenever you need to talk about your situation. My friends have helped me, and I want to do the same for you."

He cupped her face in his broad hands and gazed at her, his lips spreading into a smile.

"You're such a special woman," he said softly before lowering his lips to hers.

His kiss was gentle and sure and then became demanding as desire rose in them both.

When their kisses weren't enough, Emmett said, "Do you want to go inside?"

Crystal knew he was asking more than that. It's what they'd both wanted from the beginning.

He held out his hand, and she took it.

Emmett led her into the kitchen through a temporary door where a glass sliding door would eventually be placed. They stepped through the construction area, into the living room, whose interior walls had been removed, and walked up the stairs to one of the guest rooms.

At the doorway, Emmett studied her. "Are you sure?"

Heart pounding with anticipation, Crystal said quietly, "Yes."

Smiling with delight, Emmett picked her up and carried her over to the bed. Gently, he lay her atop the covers and climbed onto the bed beside her.

"I intend to enjoy every inch of you," he murmured cupping a cheek in his hand and gazing at her with those beautiful eyes of his.

"Yes, all of me," whispered Crystal as his lips met hers.

As they lay close, Crystal marveled at how well they fit together. She was overcome with the thought that she'd found her true home in his arms. When kisses were not enough, they eagerly removed their clothes to discover what else they could about one another.

Crystal woke suddenly, and realizing where she was, she nudged Emmett. "Wake up! It's late, and I need to get home. Misty is there and I have to get up early."

Emmett opened his eyes sleepily and smiled at her. "Ah, fantastic woman, your wish is my command. First, another kiss."

As his lips played with hers, Crystal reminded herself that

she couldn't stay, even though the thought was tempting. Making love with Emmett was soul-satisfying. More like a spiritual reunion.

She forced herself out of bed and tugged on his arm. "Sorry, but you have to take me home."

Emmett got up and dressed as quickly as she. Crystal assumed that skill was part of being a doctor—coming awake easily and moving quickly.

When she walked into her apartment, Misty gazed up at her from the couch where she was watching television. "Nice dinner? It's after one o'clock."

Still riding high from the lovemaking, Crystal's lips curved.

"I'm happy for you," said Misty. "You've been alone too long, and even with a lot of friends, it's nice to have someone special in your life."

"Emmett is ... well, wonderful," said Crystal. "Surprisingly, our backgrounds mesh, and we understand one another. In addition to that, being with him is perfect." She took a seat next to Misty. "How are you doing?"

"I've gone ahead with the move. I've been released from the lease on the apartment in Florida, turned in my letter of resignation, and applied for a teaching position here in town. Everything has come together so quickly, I'm sure it's the right move for me."

"That makes me very happy," said Crystal. "I wish I'd known earlier that your situation in Florida wasn't healthy."

"I appreciate that, but I'm a big girl who can take care of my problems. It's just nice to know I have a home to come back to."

"We'll take it one day at a time to see how you're doing before I push you out of the nest," said Crystal. "But you can stay as long as you need." She hugged Misty. "I've got to get to bed. Another early morning."

"Maybe I can take over for you tomorrow until it's time to open at seven. No reason I can't help with the earlier baking."

"Really? You'd do that for me?"

"Sure," said Misty. "I can't just sit around and do nothing this summer."

Crystal gave her sister another hug. "You're a doll. Thanks. I'm going to let you do it. Maybe we can make alternating early mornings part of a new routine."

"Even when I'm teaching, I can help you," said Misty. "I need the extra money, and you need a break."

"Deal," said Crystal. "Have I told you lately how much I love you?"

"No," Misty said grinning. "But you can start now."

Crystal hugged her. It was fabulous to have her sister at home.

CHAPTER SIXTEEN

OVER THE NEXT SEVERAL DAYS, Crystal and other local merchants and restaurant owners in town started decorating for Summer Faire. Green and lavender flags and balloons were attached to the streetlamps in the colors of the Summer Faire. Store windows carried out the theme with decorations and signs welcoming visitors and offering Faire specials.

As the Faire weekend grew closer, anticipation grew. In its tenth year, the Faire was well organized and was yet another instance of the small town coming together. The town square was where the chili and barbeque cook-offs would be held. The town hall would house the baking contest entries and would serve as a place where visitors could cool off and buy lemonade from a church group. Their proceeds would go to the church refugee relief fund.

On Thursday afternoon, several food trucks parked along the streets connecting to Main Street, extending the town center to make room for hungry and thirsty visitors.

Crystal prepared for another cooking class, the last of the three before the Summer Faire baking contest. Two of the kids had dropped out, making it a little easier to work with the others.

For this last class, they were preparing cakes from scratch. She'd borrowed a few round cakepans from some of the mothers, so the kids could have fun covering a two-layer chocolate cake with a fluffy vanilla icing.

She focused on the kids in her cooking class and tried to imagine what her children with Emmett might look like. She hoped they'd have his beautiful turquoise eyes.

"Ready?" asked Misty, breaking into her thoughts.

Crystal laughed and nodded.

They got to work right away, so the cakes could be made, cooked, and cooled. As soon as the cakes were in the oven, the kids helped make a couple of batches of the icing to share.

While they worked, the kids chatted about their lives. Crystal listened closely, learning what children that age liked to do, wondering if she'd ever get the chance to use this information.

As soon as the cakes were cool enough, Crystal handed out special icing spatulas, hoping the spreaders would help deter the inevitable mess of icing everywhere.

It was interesting to see how each child managed his or her process. Taking care of the bottom round cake was relatively easy because there was nothing fancy about spreading the icing across the top. After the second layer was placed atop the first, the struggles began.

Crystal showed the class different ways to create swirls and designs but left them to their own devices because they'd be on their own to create something for the baking contest.

"They're doing a terrific job," said Misty, standing beside her.

"I'm impressed with their skills. It'll be fun to see how the contest goes. Something new for the Summer Faire."

"Next thing you know they'll be creating something for Chef Ramsay," said Misty, chuckling.

Crystal grinned. "I'm thinking of them as future employees of the Café."

They were still laughing when Whitney appeared. "I know the restaurant is closed, but I saw the door was unlocked and decided to see if you were here."

"Hi, Whitney. Look at what these young bakers are doing

in preparation for the baking contest at the Faire."

Whitney observed them and then pulled Crystal aside. "I understand Senator Chamberlain was in town recently. How did things go?"

Crystal shook her head. "Poor Emmett has a difficult family situation. I was able to see that for myself. The senator mentioned possibly running for president and wants Emmett's support."

"Wow, that's big news," said Whitney. I've heard rumblings about that, but I also know some in his party don't want him to run because of moral issues surrounding him. I'd be surprised if he went ahead with that idea."

"The senator is attractive and very sure of himself, but a little creepy in the way he blatantly stared at me."

"Exactly my point," said Whitney. "I haven't seen you for a while. I was wondering if you and Emmett would come to dinner at my house tonight. I know it's late to ask, but I've made lobster salad and homemade biscuits and want to share them with you."

"It sounds delightful. Let me ask Emmett, and I'll get right back to you." Crystal left Misty and Whitney to oversee the kids and went to her office to make the call.

A few minutes later, Crystal emerged wearing a smile. "Dinner tonight would be a treat. Emmett and I are happy to accept."

"After this, I may put together a party following the Summer Faire, a party to welcome Emmett and Dirk. But this will do for now for Emmett," said Whitney. She turned to Misty. "Are you sure you won't join us?"

"As I said to you while Crystal was gone, I'm still slowly easing back into my new life here. But I appreciate your offer."

Whitney gave Misty a hug. "We're glad you're back." She straightened. "See you tonight, Crystal. Shall we say seven?

Timothy should be down for the night by then."

"Thanks. It's great timing, right before the Summer Faire." She thought as she often did how lucky she was to have a friend like Whitney. They maintained a close relationship without awkwardness between them regarding Nick. She was eager for Emmett to understand that. She'd always love Nick, just not as a spouse. Maybe this evening with all of them together, he'd see that.

That night, a few minutes before seven, Emmett picked up Crystal, and they drove to Whitney and Nick's house. While she'd lived in the one-story Cape Cod house, it had been comfortable but small. Since marrying Whitney, Nick had agreed to add two new wings to the house. One wing contained a master suite and laundry room, the other, a family room, and a small office. Between them sat a screened-in porch. As Whitney mentioned to everyone who complimented them on the additions, "It's helpful to have Collister Construction in the family."

They pulled up in front of the house and got out. The evening was cooling off. In another couple of hours, the sun would end its daytime journey. The sky was already embracing a pale-yellow tinge that would eventually hold a pinkish tone.

Crystal stood a moment and inhaled the clean air. She loved living in the Lakes District of New Hampshire with its lakes, mountain views, rivers, and woodlands.

Emmett came to her and put an arm around her. "Pretty night, huh."

"Yes, I love this time of day."

Whitney opened the front door and waved them inside. "Timothy is just about ready for bed. Auntie Crystal, come say hi."

Crystal had been thrilled to be asked to be Timothy's godmother. She eagerly made her way to the door and after seeing Emmett inside, she hurried to the baby's nursery, which had once been the master suite.

When she stepped inside the nursery, a sigh escaped her. It was decorated as a baby boy's room. The blue walls were decorated with puffy white clouds and other hand-painted pictures in keeping with the theme of an airplane visiting different places and animals in the world.

"I love this room. It's very clever," said Crystal, going to the crib. She leaned over and watched the baby kicking his feet and waving his arms at her. "And this little boy? I love him, too."

She picked up the sweet-smelling baby and held him close. "Hi, sweet boy," she murmured. "It's Auntie Crystal."

He studied her, and then a wide smile spread across his face.

Crystal's heart melted. "He knows me."

"I had to show him off, too," said Nick, coming into the room with Emmett.

Emmett walked over to Crystal and gently lifted Timothy into his arms. "Hey, buddy. Looks like you're going to be a big boy."

Timothy gave him a quizzical look but as Emmett continued talking to him, he smiled and reached to touch him.

"Guess he likes you," said Crystal watching with interest.

"Most babies do," Emmett said. "Until it's time for a shot or two."

Emmett handed the baby to Whitney. "I'll leave it to you to put him down for the night."

Whitney nuzzled Timothy's neck and then placed him in the crib on his back.

Crystal and Emmett left the room as Whitney began to

croon to the baby. Nick stood by them, forming a tiny circle of new parents with their baby.

Outside the room, Emmett studied her. "I take it you want a family one day." His gaze focused on her.

Crystal tried to keep her yearning out of her voice, but after seeing Timothy, the hunger for a child was something she couldn't hide. "For years I was afraid I wouldn't make a decent mother after the example I had. But I'm stronger now, more confident that I'm my own person. I think I'm ready."

"In many ways, you've always been a mother by taking care of your sister." He gave her a sympathetic look. "That was a big job for a girl on her own."

"I suppose," said Crystal, blushing at his compliment. "Thanks."

Just then, Whitney and Nick stepped out of the nursery.

"Are you ready to relax? I've got wine and appetizers on the porch," said Whitney.

"And beer and sodas if you prefer," Nick said to Emmett.

"Lead the way," said Emmett.

Moments later, the four of them were seated outside chatting comfortably.

Crystal listened carefully as Whitney asked Emmett about his father's visit and the information on the news that he was considering a run for president in two years.

"How is that going to affect you?" Whitney asked. "I know what it's like to be in the spotlight. And I know you're trying to fit into our small community."

"When I was eighteen, I declared my independence by changing my name and studying medicine, not law as my parents thought I should," Emmett explained. "While it's not the happiest of families, I have no reason to act out and not support him. But I'm not sure thinking of running for president is enough for him to get his party's support. So, I'll just keep on doing what I do."

"Smart of you," said Whitney.

"I understand your mother made a scene at Jake's with Crystal," said Nick. "I hope that doesn't happen again."

Crystal loved that Nick was sounding protective of her, just as he had as a kid.

Whitney glanced at her and turned to Emmett. "Neither Nick nor I would want that to happen. I know you didn't like it either, but in this town, we stick up for one another."

"Believe me, I appreciate that. My mother is difficult, and she'd had too much to drink. While I can't make any promises about her behavior, I'll do my best to keep her away from Crystal or from being cruel to her."

Crystal sat in her chair listening to them and felt like a child overhearing something she shouldn't. Still, it felt satisfying to have others care about her. "I appreciate your support, but this is something I'll have to handle on my own."

"You're right," said Nick. "We just want you to know we're here if you need us."

"Let's talk about something fun," said Whitney. "Emmett, you missed our 4th of July celebration, but I think you'll enjoy your first Summer Faire starting tomorrow."

"Even though, no doubt you, like me, will be called to duty," said Nick. "But it's great for the town to host an event like this. It's a boon to the businesses here." He gave Emmett a teasing grin. "Even for doctors."

Emmett laughed. "I'll be ready. I'm finally getting the practice and office set up the way I want it, with more computerized record keeping."

When Whitney got up to serve the meal, Crystal followed her into the kitchen. "Anything I can do to help?"

"Thanks. You can fill the water goblets." Whitney waved Crystal over and placed a hand on her shoulder. "You and

Emmett are perfect together. I hope neither one of you is going to let family issues keep you from being happy."

"Honestly, I'm not sure how our relationship will endure because of his family, but I'm not going to back down from seeing where this could lead. Did you see how gentle Emmett was with Timothy?"

Whitney gave her a broad smile. "I did. He'll make a great father. That's another reason he's a match for you."

"If Emmett can be determined enough to be independent from his parents, I can certainly try to be as strong."

"Atta girl," said Whitney giving her a quick hug.

CHAPTER SEVENTEEN

As they left Nick and Whitney's house, Emmett turned to her. "Do you want to go to my house for a while?"

"I can't," said Crystal with true regret. "I have to get up especially early to help get ready for the Summer Faire. For the next three days, I'll be working double time at the Café and elsewhere overseeing the baking and cooking contests. Each day, it's something different—a baking contest for adults and kids, a chili bake-off, and a barbeque sauce and ribs contest. It's a whole lot of eating fun for the crowd and total, exhausting chaos behind the scenes. But like Nick says, it's great for the town. People come from all around."

"I guess I'd better get a good night's sleep too. Dr. Johnson warned this was a busy time for him too."

He drove into the parking lot behind the Café, pulled into a spot, and turned off the engine. Facing her, he said, "I'm falling for you, Crystal. I hope you're going to give me a chance."

"No promises about anything, but I do want to keep seeing you. You're the first man I've been with in a long time, and that's something I don't take lightly. I hope you don't either."

He moved quickly, unbuckling his seat belt and hers. Then he took her in his arms. She liked that he proceeded with assurance yet wasn't aggressive. As usual, she felt both safe in his arms and deeply aroused, allowing her to respond easily. The world around them seemed to melt away as they kissed. And when his hands met her breasts in sweet caresses, she sighed happily.

Later, when she walked into her apartment, Crystal did her best to brush her hair away from her flushed cheeks and to straighten her blouse. But she knew all Misty had to do was look at her face to see her happiness and know she was a woman in love.

"Another pleasant evening?" asked Misty.

"A very nice evening. Something to get me through the next three days or so. Are you ready to join me bright and early tomorrow morning? We're offering free coffee or tea with breakfast for anyone."

"I've already organized that area of the kitchen. We shouldn't have any problem keeping up with the crowd."

"Thanks. I'm glad you're here to help. I'm off to bed. See you in the morning."

Crystal went into her room, her body languid just thinking of how Emmett had kissed her. She knew he was as aroused as she, but she was glad she'd fought the urge to go to his house as they both wanted.

Even later, as she lay in bed, she recalled the way his eyes had grown greener in color as he caressed her cheek and told her he was falling faster and harder than he'd thought possible. She felt the same but hadn't voiced her feelings. Even now, she replayed his words in her mind, unable to verbalize exactly how she felt.

The alarm sounded like a screeching cat to Crystal's ears as she was abruptly awakened. Grumbling to herself, she turned off the alarm and sat up in bed. She'd been dreaming about Emmett and her taking a cruise, and she wanted to go back to sleep.

Huffing out a breath, she forced herself out of bed. Today was a Summer Faire day, and she'd need all her energy to help get it off to a good start.

The weather forecaster had promised a nice day. She was anxious to see that the Café was ready.

In the kitchen, the aroma of baked bread filled her nostrils, warming her insides.

She went out to the dining room to check the decorations. Each table held a bud vase with green silk leaves and purple lilac blooms. Outdoors, the railing around the patio was wrapped with a woven string of leaves and lilac blooms. That, coupled with bud vases on the tables duplicated the colors and made the space very festive. She breathed in the cool air, relishing its crispness before the temperature rose. Though the lilac blooms had long since died, she imagined she could still smell their perfume.

When she went back inside, the kitchen staff was arriving and wearing the special T-shirts and aprons with the Café logo she'd provided for the occasion. Baseball hats, aprons, and T-shirts were displayed for sale near the cash register.

"Going to be a busy three days," Crystal told her staff. "We'll stick to our normal schedule, but if you see there's a need to work beyond your shift, I hope you'll stay and pitch in."

"Are we going to have a party Sunday night as usual?" asked one of the staff.

"Oh, yes," said Crystal. "We'll all need to let loose by then." She grinned at the cheer that went up. As a thank you to their staff, all the merchants in town pitched in to pay for food and entertainment in the parking lot behind the row of stores and restaurants on the final night of the event.

Crystal posted a sign by the cash register and put one up on the front door announcing that coffee was free with every breakfast served. Seeing that all was in order, she went to the kitchen to help just as Misty arrived.

"I'd forgotten how exciting Summer Faire could be," Misty said, putting on an apron.

"It's a ton of work but a lot of fun," said Crystal. "I'm looking forward to seeing some of my summer regulars." At the sound of customers arriving, she hurried to the dining room to greet people and oversee staff. Quick service, along with excellent food, had made the Café a popular choice.

When a lull came in the morning activity, Crystal slipped out of the Café to see how the other business owners were doing.

She was talking to Estelle Bookbinder, owner of the bookstore, Pages, when she heard someone call, "Diana, dear, is that you?"

Estelle looked up and Crystal turned around to see Emmett's mother rush toward her, arms outstretched, before coming to a surprised stop.

"I'm sorry, I thought you were someone else."

Crystal waited for her to recognize her and realized Emmett's mother never really saw her beyond her purple hair. She said goodbye to Estelle and went on her way. She had no desire to talk to Emmett's mother.

Instead of going directly back to the Café, Crystal went to Bullard's Hardware Store to check on things there. Crystal and Sarah Bullard had been friends growing up, and Crystal was hoping she'd come back to town for Summer Faire.

She went inside the store and was pleased to see a crowd milling around for bargains.

Sarah's mother, Edie, beckoned to her. "How are things going at the Café?"

"We're swamped," Crystal said. "I'm just taking a break. Did Sarah come back for Summer Faire?"

Edie shook her head. "Since her husband died unexpectedly, she's been staying close to home with the girls.

We're trying to talk her into moving here, though, and I think we might be making progress. The twins are four now, and Sarah needs help raising them."

"I'd love it if she came back to town," said Crystal. "More and more of the summer gang are returning."

"That's what I keep telling her. She'd have a lot of friends here to support her as she deals with her grief."

A customer interrupted them, and Crystal took advantage of the moment to leave.

As she was walking back to the Café, she bumped into Melissa and Ross.

"Are you taking some time off from cooking?' Crystal teased.

Melissa laughed. "Not for long. Ross stopped by my house to see if I was going to the Faire. It's his first time, and I'm giving him a tour. But I'll be back at the restaurant this afternoon, helping to prep for dinner."

"Nice to see you, Ross," said Crystal. "Be sure to stop by the Café. I'm offering free coffee to those who order food." She gave them a wave and hurried back to the Café where people were waiting to get inside.

A short while later, Dani and Brad walked into the Café. Crystal greeted them and found a table for them on the patio.

"We saw Ross and Melissa hanging out together," said Dani. "Do you think they're dating?"

Crystal shrugged. "I'm not sure. They're next-door neighbors. I imagine they've simply become friends."

"We'll see," said Dani, giving her an impish grin. "Nothing is secret in this town."

"Guess who I saw this morning? Emmett's mother. She didn't recognize me. She thought I was Diana until I faced her."

"Hmmm, there are some similarities. Did you speak to

her?"

Crystal shook her head firmly. "No. I don't want to be part of any chaos with that family."

"Wise of you," said Dani, placing her order.

After getting Brad's order, Crystal left them, her mind on Emmett's mother. She wondered how long Natalie would be in town and hoped she wouldn't have to see her again.

By the time the Café closed at six, two hours later than usual, Crystal was exhausted but satisfied with how well they'd done.

"Enjoy but be sure to be ready for tomorrow," she said to her staff as they headed out for an evening of fun.

Crystal went back to the kitchen to prepare for tomorrow. Misty helped her refresh all the tables with salt, pepper, ketchup, and hot sauce, and then, together they swept and mopped floors. Crystal urged Misty to go and have fun and took her receipts and cash up to her office to reconcile daily earnings.

She was finishing up when her cell rang. *Emmett.*

"Hi, Crystal. My mother is in town, and I'd like you to join us for dinner at Fins."

Crystal didn't hesitate. "I'm sorry. I can't. I'm just going to go to bed so I can get up extra early tomorrow."

"Is this how it's going to be?" Emmett asked. "You and my family not able to get along?"

"Oh, Emmett, I do want to get to know them better if your parents will allow it. But I don't think meeting me is part of their plans. Especially if your father is thinking about running for president."

"That's exactly why I want you and my mother to meet. I want her to see you for the wonderful person you are."

In your dreams. "She ran into me earlier and thought I was

Diana until I turned around. Then, she didn't recognize me. I just let the opportunity go."

"If not tonight, how about joining us for dinner tomorrow?" said Emmett. "I want to make our relationship work."

If it was that important to Emmett, she'd give it a try. "Okay, but I don't want any scenes. Promise me that won't happen. You know how I've been judged in the past."

"I promise to do my best. I've already talked to my mother about her behavior when she was here last time. I never want anyone to hurt you."

The sincerity in Emmett's voice touched her. "Alright, let's do this. I can't allow your mother to intimidate me. I may see you around town tomorrow. Have fun." Crystal ended the call and then sat back with a sigh. Natalie Chamberlain was intimidating. Crystal decided to go to The Woodlands for a chat with GG for a pep talk.

Pulling up to the main building, Crystal was struck by the beauty of the twinkling lights wrapped around the railing of the porch and repeated around the front entry. Unlike some assisted living places, The Woodlands went all out to make their residents feel pampered. Inside, in the card room to the right of the entry, several couples were playing games. Crystal searched for GG but didn't see her.

She signed in at the reception desk and told the woman who she was visiting.

The woman smiled at her. "Go on down the hallway, Ms. Wittner's in her room."

Crystal filled with anticipation as she approached GG's apartment. She always felt better and stronger after talking to her.

She knocked on the door, and when GG called to her to

enter, Crystal opened it and walked inside.

When she saw her, GG's face lit up with pleasure causing Crystal's eyes to sting with tears.

"Crystal, what a surprise. It's lovely to see you," said GG. "Come sit down and tell me what's going on."

"First of all, it's Summer Faire. Are you planning to attend?" asked Crystal.

GG nodded. "I went for a short while this afternoon. Everything looks beautiful decked out in green and lavender. Whitney is going to pick me up and take me to the band concert tomorrow afternoon. I doubt I'll make it to the canoe races, but the weather is holding, and it should be great business for the Lilac Lake Inn. I understand the new owners are offering viewing places, along with food and beverages."

"I know Ross is back in town. As one of the new owners, he must be taking part in that. He and Melissa Hendrickson are becoming friends, what with him living next door to her and all."

"Another romance, perhaps?" GG said. "With all you young folks back in town, I suspect a few may crop up. How are things going with you and Emmett?"

Crystal sighed. "Emmett and I are fine. With his parents, not so much. His father came to see him and now his mother is in town. His father told us he's considering a run for president of the United States in the next election. Emmett doubts that will happen, but it still affects us." She hung her head.

GG leaned forward and studied her. "If you're inferring that they'd consider Emmett dating you as unacceptable, you're going to have to stand up to them. You have nothing to apologize for. You're a good, kind, bright woman. No one can take that away from you."

"I know, but it isn't like I have a normal family with a

mother and father who are decent people. I don't even know who my father is. Frankly, I don't want to know." Crystal emitted a heart-rending sigh.

"Seeing who you are and what you've accomplished is more noteworthy than anything else. Besides, I happen to know that Natalie Chamberlain came from a humble background, and we all have read stories about Senator Chamberlain's behavior. Keep that in mind should you feel insecure about your place."

Crystal studied GG's earnest expression. "You're right. I'm proud of what I've done with my life. I can't let someone destroy that."

"And I'm guessing Emmett will protect you," said GG. "Am I right?"

Crystal's lips curved for the first time that evening. "Yes, I believe he will. He wants us all to get along."

"Well, then, just be yourself. It'll work out in the end," said GG.

Crystal got up and kissed GG's cheek. "Thanks. This is what I needed to hear. You always know the right thing to say to me."

"Okay, then, care for a cup of coffee or tea?" said GG.

"I'll have a cup of decaf coffee. Can I fix one for you too?" she asked.

"Thanks. That would be lovely." GG held up the baby blanket she'd been knitting. "Don't tell Dani, but I think she'll be next to add to the family."

"I won't say a word." She laughed. "What about Taylor?"

GG's impish grin was amusing. "I'm knitting two blankets. One in pink and one in blue. In time, we'll see who gets which one. I figure I have a fifty-fifty chance of being right."

All her normal disposition restored, Crystal headed for the kitchen to make the coffee.

CHAPTER EIGHTEEN

THE NEXT MORNING, Crystal arose with a sense of excitement. Yesterday had been very profitable for the Café, and she'd heard from other owners that they'd been successful, too. The baking contest was to be held in the town hall at noon, and she was wondering how her students would do. The idea of creating something others would enjoy was a deep-rooted motive for her to run the Café.

She dressed for the day and went to check on Misty. "You almost ready?" She'd been late getting in last night.

Misty groaned and got out of bed. "Sorry. I intended to make it an early night, but I couldn't resist staying to hear the band at Smokin' Joe's Fish Shack. Ross's friend, Mike Dawson promised to take me home whenever I was ready."

"Mike's a great guy. I'm glad you're getting to meet some of the newer members of the gang."

"They all seem pretty secure in what they're doing. Mike is talking about opening tennis clinics here in the area. Maybe do a deal with the Lilac Lake Inn. It sounds exciting."

"Lilac Lake is becoming *the* place to live," said Crystal. "I hope we can keep the small-town feel to it."

"Me, too. I'd forgotten what it's like to have people know and care about you just because you live in the same town."

"It's certainly helped me. Now, get moving. We have a busy day ahead of us."

Memories of Crystal prodding Misty to get ready for school made her lips curve. Misty was not a morning person.

Downstairs, some of the staff appeared to be hung over.

She knew Sunday would be even worse. As hard as the younger people worked, they also played hard. And Summer Faire was a time of fun for all ages.

Crystal got coffee and hot water started, and plated fresh cinnamon rolls, a variety of muffins, and cookies for the counter display in the dining area. The staff wiped down the moisture that had accumulated overnight on the patio chairs and tables.

When she was ready, she opened the door just as the first customers arrived. It always thrilled her to see her place fill up. This morning was no exception. Today, most of the early customers appeared to be visitors. A campground a couple of miles away to the east brought new people into town. And for this weekend, every local B&B, AirBnB, cottage, motel, and campground had been booked for weeks and months.

When Taylor and Whitney arrived together mid-morning, Crystal noticed how much attention they got. But then, they were well-known to TV viewers or romance readers. She went over to them.

"Taylor, it's great to have you back in town. I heard you were going to stay for the rest of the summer. Is that true?"

Taylor gave her a hug. "I've got to finish this last book in the series, and I've been struggling with it. Cooper suggested we come to Lilac Lake to refresh my creativity. This is much better than staying in New York or going to Long Island for a few days at a time."

"I'm delighted she's here," said Whitney. "Timothy needs some time with Auntie Taylor and Uncle Cooper. And Nick will love having Cooper go fishing with him. By the way, we're inviting a few people to the Lilac Lake Cottage for a barbeque Sunday evening. I hope you and Emmett will join us."

"That sounds perfect. What can I bring?" asked Crystal, delighted to be included.

"How about those molasses cookies GG loves," said Whitney. "They're delicious."

"Speaking of GG, I think she's hoping that Timothy will have cousins," said Crystal. "I visited her last night."

"I know. She's knitting baby blankets," said Whitney, elbowing Taylor.

Taylor waved the suggestion away with a sweep of her hand. "Dani can be next. I've got too much to do to think of starting a family so soon. But Cooper and I want children someday." Taylor turned to Crystal. "What about you? Whitney tells me you're ready to settle down and have a family. You and the new doctor in town?"

Crystal felt the heat in her cheeks rise but was helpless to stop it. "We're just friends."

"I hope it all works out for you," said Taylor.

Seeing new customers arrive, Crystal said, "Better go ahead and find seats. I'll catch up with you later."

The pace kept steady until Crystal was due to go to the town hall for the baking contest. At noon, the tasting would take place, and after winners were announced, pieces of the various entries would be offered for sale to benefit the community center.

Crystal arrived in the auditorium of the town hall to find a crowd milling around the long, cloth-covered tables displaying the various items to be judged. Pies, cakes, and fancy desserts were displayed together. Descriptive tags were placed in front of each one. Crystal could already guess one or two entries that appeared to be prepared by kids, but the array of offerings was very impressive with its professionalism.

Two selectmen, Melissa, and Emmett were chosen to help Crystal judge the entries. They'd already decided to divide the items into four sections to avoid tasting them all and getting sick. When the top three of each group were chosen, the other judges would taste to decide the winners.

"Are you ready to begin?" Crystal asked the judges.

"Oh, yeah. I've been waiting for this all morning," said Emmett, winking at her.

Crystal walked over to the microphone stand that had been set up for her. "Welcome, everyone! I'm happy to see so many participants and supporters of the baking contest. This is the first year we have a prize for children twelve and under in the hopes of encouraging more kids to consider the hospitality industry. First prize for them will include a hundred-dollar gift card to the kitchen supply store in Portsmouth, courtesy of Eugenia Wittner. The prizes for the adult winners will be blue, red, and yellow ribbons. I want to give thanks to our two selectmen, as well as Melissa Hendrickson and Dr. Chambers, who all have graciously offered to help me judge. We hope to have the winners announced within the hour. Good luck to everyone, and many thanks for your participation."

Crystal started in her section with the pies. She considered presentation foremost. Then studying them, she broke a small piece of the pie crust off one of them and tasted it. Liking it, she then cut herself a small piece and plated it before tasting the huckleberry filling. Sighing with pleasure, she studied the small, blueberries that were famously grown in Maine. Out of the twelve pies, she sampled eight crusts and six fillings and marked down her three ribbon winners in proper order.

Because it was her special project, Crystal went to the kids' collection and quickly chose a chocolate cream Bundt cake, iced butterscotch brownies, and an apple pie as her top choices.

When all the sampling and judging had taken place, Crystal went to her microphone to announce the winners. The crowd had thinned during lunchtime, but several people were standing by to hear the results, including all of the children.

"As you know, we appreciate every one of the entries. I believe sharing baking treasures with family and friends is a true form of love. We all appreciate your individual talents." She smiled at each of them. "Any time one of you wants to come to work for me, just let me know." Laughter followed. "And now on to our winners."

She started with the kids who were anxiously standing by. "You all deserve a ribbon, but we have only three to hand out. She handed out the third and second place awards and then announced, "And the first place winner of a blue ribbon and the gift certificate is none other than Elissa Sawyer. Your chocolate cream Bundt cake is a delight—moist and rich with a dramatic chocolate cinnamon glaze."

Among the applause that followed, Crystal caught Pam Sawyer's attention and they exchanged smiles. Crystal was pleased with the outcome. Her daughter loved to cook.

By the time Crystal finished handing out ribbons, she was filled with satisfaction. The public's interest was sincere, adding to the suspense of each announcement. More than that, the community had come together not only to support the bakers but also to support the Community Center, which was the recipient of each entry fee. Through the center, she hoped to provide cooking classes for all ages.

"Nice job," said Melissa coming over to her. "Next year, I'd be happy to help judge again. It's such a worthy cause and loads of fun." She looked around. "Have you seen Dirk?"

"No, I haven't. By the way, I'm coming to Fins tonight for dinner. Can't wait. The restaurant always has such delicious food."

"Thanks," said Melissa. "We just got a fresh load of seafood delivered. It should be delicious."

They walked out of the town hall together.

Melissa saw Dirk in the distance and hurried towards him.

As Crystal headed back to the Café, the street was full of activity with people shopping, eating at food trucks, or watching a juggler. She was pleased to see it. With Misty so willing to help, it gave her a chance to have a little free time.

Crystal was alone in the Café preparing for the final day of Summer Faire when Emmett showed up and knocked on the locked door. Smiling, Crystal went to let him in.

"How's it going?" he asked.

"Business has been booming. How about you?"

"A case of heat exhaustion, a couple of scraped knees, and a sprained ankle."

"Thanks for helping with the baking contest. Everyone was really into it—clapping for each winner and then lining up to buy goodies for sale. I think we raised a lot of money for the Community Center. I'm glad we did it."

"Me, too. All the store owners I talked to seemed pleased by the business. I couldn't make it to the canoe races, but I heard they were fun. This whole weekend is a real small-town adventure."

"It's one of the town functions I love," said Crystal. "By the way, I talked to Whitney and Taylor this morning, and we've been invited to a barbeque at their cottage Sunday evening. Do you want to go with me?"

"Sure. Sounds like a good way to end the weekend. Are you set to meet my mother and me for dinner at eight?"

"Yes. Will you pick me up?" asked Crystal already nervous about it.

"Of course. I'd better pick you up at 7:45 to give us time to make it to the inn on time. My mother doesn't like it if I'm late."

"Okay," said Crystal, suddenly aware she'd set aside the

wrong dress to wear. This was going to be a more formal affair than she'd thought.

Emmett drew her to him. Wrapping his arms around her, he whispered into her ear, "Everything will be fine. Just be yourself. You're perfect."

Crystal closed her eyes as his lips met hers. She loved the confidence he had in her. It made her feel worthy of him and his cold family.

When they pulled apart, Emmett smiled at her, adding light to his eyes. "You make me happy." He sighed. "I'd better go. See you later."

She let him out and locked the door behind him, leaning against it a moment to let her racing pulse slow. The chemistry between them was on fire. She clasped her hands together thinking of what the future might bring.

CHAPTER NINETEEN

CRYSTAL STUDIED HERSELF IN THE MIRROR. She'd finally decided to wear a simple, black-linen, sleeveless sheath adorned only by a gold chain necklace holding a small single diamond that matched the small diamond studs in her ears. Both were graduation gifts from GG—one for high school, the other for culinary school. She treasured them.

She fussed with her soft blond curls. Her hair cut shorter and changed back to her natural color gave her a better look. She added another swipe of pale, pink lipstick to her full lips and sighed. Ready or not, it was time to go.

The doorbell rang, and Crystal went to answer it.

"Wow! You look nice. Very classy," he said.

She couldn't help but smile at his enthusiasm. "Thanks. I don't wear jeans and T-shirts all the time."

"I like it," said Emmett. "Now, let's go meet my mother."

The short drive from the town center to the Lilac Lake Inn was scenic. Stacked-stone walls lined the sides of the country road. She opened the window beside her and inhaled the smell of pine. She could imagine the rabbits and other small wildlife getting ready for another night in the woodlands.

"It's a beautiful area, huh?" said Emmett. "Compared to city living, life seems much easier here."

"It's a wonderful vacation spot for families, but living here is a privilege too. I haven't been able to travel much, but as long as I have this, I'm content until I can."

"I'd love to show you some of my favorite places," said Emmett.

He pulled up to the porte cochere of the hotel, and she waited for an attendant to help her out of the car.

Emmett checked his watch as they walked inside. "We'd better go directly to the dining room. We're a little late."

At the entrance to the dining room, Emmett gave his name to the hostess. Picking up two menus, she led them to a table in the corner by a window.

It wasn't until she drew close that Crystal realized that Natalie Chamberlain was sitting at the table with Diana McArthur.

" 'Evening, Mother," said Emmett. He turned to Diana. "And hello to you."

He frowned but forced a smile. "Mother, you haven't formally met Crystal Owen. And, Crystal, you know Diana."

"Yes, I do," she said stiffly, wondering what was going on.

Emmett's mother stared at her. "You're the woman I thought was Diana at the Faire." She turned to Emmett. "I thought Crystal had purple hair."

Remembering GG's words to her, Crystal straightened. "I used to have purple hair. I decided it was time to go back to my natural color."

"Well, change was needed." She took hold of Diana's hand. "And this young lady has grown into a beauty. She always had a special thing for Emmett. Isn't that so?"

Diana's cheeks flared with color, but she gazed at Emmett adoringly.

A waiter hurried over to them and helped Crystal into her chair and then helped Emmett. They were seated next to one another, allowing Diana to face Emmett while Crystal was forced to sit opposite Natalie.

"As long as Emmett was finally able to give me a little of his time, I thought it a perfect opportunity to invite Diana. With my husband considering a run for president, it seemed like a wise move. We'll want to present a united family picture."

Crystal heard all the innuendos in Natalie's talk and though a part of her wanted to flee, she forced herself to speak calmly to Diana. "Dirk seems to be settling into the dental practice nicely."

"Yes. He's renting a house, but he's looking for a place of his own," said Diana. "He's loving the area."

"It's great for outdoor sports year-round," said Crystal. "And we're growing so fast, another dentist is very welcome." Aware that Emmett's mother was staring at her, Crystal stopped talking and turned to Emmett.

Emmett picked up on her cue and said, "How did you like the Faire today, Mother?"

"The canoe races were fun to watch, but I invited Diana to join me for a spa afternoon. We spent most of it inside getting pampered. It's lovely to have a young woman whom I know and respect do things like that with me. How about you, Crystal? How did your day go?"

"I was very busy. For the first time, the baking contest included entries by kids twelve and under. It was very exciting for them."

"Oh, yes," said Diana. "I bought a piece of apple cake for Emmett." She flashed him a dimpled smile. "Was it as delicious as I thought?"

"It was very tasty," said Emmett tersely, and Crystal knew he was as upset as she was over his mother including Diana in a dinner meant for the three of them.

Crystal hoped she could get through the evening without either crying or shouting at Natalie and Diana.

Emmett's cell rang. He clicked on the call and listened. "Okay, I'll be right there." He ended the call. "Emergency. A little boy has broken an arm. I've got to leave."

"I'll come with you," Crystal said, placing her napkin on the tabletop.

Emmett studied her. "Okay, let's go." He turned to his mother. "We'll have dinner another time, Mother. Goodnight to both of you."

He helped Crystal out of her chair, and she gave his mother and Diana a bob of her head before turning and following Emmett out of the room.

As they were waiting out front for the valet to bring his car, Diana rushed out to them. "Emmett, I'm sorry. Please don't be mad at me. I just wanted to have some time with you."

"I'm on a date with Crystal. We can talk later," he said as his car was driven up to the front. He helped Crystal down the stairs to his car, and after getting in himself, they took off with a roar.

"What was that all about?" Crystal asked. "You didn't know Diana was going to be there?"

"My mother suggested it, but I told her no, that I wanted her to get to know you. I'm sorry. She can be so irritating, hurtful."

"That was humiliating."

Emmett reached over and took hold of her hand. "You handled yourself well. I'm just sorry you had to go through another terrible scene with my mother."

"Maybe we'd better cool it," said Crystal. "It's obvious I'll never be acceptable to your family, your mother in particular."

"It's my life, not theirs," said Emmett quietly but firmly. "Do you understand now why I've done what I did by changing my name, educating myself, and demanding independence?"

Crystal nodded but it didn't make her feel any better.

"I'm going directly to the clinic. Do you want to go with me?" he asked.

"Yes," said Crystal. "If we have time after that, I can whip up dinner at my apartment. Then the entire evening won't be wasted."

"Sounds like a plan," said Emmett driving to the outskirts of town where his practice was located.

When he got there, a mother was waiting in the car with her eight-year-old son who was crying.

"I'll open the office. Will you help them get inside?" Emmett said to her.

"Sure." Crystal got out of the car and walked over to them.

The mother was sniffling as she helped a crying boy out of the car.

"Hello, I'm Crystal, here to help Dr. Chambers. He's getting ready for you inside. Please come with me and he'll get you all fixed up." She knelt in front of the boy. "It's going to be all right."

Crystal led them inside where Emmett had turned on the lights and was waiting for them.

"Hello," he said. "I'm Dr. Chambers."

With tears still wet on her cheeks, the woman said, "Hi, Dr. Chambers. I'm Samantha Butler, and this is my son, Jeffrey."

Emmett knelt in front of the boy. "Hey, Jeffrey, we're going to take a look at your arm and then get you fixed up." He looked up at the boy's mother. "Tell me what happened."

"We were having a picnic at one of the lakeside parks, and the kids were all running around like crazy. I called to Jeffrey to tell him to stop, and when he turned towards me, he tripped on a toy truck and fell." Her eyes welled with fresh tears.

Emmett stood. "Things like this can happen, especially with active young children busy having fun. He's not a regular patient of mine. Is there any medical information I should be aware of? Is he up to date on a tetanus shot?"

"He's up to date on all medications," Samantha said. "I tried to tell him to be careful ..."

Crystal walked over and put an arm around her. "Don't

blame yourself. I remember when something similar happened to my sister. I felt terrible, thinking it was my fault. But kids are bound to have accidents from time to time. It's how we all learn."

Emmett glanced at her and smiled. He turned to Jeffrey. "We're going to get a picture of your arm. Why don't you come back with me, and I'll show you how we're going to do it. Mom, you might want to join us."

"I'll wait here in case you need me," Crystal told Emmett.

Crystal sat in the waiting room. It was interesting to see the changes Emmett had made to the space, including painting the walls a sunny yellow and updating the dark wood chairs lining the room with bright colors. It gave the room a more welcoming feel.

A few minutes later, Emmett appeared. "Crystal, can you join us? While I set the arm, Jeffrey and his mother could use some pleasant conversation from you. And then you can help me keep them both calm while I take care of the temporary cast."

Flattered, Crystal rose and followed him into the examination room.

"I have a clear picture of the arm and it appears the radius has a clean fracture. I'll adjust the arm a bit and then we can put a temporary cast on the arm. It's adjustable for when the swelling goes down but don't worry about that. You can bring Jeffrey in this week to have me take another look at it and adjust the cast."

"Sounds like an easy plan, huh, Jeffrey?" Crystal said cheerfully. "Want me to tell you a story about my sister and the purple cast she wore once?"

Jeffrey gave her an unenthusiastic nod.

Crystal began with, "My sister's name is Misty, and she was nine, I'm guessing a little older than you when she broke her arm. The doctor put a cast on her arm, covered in purple, and they made up a story about how she saved a whole family of fairies by doing battle with a mean gardener who was about to destroy their little garden kingdom. We can make up a story for you, too. Would you like to do that?"

Jeffrey's eyes lit with interest. He nodded, unaware of the adjustment Emmett was making to his arm.

"What do you want to do? Take on pirates? Spacemen? What?" she asked him, noting how pleased the mother seemed at the way Jeffrey was smiling.

"I want to fight sea monsters," said Jeffrey. "Big ones, like dinosaurs."

"Okay, let's begin. Once there was a boy named Jeffrey. And he lived by the sea...where?"

"In Florida," said Jeffrey.

His mother laughed. "We recently visited Disney World."

"Okay, Florida," said Crystal. "And the little boy Jeffrey one day saw a monster rise out of the sea. What did he look like?"

"He was big and green with sharp teeth like a shark," said Jeffrey, hardly noticing Emmett tightening the temporary cast around his arm.

"And then what happened?" Crystal asked. She loved children's imaginations.

"Then Jeffrey told the monster to go away. People wanted to swim. But the monster said, 'I want to swim too. So, Jeffrey said, 'Okay, but you have to give us magical rides in the water."

"Oh, what fun! Did he give everyone rides?"

"Yes. Even Betsy Dooley. She's not my girlfriend."

Crystal worked not to laugh. Jeffrey was such a sweet boy. Poor Betsy Dooley.

Emmett's eyes were twinkling with laughter, but he said seriously, "Okay, Jeffrey, I'm glad you got the monster under control. Guess what! You're almost ready to leave. You and

Crystal can keep talking while I give your mother instructions for taking care of the arm."

"Okay," said Jeffrey looking at the cast. "I want a blue color."

"Remember that when it's time to choose," said Crystal.

His mother returned to get him.

Crystal helped him off the examination table. "Goodbye, Jeffrey. It was fun to hear your story. I hope your arm heals fast."

Jeffrey waved to her before he turned to leave.

"Thank you for your help," said Jeffrey's mother.

"I'm glad I could be of help," Crystal said, following them to the front door.

Emmett met them there. "Call my office on Monday to make an appointment. We'll want to check on the swelling and go from there."

"Thank you, Doctor. I'm glad we were able to get help quickly." She turned to Crystal. "And thanks for helping both Jeffrey and me. I've noticed you're both dressed up. I'm sorry to have disturbed you."

"That's not a problem." Crystal watched them leave and turned to Emmett. "You have an easy way with children. I'm impressed by how quickly and calmly you got the work done."

Emmett threw an arm around her shoulder. "Thanks to you. You're a natural nurse. 'Sure you don't want to come work for me?"

Crystal laughed. "No thanks. You know the old dating rule—no fishing off the company pier."

"Yes, it might become a big problem because I'm always thinking of you." He clasped her face in his hands and gently, slowly kissed her, savoring the taste of her.

Reaching up, she drew him to her, never wanting to let go. When they finally pulled apart, Crystal sighed with pleasure.

"What about that dinner you talked about?" said Emmett. "Are you still agreeable to cooking something?"

"Your place or mine?" said Crystal.

Emmett gazed at her with a sexy smile. "Definitely mine." He crooked his arm and held it out to her. "C'mon. Let's go."

He locked up his clinic and they walked to his house. The summer evening was pleasantly cool, and as Crystal gazed up at the stars, she felt as if they were shining for her.

Inside Emmett's house, the kitchen was workable even though finishing touches needed to be made. Appliances were in place. Cabinet doors had yet to be mounted and Crystal noticed that the tile backsplash behind the counters had yet to be completed. But knocking down two walls made the kitchen much larger and open to a combined dining and living area. With the sliding glass doors in place to what would become a screened-in porch, Crystal could imagine how sunlight would fill the room.

"What an improvement," she murmured, studying the space.

"It's like a miracle, and yet Brad tells me it's all quite simple," said Emmett.

"Aaron and Brad have put together an outstanding company. They started on their own, and when they got the contract to build The Woodlands and decided to develop The Meadows, they built a fantastic team."

"Collister Construction handles a lot of the projects in this state and beyond," said Emmett. He gave her a sheepish grin. "I googled them online before I agreed to have them do the work. That, and the fact that they could move quickly, made my decision easy."

"Okay, let's see what you have in the refrigerator," said

Crystal.

"Not much. Eggs, butter, milk, and some other basics."

"How about an omelet? I can whip one up in a hurry."

"An omelet sounds perfect. Quick and easy," said Emmett, drawing her into his arms. "Or we could wait on dinner ..."

Crystal didn't answer, and, instead, lifted her face to his.

Their decision made, they headed upstairs to the guest room Emmett still used as his while construction took place.

Crystal eased her dress off, leaving the black lace bikini pants and black lacy bra she'd put on to make herself feel special when meeting Emmett's mother.

"You look fantastic," said Emmett, dropping his pants on the floor and approaching her.

Crystal hugged him tightly and then followed him to his bed and climbed on top of it, as eager as he to proceed.

He helped her remove her lacy bits. "Beautiful," he murmured and lowered his lips to hers.

Later, Crystal lay next to him, curled up in his arms. Emmett knew just how to please her, and lying there, she wondered how she could ever back away from him.

CHAPTER TWENTY

CRYSTAL WAS MIXING EGGS for the cheese omelet she was preparing. Wearing a shirt of Emmett's to cover her, she wondered if the day would ever come when this would be her kitchen, their kitchen.

Emmett appeared. Smiling, he walked over to her and nuzzled her neck. "If only this could be every night. Or morning," he added, laughing. "Guess it is another day."

"I've got Misty covering for me in a few hours. Thank God she's willing to step in."

Emmett tugged on the shirttails, bringing her to him. "The shirt's a little big on you. Want to take it off? You'd look even more beautiful."

Crystal pushed at him playfully. "Leave me alone. I'm cooking. Get some plates and silverware out. It'll be ready in no time."

"Aye, Aye, Captain," said Emmett. "I'll make some coffee. The last day of Summer Faire awaits us. I hope I don't have any other broken bones to tend to."

"Jeffrey sure was cute," said Crystal, stirring the eggs in a frying pan.

"How many kids do you want?" Emmett asked her as he set silverware on the kitchen bar.

The spoon in Crystal's hand shook. She turned to face him. "You answer first."

"Okay. Easy. I want at least three children. With a much older stepsister growing up and no one else, I want enough children to make each one feel as if they had a special friend."

He nudged her. "Your turn."

She put the eggs on separate plates, placed them on the bar counter, and turned to him.

"After raising Misty and knowing what a bad mother I had, I vowed not to have children of my own. I didn't think I could do it. But lately, I've been thinking about it, and I do want a family. Maybe two children."

He took a sip of coffee and studied her. "That's important to me. Sorry, but we're going to have to stand. Bar stools are on order, and as you can see, no table and chairs yet."

They dug into the food and then Emmett said, "Is tonight the barbeque at the Lilac Lake Cottage with all your friends?"

"Yes, it should be fun. The staff will be celebrating on their own in town, and this will be a relaxing way to end the weekend."

"My mother is leaving for Maine this morning. Again, I'm sorry about her behavior. I intend to speak to her about it before she leaves. She can't continue to disrespect you. As far as my stepfather running for president, he may announce it, but I don't think he has the staying power. He's made too many political enemies."

"Even if he does succeed, I can't change my background. Besides, I have nothing to be ashamed of." She held her breath waiting for a response.

"Of course not," said Emmett. "You're a fantastic woman, bright and capable of more than surviving on your own. You are beloved in this town, and I understand every reason for that."

Crystal let out a sigh of relief. She wanted to tell him her feelings, but she held back. Though she knew he felt that way toward her, he had yet to say those magical three words to her.

After eating their early morning supper, Crystal hurried to get dressed so Emmett could drop her off at her apartment.

She hoped to get a few hours' sleep before the last hectic day of the Faire.

Crystal was awakened by Misty shaking her. "Time to get up. The Café is open, but one of our cooks is out sick. Too much partying."

Startled, Crystal sat up to check the time. Eight o'clock on her bedside alarm. She stretched. "Oh, Misty, you should've woken me up earlier. But bless you for letting me get some sleep."

"Well, we need you now. You'd better get moving," said Misty, reminding Crystal of herself.

She got out of bed, took a shower, and dressed in record time.

Downstairs, the kitchen was backed up. She grabbed a cup of coffee and went to work prepping salad fixings for lunches. Brad's family owned the Collister Farm Stand. Crystal sent Misty there for fresh greens and vegetables. Though they were running low on some supplies, Crystal figured they could make it until Monday when her normal food delivery would arrive.

While Misty was gone, Crystal handled the front, greeting customers, and helping with the flow of dishes to and from tables. Her waitresses were of varying ages. Brenda Thomas was the oldest at a spry seventy. Crystal had made sure it was a pleasant place to work, and most of her staff front and back had been with her since she'd first opened.

She was carrying a stack of dirty dishes to the kitchen when Emmett's mother and Diana walked into the Café. Crystal bobbed her head at them and continued walking. After dumping the dishes into the dirty-dish bin, she wiped her hands on her apron and approached them.

"Welcome to the Lilac Lake Café. As you can see, we're busy, but I believe a table might be available out on the patio. Will that do?"

Emmett's mother studied the room. "I see you have one table reserved."

"I'm sorry, but that's taken for the Governor and his wife. They're regular summer customers of mine."

The look on Emmett's mother's face was priceless. Crystal would have given anything to be able to take a photo of it.

"So, the outdoor table will do?" asked Crystal.

"Yes," said Emmett's mother. "Come, Diana. Let's see if the food is as delicious as you say."

Crystal led them outdoors and to a table under an umbrella. "Your waitress will be here shortly. Enjoy."

In the main room, she signaled for Brenda to join her and explained the situation. "It's important that Mrs. Chamberlain and her guest get excellent service. I know I can trust you to provide it."

Brenda grinned. "I know who she is, and I promise to do my best even though she's known to be a stingy tipper."

Crystal wasn't surprised that Brenda knew such a thing. It was a small town where staff members of various businesses talked to one another. Still, she wondered if Natalie Chamberlain was aware of her poor reputation.

"Don't worry, Brenda, I'll make it up to you by assigning you the Governor's table."

"Thanks. That makes it even," said Brenda. She brushed at her apron, straightened, and headed outdoors to do the job.

A short while later, Governor Simon Mitchell and his wife, Jaynie, showed up. Crystal shook hands with him and accepted a hug from Jaynie. Crystal and Jaynie had worked together on a tourism project, and Jaynie had taken Crystal under her wings, treating her like one of her daughters. Still hugging her, Jaynie said, "I love your hair. You're back to your natural color."

Before she could answer, Crystal heard a voice behind her say, "Jaynie Mitchell, I thought I recognized you and Simon."

Emmett's mother held out her hand to Jaynie, forcing her to relinquish her hold on Crystal.

"Oh, yes. Natalie Chamberlain." Jaynie shook hands with her. "I thought you were spending the summer in Mt. Desert."

Natalie nodded and smiled. "I'm here visiting my son. He's the new doctor in town."

Jaynie frowned. "Oh, you mean Emmett Chambers. We were delighted that he agreed to take over for Dr. Johnson. I keep an eye on such things as doctors, especially rural doctors, who are in such shortage everywhere. We were lucky to get him."

"Indeed," said Emmett's mother. "Perhaps we can get together sometime soon. Everett is considering a run for a higher office, and it would be helpful if we could spend some time with you and Simon." She turned to him. "Simon, nice to see you. I love this little town."

"So do we," he replied. "Especially this Café and Crystal's excellent food. We're big fans." Sensing Crystal's discomfort, he put an arm around her shoulder.

Natalie's eyes rounded. "Oh, yes. Well, I hope to be able to chat with you later." She turned and walked away.

Jaynie studied Crystal. "Okay, what's going on?"

"Let's talk later," said Crystal. "Right now, Brenda is waiting to take your orders."

"Okay," said Jaynie. "But I know you well enough to understand you're troubled. We visited The Meadows, and I heard from Dani Collister that you had something going with a new man."

Crystal sighed. "I need your opinion on something."

"All right, sweetie. Now, I'm ready for some of your biscuits." Jaynie followed Crystal to their table and smiled at Brenda who was waiting to serve them.

Shaken by the undercurrents between Jaynie and Emmett's mother, pleased by the support both Simon and Jaynie had shown her, Crystal retreated to the kitchen to catch her breath. It was going to be a long day. Thank goodness she had the barbeque to look forward to.

A few moments later, as Crystal emerged from the kitchen, she saw Emmett's mother and Diana preparing to leave. She hesitated and then decided not to be intimidated by the woman.

"I hope you enjoyed your meal," said Crystal approaching them.

"It was delicious," said Diana. "With Dirk living here, I intend to eat here whenever I visit. Right now, I'm working for Senator Chamberlain's campaign."

"A great opportunity for you following college graduation," said Crystal keeping a noncommittal expression on her face.

"I had no idea you knew the Mitchells," said Emmett's mother.

"Yes, they're good people," Crystal replied. "We have several well-known people visit Lilac Lake. It's become a popular resort area."

"I've heard that Whitney Gilford lives nearby," said Emmett's mother.

Crystal hesitated, then said, "She's my best friend. Emmett and I are going to a barbeque at the cottage she shares with her sisters. Courtney Castle, the pen name for Taylor Gilford, is one of her sisters."

"Well, I ... I don't know what to say," said Emmett's mother, looking flustered.

"Enjoy your trip back home," Crystal said to her. "Goodbye,

Diana."

Crystal walked away, satisfied with the way she'd handled herself. Normally, she'd never mention Whitney or Taylor, but it felt right to be able to do so. Somehow, she knew GG would approve.

Later, as Jaynie was finishing her breakfast, she waved Crystal over. "C'mon, girlfriend, let's go outside where we can talk."

Crystal followed her outside and to the town green to one of the benches placed along the edge.

"What's going on with you and Natalie Chamberlain? Is it her son?"

Crystal sighed. "Emmett and I are dating. His parents, his mother in particular, have been very critical of me, even making a scene inside Jake's restaurant where I was sitting with friends. She'd seen a picture of us on the local news when we had an accident on Route 1 in Maine."

"Oh, I remember that. It became part of the discussion about widening that road. But you weren't hurt."

"Emmett's nose was broken, but other than that, both of us came out of it okay. My car had damage, of course, but I was glad nothing worse happened."

"Was that the first Emmett's mother had heard about you?" Jaynie asked.

"Yes, she was furious he was with me and treated me like I was a gold-digging whore because of my purple hair. I thought I'd keep the color to spite her but then decided it was time to change it back to my natural color anyway."

"I love you no matter what color your hair is," said Jaynie, giving her a quick hug. "What did you want to ask me?"

"Since Emmett's father might be running for president, do

you think I should step away from him for a while? He has problems with his family. I don't want to add to them."

"Absolutely not," said Jaynie. "First of all, you don't owe his parents anything. Second, if you become part of the family, you'll have to put up with all kinds of comments like the rest of us in politics. But I don't believe Everett Chamberlain has a chance in hell of winning a nomination from his party. He would be running against a well-respected man, which is saying a lot." She shook her head. "I don't understand why some men can't be satisfied with the job they're doing. Simon and I decided long ago not to pursue the route Everett is choosing."

"But Simon is someone who could do an outstanding job as president," countered Crystal.

"We're proud of the job Simon's doing for New Hampshire, but that's it. We don't want to deal with the intrusive media and the circus that comes with that much attention. We believe in public service, but we've done our duty. Simon and I want a peaceful life. That's why we were looking at houses in The Meadows."

"Oh, nice. It's beautiful there."

"Listen, I know enough about both Natalie and Everett Chamberlain to tell you to relax. You and Emmett go about your business, and if things go smoother for Everett than I think, then you can face how you want to deal with it."

"Emmett's father already has a campaign committee because the young woman Natalie was having lunch with is working on it."

"M-m-m, interesting. I still don't think you have anything to worry about. And, for heaven's sake, Natalie has no reason to try to belittle you. She has problems of her own."

"Thanks for helping me put things in perspective." Crystal gave Jaynie a hug.

"You're a lovely woman," said Jaynie. "Remember that."

They started walking back to the restaurant.

"Now it's your turn to talk," Crystal said to Jaynie. "Tell me about your granddaughter. She's two now. Is she a terrible two?"

"She's a terrific two," said Jaynie acting the proud grandmother. "When her baby brother arrives, she might turn terrible. But in the meantime, I adore her. It's another reason for Simon and me to not want to seek a higher office. I want time to enjoy both grandchildren. And with my other two daughters engaged, it's going to be a few busy years ahead."

"It sounds perfect for you. I've always loved that you've been very warm and welcoming to everyone. I'm sure your future sons-in-law feel the same way about you."

Jaynie smiled at her. "That's sweet of you to say. The truth is you love your kids and theirs in different ways—all with an equal amount of love, just differently."

Simon stood outside the Café waiting for them to approach.

"It will be wonderful to have you living here year-round," said Crystal. "And I know Dani, Brad, and Aaron must be thrilled to think of you living at The Meadows."

"I think it's going to be just what we want," said Jaynie. "We'll live here at least part of the year after Simon is free from his job. Summers here are delightful."

"Ready?" said Simon, smiling at them both.

Crystal and Jaynie glanced at one another and nodded. They hugged goodbye and Crystal returned to the Café. Today, they would close promptly because an evening with friends was ahead.

CHAPTER TWENTY-ONE

AFTER CLOSING UP THE CAFÉ, Crystal hurried up to her apartment to shower and change for the barbeque. It seemed like a long time since she and her friends had hung out at the lake. She was anxious for Emmett to see how much fun it could be. While she was growing up, many summer days were spent at The Lilac Lake Inn with the Guilford girls and their circle of friends. Now that the women had taken over the cottage, it was even better.

Because it was a hot day, Crystal wore a pair of denim shorts, a yellow print halter top, and sandals. It felt great to be out of her workday attire of jeans and T-shirts with the Café logo.

Misty had gone ahead to the barbeque, so Crystal was alone when Emmett picked her up. His lingering gaze flashed his approval. "You look fantastic."

"Thanks. You're looking quite handsome yourself," she replied, admiring the way his blue golf shirt showed off his muscles and brightened the color of his eyes.

He put his arms around her and lowered his lips to hers. "We could be late to the picnic," he murmured rubbing her back.

Laughing, she pulled away. "No way. I've been looking forward to this all day. But after we leave there, we can go to your place ...

"Okay," he said, giving her a sexy grin as he squeezed her, "Then we won't be rushed."

"I know the way. Shall I drive?" she asked. "I won't have

anything alcoholic and will be the designated driver."

"Perfect. I'd like a beer or two."

Happy with their solution they headed to her car.

As they drove, Crystal filled him in on the history of the cottage. "Two years ago, Whitney, Dani, and Taylor's grandmother, GG, gave the cottage to them with the understanding that the cottage would be renovated. That's how Dani and Brad met. Dani designed the improvements to the cottage. But, in renovating the cottage, the three women had to resolve the story that the cottage was haunted. They were able to figure out who the ghost was, and she has since disappeared."

"A ghost? Really? It sounds interesting," said Emmett.

"Pretty scary, if you ask me," Crystal retorted. "Anyway, the women own the cottage for as long as they live in it at least six months of the year. Otherwise, the owners of the Inn have the right to buy it."

"That will keep everyone in the family connected to Lilac Lake. That's a cool way of ensuring the family stays close."

"Yes, I think GG had something like that in mind. Her family has owned the land on which the Inn sits for years. You now know Dani and Brad, Whitney and Nick. I don't think you've had much of a chance to know Taylor or to meet her husband, Cooper, an editor with Pritchard Publishing in New York. You'll like them. Taylor writes romances under the name Courtney Castle."

"Seems like everyone in this small town is interesting," said Emmett. "I'm glad more and more of your friends are opting to live here year-round. That makes it nice for everyone."

"Yes, it was pretty lonely for a while when everyone was off to college and new jobs leaving just a few of us behind in town. I think that's why Nick and I ended up together for a while. Now, he's where he should be, with Whitney, and I'm free to be with you."

Emmett glanced at her. "I hope so."

"What do you mean?" Crystal asked, alarmed by his words.

"I just meant I hope you can be patient with my family. They're pretty difficult."

"Let's just take it one day at a time. A dear friend suggested I simply wait to see how things unfold."

He grinned. "Are you talking about me?"

"I needed some advice. That's all," she said. "I don't want to make any mistakes."

Emmett sobered. "Neither do I. Simply put, I don't ever want to hurt you."

Their conversation ended when she pulled into the driveway of the cottage and parked by other cars. Painted gray and attractively landscaped, the cottage that had seemed so forlorn now looked beautiful with its wide windows and open view of the lake.

Dani came to greet them.

Crystal got out of the car and handed a basket of cookies and cake to her. "It looks like a perfect evening for a barbeque picnic."

"And with the slight breeze, the bugs aren't a problem. Come on around to the front."

Crystal and Emmett followed her to the sweeping lawn in front of the house. The grass met the shoreline. Sitting in the water was the mammoth rock where they'd sunbathed each summer. A group of ducks paddled about in the shallower water near the rock.

Inhaling the aroma of pine and the distinct smell of lake water, Crystal let out a contented sigh. She could already feel the tension of the day ease from her body. Being at the lake always did this for her.

A crowd was already standing around, drinking sodas and

beer, and chatting in groups.

Crystal was pleased to see so many friends. She noticed Dirk. It wasn't until he moved that she saw Diana. Before she could mention it to Emmett, Diana jogged toward them.

"Emmett, I'm glad you're here. I know you were upset with your mother and me at the Inn last night, and I want to say I'm sorry. As your mother may have told you, I'll be working with your father's campaign and helping her. I already feel like part of the family."

"I think you owe Crystal an apology too. It was supposed to be a dinner for my mother to get to know Crystal better."

Diana bit her lip before turning to her. "I'm sorry, Crystal. Natalie asked me to accompany her. I didn't understand."

"Thank you," Crystal said, unsure what to say next.

Diana smiled at Emmett, lifted herself onto her toes, and kissed Emmett on the cheek. "There. I don't want anything to ruin our relationship."

Emmett patted Diana awkwardly on the back before stepping away from her. "Okay, now that that's out of the way, let me enjoy myself with Crystal."

As they walked away, Crystal looked back and noticed how intensely Diana was studying them. An uneasy feeling entered her. Diana was interested in Emmett as more than a family member. And if Crystal wasn't mistaken, she was being encouraged by Emmett's mother.

She was jarred back to the moment when Taylor approached. "Crystal, I'm happy you came." She turned to Emmett. "And you too, of course. I'm glad to see you here with Crystal."

Certain Taylor was going to gush more about their being together, Crystal said, "Where's Cooper?"

Taylor took her elbow. "Follow me."

She led them to the far edge of the lawn where two men

were in deep discussion.

"Cooper and Aaron are talking about a possible project, but we can interrupt them," said Taylor.

Aaron turned as they approached. Tall, with black, straight hair, brown eyes, and tan skin, he had classic features. He smiled at her, and Crystal easily gave him a quick hug hello.

"I haven't seen you in forever," she said. "Where have you been hiding?"

"At The Meadows. While work is being done on Emmett's house, I've taken over running most of the development." He shook hands with Emmett.

"Cooper, darling," said Taylor. "You've met the new doctor in town, Emmett Chambers. And you know Crystal."

"Of course. Nice to see you again, Crystal." He held out his hand to Emmett, and the two men shook. "I understand how happy Lilac Lake is to have you here. Are you enjoying the area?"

Emmett glanced at her and back to him. "Yes, I am. Everyone seems friendly, and I can practice medicine on a personal level I like."

"I heard you're the son of Senator Chamberlain. How is that working in a conservative state?" Cooper asked. Crystal realized that he wasn't being rude, but was simply interested.

"I've maintained my independence for some time, so it isn't an issue, especially with the name change. I'm sure you've experienced some of that same need working in the family publishing company."

Behind his horn-rimmed glasses, Cooper's blue eyes sparkled. "Touché. I like you, Emmett. I hope we can spend some time together. Do you enjoy fishing?"

"I haven't tried it, but I'm sure I'll like it. Just being on the water is soothing." Emmett turned to Aaron. "How about you? Do you ever get a chance to relax?"

"Evenings often find me on the lake in my canoe. That's when nature quiets for the night. A perfect time."

Emmett grinned. "With my house on the river, I guess I need to get a canoe."

"You're welcome to use mine until you do," said Aaron. "Are you interested in doing anything with maple sugaring? I'll need help in the spring."

"I haven't done it, but it sounds like something I'd like to try," said Emmett.

Pleased, Crystal listened to the exchange. As Emmett had mentioned, everyone in town was welcoming, and it felt so wonderful to be part of it.

Dani walked over to them. "We need some badminton players. C'mon, join us."

"I will in a little bit. Right now, Emmett and I need something cool to drink."

Taylor took her arm. "Let's get some sodas and beers for our ... dates."

Crystal laughed. "I wondered when that would come up."

"Emmett's adorable, and you two look perfect together," Taylor said.

"Well, Diana is very interested in Emmett, and I believe his mother is encouraging her. So, we'll have to see how it all plays out. Right now, Emmett and I are enjoying one another. But where it goes from here is unknown. Funny, I wanted a family for so long, and now, I find myself having to deal with one I don't necessarily like."

"Life is like that, isn't it? It sometimes takes a sense of humor to understand all of it," said Taylor. "It's those kinds of quirks that I like to place in my books."

"How is your next novel coming along?"

Taylor laughed. "Speaking of needing a sense of humor ..."

"I know you'll make this time at the lake working on your

novel succeed. You always do."

"I hope so," said Taylor as they approached Brad who was refilling a wheelbarrow with ice and canned drinks.

"Hey, Crystal, I didn't see you arrive. What'll you have?" asked Brad.

"A coke and a beer for Emmett."

"Here you go," he said, handing them to her. "What about you, Taylor?"

"I'll just have a coke," she said. "But I'd better take a beer for Cooper."

Crystal and Taylor carried their drinks back to the three men talking together. Crystal handed a beer to Emmett and then asked Aaron if he wanted her drink.

"No thanks," he said. "I need to talk to David about some landscaping at The Meadows."

Crystal waited until the men appeared to be finished talking, then she nudged Emmett. "Come talk to David Graham. He and his father own Graham Landscaping, and he's a nice guy."

As they crossed the lawn, Crystal waved to Beth and Garth Beckman who'd brought their toddler daughter to the gathering. The mix of adults, children, and dogs was pleasing.

Mindy, Whitney's black-and-tan dachshund, roamed the area nose to the ground, no doubt looking for snacks.

David was talking to Aaron and Diana. Crystal studied him. A tall, lanky man with sandy-colored hair and an easy smile on his handsome face, he'd always been on the quiet side. But he was someone you listened to when he spoke because he knew a lot about many things.

Crystal quietly told Emmett that David's older sister had died in a boating accident when she was still in her teens. "David faithfully maintains a small memorial garden in town in her memory. He and Aaron, with their love of outdoors and growing things, have always been friends."

"Interesting." Emmett studied the group as they approached.

"Hi, David," said Crystal. "It's always nice to see you."

"You might remember me. Emmett Chambers. I bought Dr. Johnson's house," said Emmett, shaking David's hand. "It's being renovated now. I'd like you to come and take a look at the landscaping. I think it's due for some upgrading."

"Be glad to do that," said David. "And I need to make an appointment with you for a checkup for my insurance company. I'm increasing my life insurance."

"That sounds very serious," said Diana.

David's facial expression changed ever so slightly as a flash of sadness filled it and disappeared. "I've learned that life can be unpredictable."

"Yes," said Diana. "But I always try to concentrate on the positive." She glanced at Emmett.

He was turning to Aaron and didn't notice, but Crystal did.

"A positive attitude is helpful," said David, looking at Diana. "But it doesn't hurt to be prepared."

Diana laughed. "You sound like a boy scout."

He joined her laughter as Whitney came over to them, carrying Timothy. "Hey, how's it going? Did everyone get something to drink? To eat?"

"I'm ready for something to eat," Emmett said to Crystal.

"Let's go." They headed out together.

The picnic table set up on the front porch held an array of dishes. Bowls of macaroni and cheese, coleslaw, baked beans, assorted cold salads, chips, and fruit covered most of the red-and-white checkered tablecloth. Crystal's cookies and assorted slices of cake sat with other desserts on another table with a coffee maker, paper cups, cream, and sugar.

"At these gatherings, nobody goes away hungry," said

Crystal, opting for a handful of chips before having dinner.

Garth Beckman was helping Nick at the grill cooking ribs, hot dogs, hamburgers, chicken wings, and bratwurst sausages.

Ross and his tennis pal, Mike Dawson, were climbing the rise of the lawn to the house with Misty. Dirk and Melissa called to them.

"Come with me," Crystal said to Emmett. "I want to show you the rock where I spent many summer hours sunbathing after swimming in the lake."

They walked down to the rock and climbed on top of it. The gray granite was smooth and warm from the sun. Crystal sat down and then stretched out on her back along its surface. She turned to Emmett. "This is how we play games with the clouds."

He lay down beside her facing the sky. A willing participant, he looked up and said, "Okay, what do you see?"

She concentrated on a large white cloud floating by and squinted. Staring at the shape and a long narrow strip of cloud emerging from one end, she said, "That's easy. I see an elephant."

"No, it's a dinosaur. See? It's got a big body, a long neck, and a tiny head."

"Over there. What do you see?" she asked, pointing to another cloud.

"A warrior," he said. "A man with a hatchet."

Crystal chuckled. "I was going to say a woman with a bonnet and watering can."

As they laughed together, Crystal realized how different his world was from hers. But then there was the Venus and Mars thing. So, it wasn't alarming.

Whitney approached. "Mind if I join you?"

Crystal sat up. "Not at all. We were playing the cloud

game."

Whitney laughed. "How many hours did we spend doing that each summer growing up?"

"Those days seem long ago," said Crystal, unable to hide a hint of sadness.

"It's a nice memory though," Whitney said, staring out at the water. "I'm thankful GG gave my sisters and me this cottage. I want Timothy and all the little ones in our group to be able to have summers like we had. Life had taken us in different directions, and it's wonderful to be back again."

"I'm very glad you returned," Crystal said, smiling at her best friend.

Pirate, Dani's black lab, wandered over, looked at them, and then with a groan of pleasure, sprawled out on the rock next to them.

Crystal liked that everyone in the group was comfortable with one another, including Pirate and Mindy. She hoped to have a dog one day. A baby too. She gazed at Emmett still lying on the rock, his eyes closed. He was such a special friend, a generous lover.

Whitney caught her eye and winked.

Crystal winked back, happy to share the moment with her.

"Come and get it!" called Nick, waving his cooking spatula at them.

Whitney got to her feet. "C'mon. We can't keep them waiting. They've been cooking for a long time."

Crystal shook Emmett's shoulder and stood. "Time for dinner."

Emmett instantly sat up. "Whoa! I almost fell asleep. This lake air got to me."

"It's been a busy weekend for everyone," said Crystal helping him up.

He stood and put an arm across her shoulder. "Thanks for

inviting me to this barbeque. It's a needed break for me."

"I'm happy you're meeting more of my friends. They're an important part of my life."

"I can see why."

They followed Whitney up the incline.

He frowned as Diana came rushing toward them. "I've saved you seats on the lawn by me." Though she spoke to both of them, her gaze remained on Emmett.

Hiding her irritation, Crystal hoped Emmett would make it clear to Diana that they were together.

Later, as it grew dark, David got up from his seat on a blanket spread on the grass and faced the crowd with a grin. "I've got fireworks."

Everyone cheered. For someone normally quiet, David loved fireworks and usually went a little wild at Fourth of July celebrations when he and a couple of firemen presented a show for the entire town.

"While you get those ready to go, I'm getting protective headphones for Timothy," said Whitney. "Do you want to borrow one for your little girl, Beth? I've got an extra pair from the last Fourth of July."

The two women got up and went into the cottage.

Crystal stood and said to Emmett, "I'll be right back."

As she walked into the cottage, she was struck again by the changes to the building. No longer drab or worn by years of use and disuse, the interior radiated new life, openness, and comfort. She knew Emmett was going for the same feel with his house.

After Crystal finished freshening up, she went outside to find Diana sitting in her place next to Emmett.

Diana looked up at her and, not moving, patted the space next to her. "Sit here."

"No, Crystal, come over here on the other side of me," said Emmett.

Crystal sat beside him on the grass but noticed he didn't make any effort to move away from Diana.

All through the fun of watching the fireworks, Diana stayed right at Emmett's side, even turning into him at a particularly loud blast.

Crystal waited for Emmett to do something, say something, but he remained unaware of her discomfort with Diana's behavior.

After the fireworks ended and people started to pack up, Diana came over to Emmett and her. "I noticed you came with Crystal. I'm happy to take you home, Emmett."

"No, thanks. As you said, I came with Crystal."

"Oh, okay. I just thought now that I'm part of the family, so to speak ..."

Someone called Emmett, and he turned and walked away.

"You've made your intentions very clear," Crystal said to her, fed up with Diana's conduct.

Diana pulled her aside. "It's never going to work between you and Emmett. I've known him for a long time. His family approves of me. Natalie even suggested that Emmett and I should be paired together." She turned on her heel and flounced away, her white eyelet shirt a beacon of danger in the darkness.

On the way back to Emmett's house, Crystal was silent as she drove. Her mind was playing all kinds of games with her, reliving past demeaning episodes in her life, bringing out all her insecurities.

"You're unusually quiet. What's wrong?" asked Emmett.

"I'm trying to sort things out in my mind. I couldn't help noticing Diana's attention to you. She's so obvious. She had no problem taking my place next to you on the blanket and you didn't seem to mind."

"As she said, she's like part of the family because she'll be working with my parents and others on my father's campaign."

"So, will you be going out with her like she wants?" Crystal hated herself for being this petty, but she couldn't help herself.

"What? No. What's gotten into you?"

Crystal pulled up to his house and parked the car. Facing him, she said, "I thought we had something special going. I may enjoy people, and have fun with them on a social level, but I'm not someone who fools around romantically. I'm careful not to put myself in a situation where I can be hurt. This relationship with you has every indication that this is where it's headed. Your family doesn't like or respect me. Otherwise, your mother wouldn't encourage Diana's romantic interest. I see a pattern emerging. You. Me. Diana. That's one too many in a relationship. And I want no part of that."

Emmett gave her a steady look. "Are you saying you want to end it between us?"

"Not really ..."

"What the hell does that mean?" said Emmett in a sharp tone indicating his anger.

"I don't know. We've only committed to getting to know one another, but I'm afraid that I'm more invested in a future together than you are. I'm thinking maybe we should step back. Maybe this has all happened too quickly." Crystal held her breath waiting for him to deny her words.

"If that's what you want. Okay. I've tried to show you how I feel. If that's not enough, this thing between us won't work."

Crystal lowered her head. All she'd wanted was a denial from him, something that would tell her he saw them together in the future as much as she did. Why had she forced the issue?

"Goodnight, Crystal," said Emmett getting out of the car. "Thanks for the ride. I'll see you around town."

She lifted her face, but he'd already started walking into the house. Not knowing what else to do, she pulled out of the driveway and headed back to her apartment.

CHAPTER TWENTY-TWO

WHEN CRYSTAL GOT HOME, she greeted Misty watching television on the couch, and went directly to her bedroom. There, she put on a nightshirt and climbed between the sheets.

At the knock on the door, she tensed.

"Are you alright?" Misty asked.

"I will be," said Crystal in a firm voice. She'd wanted more than Emmett was ready to give. It was a lesson to her not to create something that wasn't there. Emmett could've, should've had his arm around her during the fireworks, not let Diana hang all over him. He hadn't encouraged anything, but on the other hand, he hadn't indicated any unhappiness in having Diana act that way.

Her thoughts spiraled downward, feeding her insecurity. Gravitating toward a new person in town, she'd mistakenly believed she and Emmett had the foundation of something better. He was a super lover, experienced. Surely, with his looks and personality, he would be a catch for anyone. Diana certainly thought so. On and on it went.

Crystal put a pillow over her head as if that could stop her thoughts. It reminded her of times when as a child she'd do the same thing to prevent hearing her mother rant and rave about something or nothing.

Taking a deep breath, Crystal pulled the pillow off her head. She would move forward as she usually did, keeping busy with work. Though her heart was broken, she was a strong woman.

###

The next morning, she headed down to the Café at her usual time, her mind made up to get through the day. She'd been making too much of their growing relationship, putting her own spin on it. Was it her hormones at play? She couldn't stop thinking about having a family of her own. A real family—loving mother and father, and one baby, or more.

Her day started with a crowd of locals coming in to talk and gossip about the Summer Faire. Merchants were allowing their doors to open late to catch up on the news and compare success.

Midmorning, the cleanup crew met for coffee before tackling the job of taking down banners, signs, and balloons and sprucing up the town. But it was a slower day than most, with everyone relaxed and feeling good about the event.

Her staff, some hungover, pitched in to give the Café a decent straightening and cleaning before the lunch crowd appeared.

As she was wiping down tables, Whitney appeared carrying Timothy in a front-facing carrier. Seeing his sweet face, knowing her hopes of a child might be dashed forever, Crystal fought tears.

"What's up? Why the sad face?" asked Whitney giving her a look of concern.

"I let Emmett know I was upset with the way Diana acted toward him at the picnic and why he didn't do anything to stop it. I told him I thought we ought to step away from one another."

"Wait a minute," said Whitney. "You told him all that?"

Crystal nodded, wanting to cry. "You saw how Diana was hanging all over him. She took my seat on the blanket when I went inside, and she wouldn't move. I was forced to sit off the blanket on the grass on the other side of Emmett."

Whitney shook her head slowly. "Yes, I wondered what was going on with that. She's a beautiful, aggressive young woman and she seems determined to catch Emmett's attention. What did he say when you told him how you felt?"

"He said Diana was like a family friend working on his father's campaign, that he has to be kind to her."

"Do you want to know what I think?" asked Whitney, putting the pacifier back in Timothy's mouth.

"Yes. I'm at a loss," said Crystal.

"My suggestion is for you to just leave it alone. Give Emmett time to think about things. You've told him how you feel and now the ball is in his court. No matter how long it takes."

"Diana told me it would never work between Emmett and me because his family favors her."

Whitney's cheeks grew red. She narrowed her lips. "I've known women like her. Diana is a bitch. Believe me, she won't get away with it in our crowd. Poor Dirk. He's starting to get comfortable in town and doesn't need a sister to mess things up for him."

Crystal gave Whitney a squeeze on the arm. "Thanks for being here for me. You can imagine how insecure I felt when Diana talked to me that way after his mother had been awful to me."

"Let's see how independent Emmett is," said Whitney. "I'm sorry you're having to go through this, but it might make your relationship stronger in the future."

"If there is any future with us," grumped Crystal. "I don't want to be one of those women who's jealous if her spouse even looks at another woman. But I need to know how the future is going to play out with Diana in it."

"That sounds fair to me. But remember, no contact with Emmett. He has to figure it out for himself."

"Got it," said Crystal. "It's suitable timing anyway because, for the next eight days, I'm working on a play in Ogunquit and will be gone most of the time." She waved to someone coming into the Café. "What can I get you?" she asked Whitney.

"A glass of water," Whitney said. "Timothy and I are simply going for a walk. And after gorging myself on food all weekend, that's all I need."

Crystal served her water in a paper cup. "Take this."

"Thanks. See you later," said Whitney. "Love you."

"Love you too," said Crystal, overwhelmed by the way Whitney had tried to build her up.

The day progressed with no lunch order for Dr. Chambers. Crystal shrugged and kept on moving. Whitney was right. Even if she had jumped the gun a bit in trying to find out his long-term feelings for her, she had to give Emmett time to come to his own conclusion about them. In the meantime, she hoped never to cross paths with Diana.

A couple of days later, Crystal went over the normal morning and night routines for the Café with Misty for the umpteenth time. "Thanks for taking over for me. I'll see you whenever I'm needed here. Otherwise, I'll be gone for several days." At first, Crystal had planned to leave after lunch each day to drive to Maine for the play, and then after the show that normally ended about ten o'clock late, she'd either drive back to Lilac Lake or spend the night in Ogunquit with friends. Then she realized it wouldn't be fair to Misty to do that. Especially when Misty would take care of opening and closing the Café and overseeing staff as part of a trial period.

"Take care driving," said Misty. "And don't worry about us. We'll be fine. Use this as a break from everything here, including a certain doctor."

Crystal hugged her sister. "What would I do without you?"

"It's about time I paid you back for all you did for me," said Misty. "Go!"

Full of anticipation, Crystal got into her car. She was off to her summer adventure. One that she'd enjoyed for years. She played only small parts, but it was enough to give her pleasure and keep her creative juices flowing. By now she knew the management of the theater well and a few of the touring thespians who played summer stock performing plays away from larger venues.

Located on the southern coast of Maine, Ogunquit sat in Perkins Cove and was a beautiful example of what visitors described as a picture postcard scene of the Maine coastline. The four-square-mile town was known for its sandy beaches, active art and theater scene, and dining, shopping, and lodging.

As she drove into town, Crystal smiled with anticipation. For her, it was a place to revive her love of the theater. The small roles she undertook were a means of releasing her inner creativity. The timing couldn't be more perfect. The ability to transform herself into another character was very satisfying. In this case, she would be playing a part in the ensemble of the play, *Seven Brides for Seven Brothers*. Not many people in town knew that she took voice lessons in the slower days of winter. She was content to do some ensemble work. That was enough to keep her going.

Crystal pulled up to the bungalow that her theater friends Jerry Sandler and Lance Matthews owned. It was a cute, white cape cod with black shutters within easy walking distance to Footbridge Beach.

A short, heavy-set man with blond hair streaked with pink said, "There you are," as she emerged from the car. His blue eyes sparkled. "Lance and I were starting to get worried. You don't have much time before you need to get over to the theater. But come inside and relax a bit."

"Thanks," said Crystal, hugging Jerry.

Lance appeared. Tall, with black hair graying at the temples and sporting a black goatee, Lance was the gentleman he portrayed. "Did you bring luggage?"

"I have just one bag, but it's big enough to last the week while Misty runs the Café for me. If necessary, I'll go back to Lilac Lake to take care of things."

Jerry laughed. "I get it. The Café is your baby."

Lance took the bag from her. "We'll just put this in our guest room. Come inside."

The ordinary exterior of the house contrasted with a unique, updated interior. Pale-lavender walls held an array of pictures and paintings, and the gray-stained wooden floors, and the comfy off-white furniture combined to give off cozy but interesting vibes. Thinking of Emmett's renovation, Crystal took note of the details. The lime-green, orange, and lilac pillows on the couch popped with color.

The living area opened to an updated kitchen that was a dream for any chef. Jerry had insisted on it and rightly so. He was a wonderful cook. Though you couldn't tell from Lance's thin frame, he eagerly ate whatever Jerry prepared.

"I've put your bag in the guest room. We can either stay inside or go out to the back deck. Your call," said Lance.

"I'd love to be outside and smell the salty air," said Crystal. "As relaxing as the lake is, being here by the ocean is always a delight."

"I'll fix us something cold to drink. Lemonade alright?" Jerry asked her.

"That sounds delicious," said Crystal. "Thanks."

They waited and then each carried a glass of it outside to the wooden deck behind the house. An awning kept a portion of the long deck shaded. Running the width of the house, the deck was a perfect place to stretch out in one of the lounge chairs or to eat at the umbrella-topped table. Like everything inside, the cushions on the teak chairs were color-coordinated in shades of gray, green, and brown.

Crystal chose one of the table chairs where she could converse with her friends. Jerry and Lance found seats on either side of her.

"How are the two of you?" she asked. "You both look terrific."

"I'm fine," said Jerry. "Lance had a bit of a cold in the spring before we came here for the summer. But we keep on keeping on. I've been working on a cookbook. A friend suggested I do it."

"If you have any recipes for me to use, I'd love it," Crystal said.

He laughed. "I do have one for you. Orange Chocolate Chip Pancakes. Everyone loves them."

"Sounds perfect. Thanks." Crystal turned to Lance. "How about you? Still doing consulting work for start-ups?"

"Yes. It's amazing how many people think they can simply say they're in business without laying any of the foundations behind it. The underprivileged people I work with are sometimes able to get funding from government programs, but it takes a lot of organization to put it to the best use. And a lot of patience to deal with the government." Lance had created and sold a computer program to a large company and was still getting royalties every year from it.

"Before you go back to New York, I hope to lure you to Lilac Lake."

"The fall is a good time to visit with all the rest of the 'leaf peepers'. Maybe then," said Jerry. He leaned forward eagerly. "Any new man in your life?"

Crystal couldn't stop a pink flush from entering her

cheeks. "Maybe. Maybe not. But I have met someone who interests me." She blinked rapidly. "I may be more interested than he. We had a spat, and I'm waiting to see what will happen."

"Tell us about him," said Lance sitting back and giving her a look of concern.

"Emmett Chambers is the new doctor in town. He's the son of Everett and Natalie Chamberlain."

"He changed his name?" asked Jerry.

"Yes. Everett is his stepfather, and in a show of independence, Emmett changed his name as he was about to go to college to study medicine. Everett wanted him to go into law, hoping, I think, that he'd go into politics. It was important to Emmett to separate from his family, one he doesn't much admire."

"Some of us are forced to separate from families," said Lance with a touch of bitterness.

"Yes. And some would like to forget what family they had," countered Crystal. "In this case, it's worked out well. So well, that Emmett will cooperate with his family when it's announced his stepfather is running for president. If it gets that far."

"That's a big if," said Lance. "The senator has made a lot of enemies."

"Including the gay community here," Jerry said. "I'm surprised the MeToo movement didn't bring him down."

"The senator is nicer than his wife. Emmett's mother has been rude to me and made it clear to Emmett that I'm not suitable."

"Aw, sweetie, that's too bad," said Jerry. "That can make it impossible."

"Emmett and I talked about it, but he wasn't going to let his family's opinions stop us from getting to know one another. Now, his mother is pushing a young woman at him, someone who's working on his father's campaign. She's beautiful ..."

"Stop," said Jerry. "Crystal, you're one of the most beautiful women I know. Inside and out." He gave her a teasing smile. "Even without the purple hair."

"Very Grace Kelly-like," commented Lance. "Sometimes it's best to let the situation settle for a while before any final judgments can be made."

"My friend, Whitney Gilford, said the same thing."

"How is she?" said Lance. "I haven't spoken to her since her baby arrived. She had the idea I should serve on a board of directors for a theater group she's trying to organize."

"She still intends to go forward with the idea of offering drama camps for serious students and ones for underprivileged kids as a way to express themselves."

"It's a sound idea," said Lance. "After our busy summer is over, I'll talk to her about it again."

"So, you're a member of the ensemble for the play. Have you been practicing?" Jerry asked her.

"Before Misty came back home and Emmett entered the scene, I practiced singing a lot. It's something to do when I'm all alone," said Crystal. "But I have no speaking parts, I just sing and dance a little. Nothing too showy. That's how I like it."

"It's fantastic that you've kept up with this," said Jerry. "It's wise for the theater companies to hire locals for parts like this. Saves them money."

"As a board member for the summer theater, I encourage it," Lance said.

"It's great for someone like me who wants the continued experience." She checked her watch. "I guess I'd better go. I'll eat dinner with someone from the group and will see you later."

Both men rose.

"We'll probably be out and about, but you know where the key is hidden," said Jerry.

"Thanks." Crystal hugged both men and went to her car, her stomach fluttering with excitement.

CHAPTER TWENTY-THREE

THE OGUNQUIT PLAYHOUSE, which opened in 1933, was right on Main Street. Crystal knew it was one of the last remaining summer theaters from the Summer Stock that still produced musical theatre.

The white clapboard building with green metal letters spread across the front displayed the name, while mounted above them, green and white pennants danced in the breeze. Green awnings marked the ticket window and covered the entrances on either side. She parked in the allocated space and went to join a group behind the stage, ready to go through a rehearsal.

A woman in the group smiled and waved at her. Nathan Fielding, a friend of Jerry's and the theater manager, rushed over to give her a hug. "Welcome, Crystal. I was glad to hear you're joining us for this production. It's always nice to see you."

"Thanks. For me, it's a thrill to be able to be part of any show, no matter how small the part."

"What did you do to your hair?" he asked her, standing back and appraising her. "You look fab. A lot like Grace Kelly."

"That's what Jerry said," she replied, flustered. She'd never thought of herself as beautiful.

The director came into the room. "Everyone in their places. We need to go through the two ensemble numbers." His assistant did a roll call and after he announced her name, Crystal felt her excitement grow. It took a huge effort to use her time for the few days of the show, but she never tired of her brief stints on stage. Being able to portray someone else had brought her through troubled times.

On stage, she sang and did some light dancing with other members of the ensemble, content to be in the back while others with speaking roles were in the limelight. She'd memorized the words of the songs, knew the various parts of the play by heart, and could be comfortable as they went through both big numbers.

Later, Crystal relaxed on Jerry and Lance's outdoor patio. Then she decided to walk into town to a favorite restaurant with another ensemble member for a light supper before show time.

The Lobster Trap was located on Main Street a nice walk away. Crystal's mouth watered in anticipation of the lobster rolls they served—lots of lobster pieces with minimal mayonnaise.

Ginger Allen, a woman she'd met last year, was full of good cheer as they moved along chatting about little things. Short, she was pretty with long, dyed strawberry-blond hair worn in a ponytail, and had green eyes that sparkled with humor. Her energy was unstoppable. Younger than Crystal by four years, Ginger was someone she'd always liked.

"So, how has New York living been?" Crystal asked her.

Ginger shrugged. "It's never easy. Exciting yes. But jobs are hard to find, and I'm getting tired of working a full-time gig and then as a waitress on weekends to make living there possible."

"Why don't you think of coming to Lilac Lake? Whitney Gilford is living there and is setting up a theater program for camps during the summer and for school children during the winter."

"Really? That sounds interesting. I'll think about it. Now,

let's eat. I need to go back and go over my lines once more."

They walked inside the gray weathered clapboard building to a busy scene. Tables were filling up fast at this early dinner hour. Crystal grabbed a table tucked into a back corner by the kitchen.

"What'll you have?" asked Ginger.

"A single lobster roll, and a lemonade," said Crystal, pulling bills out of her wallet. She handed them to Ginger. "And ask for a lemon slice, please. I'll grab extra napkins and silverware for us."

Moments later, Crystal bit into her lobster roll and let out a moan of pleasure. Tender lobster meat fresh from the Atlantic Ocean was a favorite seafood treat. It always tasted better in Maine than anywhere else.

That evening, on stage with the other members of the ensemble, Crystal sang and moved with them, lost in her world of fantasy and fun. Her practicing had paid off and she acted her small part with confidence.

A little after the play ended, Crystal decided to get a breath of fresh air.

As she stepped outside, she saw a crowd gathering and people rushing about.

"What's wrong?" she asked another performer.

"Some woman passed out. I think she was drunk," the man said.

Curious, Crystal stepped closer as a volunteer ordered onlookers to move back to give a doctor some room. Crystal got a glimpse of her and gasped. She stepped forward. "I know this woman. Can I help?"

The doctor looked up at her from where he was kneeling beside his doctor's bag. "I know who she is too. She doesn't appear to be hurt seriously, but I need to be sure."

"We have to get her out of here, to privacy. Let's take her to the office," said Crystal. She broke a path through the crowd. The doctor followed, helping Natalie Chamberlain inside.

"Are you traveling with her?" the doctor asked Crystal.

"No, I'm not. But I know her son, and I think he should be informed. I'm happy to make the call, but he'll want to speak to you. He's a doctor."

Natalie, more aware now, sat on a chair in the office while the doctor examined her.

"I'm sorry," Natalie said. "I skipped dinner ... and the heat of the crowd ..." She said nothing about the alcohol she'd consumed. The smell was very distinct. She noticed Crystal standing by and recoiled. "What are you doing here?"

"She helped me get you inside away from curious eyes, Mrs. Chamberlain. You owe her a debt of thanks," said the doctor. "You seem to be fine, except for tripping. You have no pain from the fall?"

Natalie shook her head. "I'm fine. Just very tired."

"I'm calling Emmett. He'll want to know," said Crystal.

Natalie gave her a thoughtful look. "Thanks. Better that he finds out from us. You think you kept this from the papers?"

"I don't know for sure, but I hope so." Crystal left the office to make the call. She punched in Emmett's number and waited and waited. She tried again and this time, Emmett picked up the call right away.

"Crystal?"

"Yes, Emmett. I'm calling about your mother. She's had a fall at the Ogunquit Playhouse. She's alright or will be when she's sober."

"What are you doing there? What is she doing there? Has she been examined by a doctor?"

"I'm doing a stint at the theater. She came to see the play and yes, she's been examined by a doctor. I'm going to hand the phone over to him so you can talk."

"Thanks," said Emmett as Crystal went back to the doctor and handed him her phone.

While the doctor went outside the office to take the call, Crystal was left in the office with Natalie.

Crystal sat in a chair and sighed. "I know you don't think much of me, but if I can help in any way, please let me know. I know enough about your condition to know how disoriented you must feel right now. Are you staying in town?"

"With a friend not far from here," said Natalie. "She wasn't feeling well and didn't want to stay, so she dropped me off. She's supposed to pick me up."

"What's her name? I'll go look for her," said Crystal.

"Eloise Harding. An old friend," said Natalie, with a quiver in her voice.

The doctor came back into the room and handed the phone to her. "He wants to speak to you."

Crystal took the phone. "Yes?"

"Thank you for all you're doing for my mother," said Emmett. "That's really kind of you considering her treatment of you. I'm going to come to Maine to talk to her. Do you know where she's staying?"

"She's visiting her old friend, Eloise Harding," said Crystal. "I'm going to find Eloise outside now. She was planning to give your mother a ride back to her place."

"Thanks. I'll take it from here," said Emmett. He paused. "I've missed you."

Crystal clicked off the call before getting into further conversation with him. She'd called him. He hadn't called her.

When she went outside, the line of traffic picking up people had dwindled to nothing but a car or two. She searched for a female driver and found a blond-haired woman driving a BMW convertible.

She walked over to the car, tapped on the window, and said, "Are you Eloise Harding?"

The woman looked startled. "Yes, I am. Why?"

"Natalie Chamberlain is inside. She's taken a tumble but isn't hurt. The doctor has checked her over, and there's nothing to worry about except a bruise on her hand where she landed. I'll help her to your car. I'm afraid she's had quite a lot to drink."

"Ah, Natalie. With the stress of a possible campaign ahead, I'm not surprised. I'll wait for you here and take her back to my house."

"Just so you know, I've called her son. Emmett will probably be phoning you."

"Thank you. What did you say your name was?"

"Crystal Owen," she said and moved away.

Natalie met her inside and Crystal walked her to Eloise's car. After seeing her safely inside the automobile, Crystal waved to them both and went to find her car. It was too late and she was too troubled to even think of making a trip home. Thank God for Jerry and Lance's open invitation.

CHAPTER TWENTY-FOUR

THE NEXT DAY, Crystal awoke in the peach-colored guest room at Jerry and Lance's house and stretched like a lazy cat. The white summer quilt had enough warmth without being hot to make a cozy night's sleep. Crystal thought over last night's episode with Natalie Chamberlain. It was sad to see her disgrace herself because of alcohol abuse. She knew only too well what damage it could cause.

She changed into shorts and a T-shirt and padded into the kitchen.

"Hello," chirped Jerry. "I've gone ahead and made the orange-chocolate-chip pancake batter. I thought you might like to try it."

"Thanks. I could use a treat this morning. You two were asleep when I came in last night, and I didn't have the chance to tell you about Natalie Chamberlain's fall outside the theater."

"Oh, honey, you're too late. I got all the juicy tidbits from a friend," Jerry said. "I gather you and the theater doctor got her out of the public eye as soon as possible, but you know something like this is going to spread quickly."

"I suppose," said Crystal. "What exactly are they saying?"

"That it's just another episode with her, that her husband is worse, and there's no way he's going to be president."

"Wow! That's pretty strong. Maybe that's why so many people tell me that Senator Chamberlain's chances of actually securing the nomination are unlikely. I've done my part to help; I'm going to step back. That family has made it clear that

I don't measure up."

Jerry placed a hand on her shoulder. "They don't measure up to you. Now, how about those pancakes?"

"First, coffee."

He laughed. "I've got some made for you."

"Thanks, you're a doll," she said.

He grinned. "Lance thinks so too."

Crystal noticed his happy smile and a pang went through her. Would she ever find someone to love and accept her? "You two are an inspiration to me. You're so happy together."

"It'll happen for you too. We love Nick, but you'll find someone better suited to you. I hope we get to meet Mr. Can't Decide."

"Who do we want to meet? Who's Mr. Can't Decide?" asked Lance coming into the kitchen.

"The man Crystal told us about. Emmett Chambers," said Jerry. "I'll know a lot about him if we ever get the chance to be introduced. Do you want some pancakes?"

Lance patted his stomach. "Just one. Your cooking is making me fat, but I love it."

While Jerry went to work on the pancakes, Crystal automatically set the table. Though she didn't see them as often as she'd like, being with Jerry and Lance was like coming home. They always gave her encouragement.

Jerry served up the pancakes and stood aside as Crystal and Lance buttered them before pouring real maple syrup on them.

Knowing he was waiting for a response from her, Crystal lifted a piece of pancake to her mouth and enjoyed the blend of orange and chocolate. She closed her eyes and let the taste settle on her tongue.

"Well?" asked Jerry, too impatient to wait.

"Perfect combination. I'll definitely steal the idea. My

customers will love it," she said.

Jerry gave her a smile of satisfaction. "Thought so. Thanks. It's the essence of the orange skin that gives it the flavor."

"I'll remember that," said Crystal taking another bite.

When at last she couldn't eat anything more, Crystal excused herself. "Don't worry about the dishes. I'll clean them up in a minute. But I want to sit outside on the deck to let breakfast settle before I do them."

"No problem," said Jerry. "It's Lance's turn to do the dishes anyway. You go on ahead."

Crystal went outside and stretched out on a chaise lounge. She closed her eyes against the sun's rays and allowed their warmth to ease into her. She loved summer days. She thought about Emmett, her need to find love and create a family, and how she'd thought he'd be the cure to the raging fever inside her.

Footsteps caused her to stir. She opened her eyes and stared in surprise at Emmett. She scrambled to sit up. "What are you doing here? How did you find me?"

"Whoa, let me explain. After your call last night, I decided to cancel appointments today and come to Maine to see my mother. But before talking to her, I need to speak to you. Misty gave me your address, and your friends kindly let me inside."

She studied him, seeing his uncertainty. "Let's take a walk on the beach. Footbridge Beach is within easy walking distance."

In the kitchen, Crystal introduced Emmett to Jerry and Lance and explained that they were going out onto the beach. Aware the men were assessing one another, Crystal noted an absence of animosity and was pleased.

Crystal grabbed her sun hat and beach bag, put two bottles of water in her bag, and led Emmett out of the house.

Though she was aware of all she wanted to say and hear,

the walk to the beach was short and quiet.

After crossing the wooden footbridge, Crystal removed her sandals and sighed with pleasure as she wiggled her toes in the soft, white sand.

Beside her, Emmett slipped off his shoes and socks and rolled up his khaki pants. "Okay, now let's talk."

They started strolling down the beach. It was low tide, making it seem as if the expanse of sand went on forever before reaching the edge of the salty water.

Emmett stopped walking and took hold of her hands. "I'm sorry I wasn't more sensitive to your feelings at the barbeque. I should've been more aware of Diana's intentions. I didn't think anything was weird until she told me last night that you and I would never make it, that my mother wanted us together." He let out a snort. "As if that would matter to me."

Crystal kicked at the sand with a painted toe. "Diana confronted me too, saying the same thing. That's why I was upset when we talked after the barbeque. And when you didn't say anything to convince me that you wanted to maintain a relationship with me, I thought, for you, her behavior was fine because you weren't that serious."

"Look at me, Crystal," said Emmett quietly. "I'm in love with you. I have no intention of our relationship going anywhere but forward. I've tried to show you how I felt."

Crystal liked the way he was gently gripping her shoulders as he earnestly stared at her. She tried to find the right words. "I let her get to me, remind me of other humiliating experiences with your family," she said. "But, Emmett, I've fallen for you too."

He drew her to him and hugged her tightly. "We can't let my family ruin what we have," he murmured before tilting her chin and lifting her face to his.

His lips came down on hers firmly, and as they kissed, she

opened her lips to his tongue and felt her body weaken with need. She wanted him pure and simple.

When they pulled apart, they stared at one another, and she met Emmett's smile with her own.

"I want you in my life," said Emmett. "Stay with me on this. We know it's what we both want. Will you trust me?"

Crystal heard the plea in his voice and nodded.

"I hope you'll help me with my mother," Emmett said. "It's time for her to get professional help, but I don't know how to go about getting her to see that."

"At some point, I'm going to suggest going to some Al-Anon meetings for you, but for now you need to understand that the choice for professional help has to be hers to make. You can, however, encourage her."

"Your mother didn't make the choice?"

Crystal shook her head. "She couldn't get off the drugs, much less the alcohol."

"I know this is a big ask, but will you accompany me to visit my mother? You'll know the right thing to say, help me keep it under control."

"My presence might upset her," said Crystal, unwilling to be caught in the middle of the situation unless he promised to support her.

"I'm going to take care of any bad behavior," said Emmett, wrapping an arm around her. "Don't worry. I'll have your back."

"Okay. This will be the biggest test of all for us," said Crystal.

"I've got you," said Emmett.

"When are you going to see her?" asked Crystal.

Emmett checked his watch. "In forty-five minutes. Why don't we walk for a while before heading back?"

"Okay. I always feel at peace here." She gazed up at the

seagulls swirling above them. "The birds, the water lapping against the shore, and the salty smell of the air are reminders of all the best things in the world. How lucky we are to have them."

"How lucky I am to be with you," Emmett said, hugging her. His turquoise eyes shone with love. "Now that we've agreed to move forward, where do you see us in a year or so?"

"I see us together. We're in Lilac Lake and we're going to get married."

"We've already talked about children," he said. "We don't want to wait."

"I agree," said Crystal. "I've been thinking about it a lot."

Emmett's eyes rounded with surprise. Then he smiled impishly at her. "Are you saying we should get married right away?"

Crystal laughed nervously. "Sooner rather than later. But we need enough time to figure out a lot of things." She couldn't hide her excitement.

"I'll keep that in mind," said Emmett, brushing his lips across hers.

"Hey! Get a room!" said one of two teenage boys marching by them carrying a frisbee.

"God! That sounds like a great idea," said Emmett, pulling away and laughing. "How long will you be staying in Ogunquit?"

"The show ends in seven days. I'm staying here with Jerry and Lance. Misty is handling the Café for me, and I want to give her a chance to prove to herself that she can do it."

"Well, when you're back in town, there's something I want to show you at my house."

"How's it coming?"

"It's almost ready for you and Whitney to help with the interior decorating. I think you'll be pleased."

"That's so exciting. I can hardly wait."

"It's important to me that I have your input going forward." He checked his watch. "Guess we'd better head back. I don't want to be late for my appointment to meet with my mother."

Emmett took her hand, and they headed back toward the footbridge, their steps in sync.

As they walked, Crystal kept glancing at Emmett. Each time she did, he was smiling at her.

Even though Crystal had cleaned up after returning to Jerry and Lance's house, she sat beside Emmett in his car, fussing over her appearance.

"You look fine," said Emmett. "As beautiful as ever."

"I'm prepared to leave quickly if your mother orders me out," she said.

"No need. I'll take care of that. It's time my family understood what you mean to me. No more nonsense from them," said Emmett firmly.

"Just as you want them to understand how you feel about me, it's important for you to let your mother know how you feel about her drinking," she said. "It's a disease that can be controlled, but only if she's willing to do the work."

They drove up to a new condo building along the beach, and Emmett parked.

Crystal got out of the car telling herself she could do this, that it was necessary to confront Natalie. But that didn't stop nerves from curling through her body, threatening a headache.

Emmett took hold of her hand, lifted it to his lips, and her nerves settled. He needed her, loved her.

Emmett rang Eloise's apartment, and she buzzed him into the vestibule where they climbed into an elevator. They reached the top floor of the building, and after the doors opened, they easily found the entrance to Eloise's condo not far down the carpeted hallway.

Emmett knocked, and when Eloise opened the door, her gaze immediately flew to Crystal. "We didn't know you were bringing someone."

"She's not someone; she's my girlfriend, Crystal Owen." He turned to her. "Crystal, this is Eloise Harding, a family friend."

"Oh, yes, we met last night. I'm pleased to see you under better circumstances," said Crystal, her attention focusing from Eloise to Natalie who was approaching them at a rapid rate.

"Hello, Mother," said Emmett. "I came to see how you were. Crystal called me to tell me what had happened at the theater."

"We can talk in my guest suite," said Natalie. "You'll have to excuse us, Crystal."

"No, Crystal's here at my request. I think she can be a help to both of us. Besides, Crystal and I have a serious relationship, and she should be part of this. Especially with Dad's political campaign happening."

Natalie thinned her lips with frustration, then led them to another part of the condo.

The guest suite had a small sitting area. Emmett helped Crystal to one of the two chairs by a window and left to get another chair.

Natalie sat opposite Crystal looking scared.

"It's going to be alright," said Crystal softly.

Natalie glared at Crystal. "What are you doing here? Have you come to gloat?"

Emmett returned with a chair. "I heard you, Mother. I told you. Crystal and I have a close relationship. In fact, I hope to marry her one day if she'll forgive my family for being so judgmental, so shallow."

"What about Diana?" Natalie said while Crystal sat still absorbing the words Emmett had just spoken.

Emmett shook his head. "That was and is never going to happen with Diana. I've never thought of her as anything other than a friend. But after discovering and witnessing how unpleasant she's been to Crystal, I'm reconsidering that."

Emmett gave Crystal an encouraging smile and turned to Natalie. "I'm here, no, *we're* here to help you, Mother. Your drinking has become a problem. It's time you stopped and did something about it."

Natalie waved away his concern. "Oh, that's not necessary. The fall was a one-time thing."

"No, Mom, it wasn't." Emmett turned to Crystal.

She cleared her throat. "I'm sure you understand that alcoholism is a disease. A disease that can't be cured but can be controlled. With help."

"What gives you the idea that you can talk to me that way," said Natalie, staring at Crystal with an icy look that sent a shiver through her.

"Hold on. Crystal's here because I asked for her help," Emmett said to his mother. "I expect you to treat her with respect. If not, we'll both leave, and I won't see you again."

Natalie pressed her lips together. She leaned back in her chair.

Crystal gripped her hands knowing she had no choice but to tell this woman who didn't like her what kind of background she had.

Emmett gave her a silent nod of encouragement.

Crystal cleared her throat. "I'm well acquainted with the disease. My mother was addicted to both alcohol and drugs. Growing up, I took care of my younger sister because my mother wouldn't or couldn't. I was eighteen when she died, and I was given custody of my sister. I know what it's like to see someone struggle, and I know what it's like to see someone lose the fight. Make no mistake, it is a battle that affects everyone in your life. You lose everything—your dignity, your ability to function well, your ability to see the problem."

"How old were you when you started taking care of your sister?" Natalie asked, sounding suspicious.

"I was eight when she was born. Even then, my mother couldn't stay sober long enough to care for her." Crystal's hands turned cold at the memories.

"Why would you help me after all I've said and done to you?" asked Natalie.

Crystal gave her a steady stare. "Because I love your son and don't want him or anyone whom he loves to go through what I had to." Crystal stared out the window trying not to cry.

"I've looked into treatment centers," said Emmett. "There's a highly respected, residential one in New Hampshire that is extremely private. I've talked to them, and they're willing to see you. Their staff is discreet. No one needs to know anything about your being away for a while."

"That's over the top. I don't need to go to a place like that," scoffed Natalie. "I'll just stop drinking."

"It's not that simple, Mom," said Emmett. "It takes a learning experience like they offer to make the necessary life choices."

"You'll get plenty of support as you change your living style," said Crystal.

"What would your father say? He'll be furious," said Natalie.

Emmett took hold of his mother's hand. "I've talked to Dad already. He's upset and finally admitted that's part of the reason he's encouraged you to stay in Maine while he gets his campaign up and running."

"He and what other women?" she grumbled.

"That's something that will have to be worked out separately," said Emmett. "Right now, I want you to get well. Crystal helped see that no photographers took photos of you lying on the ground drunk. But the situation *will* get out if it hasn't already shown up online."

Natalie hid her face in her hands. "I'm so embarrassed."

Crystal stood and patted Natalie on the back. "You can do what former First Lady Betty Ford dared to do. Get help. You have a way out. Emmett is giving it to you. He loves you."

"So, when would it happen?" Natalie asked Emmett.

"Now," he said. "You need to pack bare essentials, nothing fancy. We can have clothes shipped to you from Maine, if necessary."

"I might need a few days to think about it," Natalie said.

Emmett shook his head. "Your chance is now. The facility fills up quickly but they're saving a spot for you for this afternoon." Emmett stood, went over to his mother, and pulled her up out of her seat and into his arms. "I want the best for you, Mom. I love you."

"Oh, Emmett, I love you too, son. I'm sorry for putting you through this I'm so ashamed."

"Shame has nothing to do with it," said Crystal.

"Right," said Emmett. "I just want to help you and see you happy, Mom. The first step is getting and keeping sober."

Natalie nodded and let out a long sigh. "I've known for some time that things would have to change. I just couldn't face what it would mean." She turned to Crystal. "I've underestimated you. It took guts to come here and tell your story after all the disrespect and hostility I've shown you."

"I've been ashamed of my past," said Crystal. "But it's all part of how the disease can affect everyone."

"But you've risen above it," said Natalie. "I admire you for that." She turned to Emmett and her shoulders slumped.

"Help me get ready, and we'll go."

"While you do that, I'll stay with Eloise," said Crystal.

She left Natalie's room and went to find Eloise. "Mind if I wait here while Natalie gets ready to leave?"

"Not at all. I couldn't help overhearing some things. What's going on?"

Crystal filled her in.

"I'm glad Nat will get some help. Her drinking has continued to worsen. When I heard about last night, I knew it was time for her to get help. Emmett, bless his heart, is the only one who could convince her of it. And now, he has you to help, too."

"How long has she been staying here?" Crystal asked.

"Five days and counting," said Eloise. "It was getting more and more difficult to be with her. Natalie's already had a couple of Bloody Marys this morning."

"I understand. If she'll work the program, she can get better. I hope she'll decide to do it. The first step is having her talk to the staff at the rehab center."

"Natalie is lucky to have a son like Emmett. And they're both lucky to have you in their lives. I had no idea Emmett was engaged."

Crystal held up her bare left hand. "We're not engaged. We're just getting serious enough to consider it. I want to be sure not to pressure Emmett. He's busy getting a new medical practice going."

"I know you're from Lilac Lake. What do you do there?" asked Eloise.

"I own the Lilac Lake Café," Crystal said proudly, realizing again how far she'd come from the little girl who'd always felt as if the world was on her shoulders. If GG and others in the community hadn't helped her, where would she be?

That thought stayed with her as Crystal waved goodbye to

Emmett and Natalie at Jerry and Lance's house. Emotionally exhausted, she went inside and lay down on her bed.

Her thoughts whirled. It had taken a crisis for Emmett and her to be able to define their true feelings for one another. She let her mind float back to the moment Emmett had said he was in love with her. They were such sweet words.

CHAPTER TWENTY-FIVE

BEFORE CRYSTAL HEADED TO THE THEATER that night, she called Emmett.

He picked up right away. "Hi, I've got you on speakerphone in my car. I'm just returning from the rehab hospital after dropping Mom off."

"How did it go?" Crystal asked.

"I've never seen my mother frightened before, but she was, even more so after she decided to stay. After they'd interviewed her, we had just a moment to say goodbye. I told her how proud I was of her."

"That's important. I'm pleased she's going to do it. My mother never got that far. Sad, isn't it?"

"Yeah, I can't imagine."

"Did you mean what you said to your mother about us?" Crystal had to make sure it wasn't spoken simply from a passionate moment.

"Yes, Crystal. I meant every word of it. My mother and I talked all the way to the rehab hospital about a lot of things, including you. She finally understands my need for independence, her bad behavior, and her addiction. She's embarrassed to be in the situation she's in, but she's grateful for your help. Your truth."

"I'm glad. I meant what I said too."

"It's all a little backward right now, but we'll get it straightened out. I really love you, Crystal. I wish I could've told you under different circumstances."

"Me, too. But now that we've made our feelings known, we

can move forward."

"Yes. I don't think Diana will dare to make any more trouble after she and I have another talk. Good luck tonight."

"Drive carefully. We'll chat later." Crystal clicked off the call both elated and frustrated. She'd wanted to hear Emmett's declaration of love again, but as he said, it wasn't done at the best of times. Hopefully, there would be many other opportunities.

Crystal said goodbye to Jerry and Lance and went to the theater.

As she was chatting with people backstage, the manager came up to her. "Crystal, I want to thank you for your prompt response to Mrs. Chamberlain's difficulty."

"You're welcome," she said, eager to leave it at that.

"Are you enjoying the show?" he asked.

She smiled. "It's always fun for me to be able to do this. Thanks."

He bobbed his head and left to take care of a problem with the curtains.

Crystal walked outside for a breath of air, her mind whirling. Everything with Emmett was now happening at a fast, emotional pace.

The next morning, she was sitting on the deck reading when her cell rang. She picked it up with a surge of happiness.

"Hello, Doctor. What can I do for you?"

Chuckling, he played along. "I need a cure. There's this woman who insists on being in Maine when I want her here. It's about killing me."

"Take two aspirin and call me tomorrow," she said and burst out laughing.

"Fine," he said with pretended indignity and then became serious. "Good morning. I called to update you on the situation. I talked to my father last night, and he was very grateful for your interference at the theater. He thinks you're savvy and beautiful."

"And what about your mother? Is he happy she's going to work to get well?" Crystal asked. She didn't give a hoot that his father thought her beautiful.

'Yes and no. He's not happy about the situation. He thinks it might hurt his run for president, but he's trying to make the best of it. With Betty Ford's issues and subsequent turnaround, he's hoping it'll add a bit of humanity to his campaign."

Crystal's stomach knotted. "I'm not talking about his campaign. What does he think about Natalie? Is he going to support her? I've done some research on the rehab facility, and it's recommended that family members become part of their program at different times. Is he going to do that?"

Emmett sighed. "He said he'd try. That's all I can do for the moment."

Crystal hid her disappointment. "One day at a time, as they say. Somehow, things will work out."

"They might not. My mother may not want to continue living with "the Senator". That's between them, but I must admit, I wouldn't be sorry if she left him."

"Did you mention our situation with your father?" Crystal hated to ask, but discussing Emmett's declaration of love for her with his father was a big deal.

"I told my father we were in love and wanted to plan a future together."

"And what did he say?"

Emmett snorted with disgust. "He thought it would be helpful to his campaign."

"I see now why your mother has been very unhappy," Crystal said. "And why you decided to become independent.

He seems such a shallow man."

"A determined man. I understand some of his advisors are telling him not to make the run, that his reputation will become ruined by those he's treated badly, including a slew of women. But he won't listen to them."

"What are you going to do about it?" she asked.

"I'll carry on doing my job and loving my life with you in Lilac Lake. That's all I can do."

"Okay. I'll see you at the end of the week. Our last performance is on Sunday. I hope you'll try to make it. I've decided to stay here for the duration. Misty is very proud of handling the Café, and I want to let her do it without my interference. I'm hoping she'll agree to continue to share some of the duties to enable me to work at the Café less than I am now doing."

"Guess I'd better take more than two aspirin," teased Emmett.

She laughed, loving the idea of being able to be playful with him.

"I am going to miss you. I've got a busy week, but I'll come there to see the show over the weekend," said Emmett.

"That sounds perfect. In the meantime, we can talk. There are so many things to think about."

"Yes," said Emmett. "It's important."

As she ended the call, Jerry came out to the deck. "Did I hear you say you're spending the rest of the week with us?"

"I've changed my mind about trying to drive back to Lilac Lake to occasionally check on Misty. I hope my staying here won't be any trouble."

"Aw, sweetie, you know we love having you," said Jerry. "Are you up for some shopping? I'm looking for a special platter, and you know I love to browse the stores."

"That sounds like fun," she said, remembering that the

automobile accident with Emmett meant they hadn't been able to complete their shopping.

"I'll drive," said Jerry and winked at her.

Crystal laughed, grateful to have such a dear friend. She'd been tempted to call Whitney and fill her in on all that had happened but decided to wait until she had things settled in her mind.

The week flew by for Crystal as she relaxed and worked in Ogunquit. Trips to the beach, eating out, and shopping worked their magic, even as her mind spun.

Early evening talks with Emmett were helpful. They opened up to one another. At first shy, Crystal learned she could say anything to Emmett without judgment. That, and his willingness to share thoughts of his own made her comfortable about her decision to move forward with him. She wasn't an admirer of his father and probably would never be, but she felt she'd made enough strides with his mother to think they might one day have a satisfactory relationship.

She received a call from Whitney. "How are things going?"

As if she'd stored the words for such a call, the entire story came tumbling out.

"A lot to think about, just as you say," responded Whitney. "I called to tell you that Dani, Taylor, and I have tickets for Saturday night's show. We thought we'd come early that morning to spend some time with you. Is that okay?"

"Okay? That's perfect," Crystal said, her eyes smarting with the sting of tears. It was wonderful to have such supportive friends. And Emmett was coming on Sunday.

CHAPTER TWENTY-SIX

ON SATURDAY MORNING, Crystal felt like a child waiting for a birthday party. It was rare that she could get together with the three Gilford women, especially now that they were married. And with Whitney having a baby, time with her was even more precious. Even though the sky was gray with the promise of rain, nothing could dampen her enthusiasm.

Jerry and Lance had met the women when they'd visited her in Lilac Lake. In their honor, Jerry had made breakfast scones for their arrival.

"We'll say hello, and then give you women your space," said Lance, taking a bite of a scone.

"We're going to meet friends in Portland today," Jerry said, before sipping his coffee. "Hopefully the sun will appear this afternoon. In the meantime, this is a great place for you all to stay inside and be cozy."

"It's perfect," said Crystal. "Thank you so much. I hope to repay you when you come to Lilac Lake as you promised."

"Definitely," said Lance. He wiped his mouth with his napkin and looked up at the sound of a car in his driveway. "I think they're here."

Crystal hurried to the door, flung it open, and ran to the car. Dani got out, followed by Taylor and Whitney.

One woman, then another, and another hugged her while the two men studied them from the front entry.

Crystal re-introduced the women to them and announced, "Jerry and Lance have given us use of their house while they travel to Portland up the coast."

As Jerry ushered them inside, Lance spoke to Whitney. "I got your email and would like to talk to you about the theater program some other time. We've promised Crystal to come to Lilac Lake this fall. Maybe then?"

"That would be wonderful," gushed Whitney.

Jerry served them coffee and set a plate of scones in the middle of the kitchen table. "Enjoy! We'll see you later."

After they left, Crystal said, "It's cool and cloudy, how about staying here as Lance and Jerry suggested?"

"Fine," said Dani. "I need a day to simply relax. Collister Construction has been very busy."

"I've tried to talk Dani into starting her family so Timothy has at least one cousin to play with," said Whitney, grinning at her sister.

"I'm not ready," said Dani. She turned to Crystal. "But give us the lowdown on you and Emmett."

Crystal faced Whitney. "You told them about us?"

"I told them that you and Emmett were serious. That's all. With the three of us in a car alone without any interruptions, we all caught up on a lot of stuff."

"Including the sudden departure of Diana McArthur," said Taylor. "I'm not sure what happened, but she left town, and her brother told Cooper he was happy she'd gone. Something about the way she'd been acting."

"I did mention to Dirk what had been going on," said Whitney. "I thought it was only fair."

Crystal chuckled and shook her head. "Okay, what's going on with you, Taylor? How's the book coming?"

"Slowly, but it's alright. I've been thinking of turning it into a trilogy. I'm creating a story bible for it." Taylor smiled. "It might mean staying in Lilac Lake a little longer. Cooper can do a lot of his work away from the office, so being in Lilac Lake can work."

"That sounds terrific," said Crystal. "Nice things always seem to happen when the three of you are in town. I bet GG loves it."

"She does," said Dani. "By the way, Crystal, GG has decided to start a third baby blanket. She thinks you're in the running to be the next winner."

Crystal's cheeks grew hot. "Someday."

"Seriously, what's happening between you and Emmett now?" asked Whitney.

"We're spending this time away from one another thinking about what each of us wants out of life, talking about anything and everything. It's been good."

"How's his mother doing?" asked Dani. "We heard about her episode."

"It's only been a few days since she checked into rehab. In a few more, Natalie will be able to make phone calls. That's when Emmett will know. Until then, we hope she's following the program."

"She was nasty to you, Crystal. I'm impressed by how you're handling her. You've been very gracious," said Whitney.

"She's important to Emmett. Even though he and his father don't get along, he's important to Emmett too. I must respect that."

"Well, I for one, love to see romance conquer all," said Taylor with a dreamy expression.

"No wonder readers love your books," Crystal said.

It was delightful to be able to relax and chat with her friends. The sound of rain hitting the windowpanes gave them a sense of comfort. Crystal poured more coffee and refreshed the plate of scones, and they settled down for a morning of girl talk. Though it was a usual scenario for the three sisters to do this, Crystal reveled in being part of it.

#

The rain stopped, and the sky brightened. The cool offshore breeze seemed to dance with joy, pushing the gray clouds out over the ocean.

Crystal and her three treasured friends walked down the street to an Italian restaurant for lunch. She didn't know about the others, but the thought of a hot soup was enticing. Mama's was known for their Italian sausage and orzo soup, a nice change from seafood chowder.

As she ate, her thoughts flew to Misty. Since she'd come home, Misty had seemed happier and more relaxed. She hoped it was enough to make her want to stay for more than a year's trial period.

Later, while the women got settled in their hotel room, Crystal took a moment to call Emmett. They'd talked a lot over the past few days, discovering more to like about one another. More than that, they'd become real friends.

Now, just hearing his voice, she filled with anticipation. She could hardly wait for tomorrow when they'd have the entire day together before her last show.

The next morning, Crystal eagerly dressed for the day. She'd just finished fussing with her hair when her cell phone rang. *Emmett.*

"Hello," she chirped happily. "Are you here already?"

"I'm sorry, Crystal. I really am, but I can't come. I got a call from the rehab hospital, and there's been some sort of breakthrough with my mother in her counseling sessions. They want me to drive there this morning and stay for two sessions with her. I couldn't say no."

"Of course not," said Crystal blinking rapidly, glad he couldn't see her tears of disappointment.

"You're coming home tonight, right?" said Emmett.

"Maybe not. I might stay for the wrap-up party now that you won't be here. I'll rest overnight and return to Lilac Lake early tomorrow. I hope things go well with your mother and she's doing better."

"Thanks. It sounds as if she's working on several issues," said Emmett. "Let's have dinner at my house tomorrow night. Okay?"

"Yes. Don't worry about a meal. I'll come up with something simple. The most important thing is our being together."

"I wish I didn't have to go to the rehab hospital today, but I promised my mother I would be there for her."

"You're doing the right thing," said Crystal. "We'll make dinner tomorrow special."

"Okay. I've got to go, or I'll be late for the morning session. Thanks for understanding, Crystal. It means a lot."

After they ended the call, Crystal sat on the bed staring out the window. She hadn't given it too much thought, but living with Emmett would always mean interruptions to plans, whether it was a patient or a family matter. Without having those obligations herself, it was easy to forget that.

She went into the kitchen and told Jerry and Lance that Emmett wasn't coming after all.

"Aw, sweetie, I know you're disappointed," said Jerry. "Make yourself at home. Lance and I are meeting friends in Portsmouth. You're welcome to come with us."

"Thanks, anyway. If you don't mind, I'm going to hang around on the deck and read and relax. This is my last day before my usual rat race at the Café will resume."

Later, alone on the deck, Crystal lay back on a chaise lounge and thought about a future with Emmett. It would have its ups and downs like most marriages, but every time she thought of what the future might hold with him, happiness filled her. She couldn't deny the chemistry between them. It was at a level she'd never experienced. More than that, she liked Emmett—his personality, his goals, his innate kindness.

She let her mind drift and soon was asleep.

At the sound of her cell ringing, Crystal awoke with a start. She groped around for it, hoping it wasn't Misty. She'd left her sister pretty much alone for the week, giving her the respect that she deserved.

"Hi, Crystal."

"Hi, Emmett," she said, sitting. "What's up?"

"There's someone who'd like to speak to you," said Emmett.

She was surprised to hear Natalie's voice. "Hello, Crystal. I just wanted to apologize for my past behavior to you and want you to know I approve of any plans you and Emmett make together. I've learned a lot about myself this week. I hope you'll agree to meet with me in the future."

"I'd be pleased to do that, Natalie. I'm proud of you for working the program. I wish my mother could've been that strong."

There was a pause, and then Emmett's voice came on. "Thank you, Crystal. See you tomorrow. I love you."

"Love you too," Crystal said, ending the call and bursting into tears for what might have been with her mother and for the fabulous possibilities that lay ahead with Emmett.

That night, Crystal bowed with the other performers as applause filled the theater. It was exciting to have this small part as one of the townspeople in the special production of *Seven Brides for Seven Brothers*. She brushed at the skirt of her costume sorry the play had ended.

Looking out at the audience clapping, she understood why some people dedicated their lives to acting. However, traveling and constantly being under pressure to learn different parts and routines were not for her.

The curtain closed, and she and the rest of the cast changed out of their costumes. Then she joined them at the Blue Lobster Bar for a party.

There, Crystal sipped on a glass of red wine and watched as a couple of cast members sang dirty ditties. It was a fun group, and she laughed with the others.

Ginger Allen came over to her. "Are you sorry to be leaving to go back to your work at the Café?"

"Not at all. Though it's always fun to be here, home is where I want to be. I'm sincere about asking you to come visit me in Lilac Lake. You might decide to move there if you're sick of New York. It's a very nice lifestyle."

Ginger's green eyes sparkled as she fingered her strawberry-blonde hair. "I just may take you up on it. It's time for a change for me. And with Whitney Gilford working on a project there, maybe I can do something to help her."

They hugged, and before she left the party, Crystal went around and talked to both actors and management, thanking them for the opportunity.

"It's always great to have you here," said the theater manager. "Maybe next year?"

"Maybe," she said and wondered what the year would bring.

CHAPTER TWENTY-SEVEN

DRIVING INTO LILAC LAKE, Crystal felt her spirits lift. She'd never grow tired of seeing the lake, the rock she and her friends had always loved, and the scenic little town. The smell of pine filled her nostrils, and she drew in a breath and let it linger inside her as long as she could.

At this early morning hour, joggers were out running, and regular traffic was almost non-existent. She drove past the church, the town square, and onto Main Street, and parked her car behind the Café next to Misty's red coupe.

When she walked into the kitchen, Misty looked up at her. "Home again? Where has the time gone?"

"Thanks for sending me evening reports," said Crystal hugging her. "You've done a fantastic job of running the business while I've been gone."

"You're welcome. I appreciate your letting me do it on my own. I was thinking if you ever want to take on a partner, I'd be interested. I could do some work before going to school in the mornings and help on weekends."

"It's something I've begun to think about. We'll talk about it in time. Right now, I'm not sure what's going on with my life." She stopped talking when staff members appeared, and she turned to them.

"Thank you, everyone, for the help you gave my sister while I was gone. I really appreciate it." Seeing the faces of those who worked for her, Crystal's eyes grew misty. They were such decent people.

"Okay, the pies for today are apple and lemon meringue,"

said Misty. "We need to get going on them and prepare for breakfast and lunch."

"Let me dump my things upstairs and get changed," said Crystal. "I'll be right back to help." If she was lucky, she could snatch a couple of pieces of pie for dessert at Emmett's house.

It felt wonderful to greet people as she usually did when they walked into the Café. In a way, it was like welcoming people to her home. And, of course, it was good to catch up on the local gossip. When Dirk stopped in for coffee, he caught sight of her and came right over. "Hey, I'm sorry again for the mess my sister made between you and Emmett. I hope it won't affect our friendship."

"Not at all," she said. "It's over and done with."

"Good, because I like living here and being part of the 'summer group.'"

Dani came in to pick up coffee for the crew working at Emmett's house. She gave Crystal a sly smile. "How was yesterday with Emmett?"

Crystal shook her head. "Emmett couldn't make it to Maine. He had to do something to support his mother."

"Aw, too bad. Can you guys make it to Jake's tonight?"

"No, I'm going to have dinner at Emmett's. How's his house coming along?"

"Close to getting done inside. You and Whitney need to choose wall paint colors. We're ready for it in the main areas of the house. I'm not sure what you're doing with the upstairs. The bathroom has been redone but no work has been done on the three bedrooms. I'm not sure they need it."

"Maybe I can get Whitney to help me tomorrow. I know Emmett appreciates your fast work."

"It's important to keep our crews busy," said Dani, "so, it works both ways."

###

That evening after finishing the closing routine for the Café, Crystal went upstairs to get ready for her dinner date with Emmett. She'd prepared a meal of chicken salad, fresh tomato slices, deviled eggs, pickled green beans, and lemon pie.

She wanted to look her best for what she hoped would be a very romantic evening. She lingered in the shower, letting the water sluice over her skin as she washed and conditioned her hair. Then, stepping out of the shower, she dried and worked on her curls, taming them into a satisfactory style. She didn't usually wear a lot of makeup, but tonight, she added eye shadow, mascara, and eyeliner.

Stepping away from the mirror she saw how the makeup added dimension to her eyes and decided to wear it more often.

She dressed in a light purple sundress and put on comfortable sandals. It was a relief to get out of the sneakers or heavy-duty shoes she usually wore on her feet for support.

At the last minute, she added a silver heart necklace for luck.

Satisfied she was ready, she picked up her purse and the small box of containers holding their dinner, headed to her car, and climbed in, her nerves tingling with excitement.

As she pulled into the long driveway to Emmett's house, she studied the landscaping. It needed dressing up and the replacement of older plants. David Graham would be on the job as soon as the work on the house was done and the construction site cleared away.

As she got closer to the back of the house, she stared in surprise. A large screened-in porch had been added to the structure. She got out of the car and went around to get a closer look at it. Emmett had talked of adding on, but seeing the size of it, she was impressed. This was like an additional room to the house.

She searched for him at the dock, but he wasn't there. She grabbed her box of dinner, went to the front door, and knocked.

Emmett opened the door, his hair still wet from a shower. The aroma of spice and lime surrounded her as he kissed her hello. She inhaled it with pleasure.

"M-m-m, what's in the box? Looks like our supper is going to be tasty," he said. "I'm glad. It's been a busy day." He took the box from her. "Come in, and I'll show you around. I've already got a bottle of wine open."

She followed him into the large open space serving as a living area which opened to the kitchen dining area and into the screened-in porch. Without the interior walls that had been removed, the openness was spacious and inviting.

"I'm meeting with Whitney tomorrow to go over paint colors. Dani said we had to get that done. Things are moving fast now."

"Yes. The kitchen is all but done, the master bath and powder room are done, and the master bedroom just had the skylight installed. I need you and Whitney to help choose the outside color of the house. I'm thinking gray."

"That sounds nice," said Crystal. "Give us a chance to see what different shades of gray we can find." She gazed around, liking what she saw. "Collister Construction did a remarkable job in getting this done for you this quickly."

Emmett laughed. "It was like watching an army of ants going to work, with everyone busy doing their own thing. And Dani's great at supervising."

"Oh, yes. She's very talented," said Crystal.

Emmett wrapped an arm around her. "I'm happy you like it. You helped Whitney order some furniture, and now you can put the finishing touches on that, too."

Crystal wasn't sure what to say. Did he envision them living here together?

He drew her closer and stared down into her eyes. "I missed you. I thought we'd have time to go on the beach together in Maine, but that didn't happen. Let's walk out to the dock."

Before they could head outside, the sound of a car pulling into the driveway caught their attention.

Emmett frowned. "I hope this isn't a patient." He went to the front door, opened it, and stepped back as a man stormed into the house.

"Dad! What are you doing here?"

"We need to talk, son. Word has gotten out that Natalie is in a rehab center, and now I'm being accused of despicable things in a 'me too' smear. My reputation is being ruined. It all goes back to your mother and her weakness."

Crystal felt her mouth open but said nothing. *'His reputation ruined? He's already done a masterful job of ruining it. And now he was blaming Natalie?'*

While his father continued to rant, Crystal waited to hear what Emmett would say.

Emmett stood tall, his feet planted firmly apart as if preparing for a fight. "Mom being in rehab is brave. And necessary. There's nothing to be ashamed of. It will help her find herself and overcome an addiction. Why would you be upset about it? As her husband, you should be proud of her."

Senator Chamberlain's lips thinned. He shook his head like a stubborn child. "It's ruining everything. Now, there's talk of a divorce just when I'm trying to present myself as a family man."

Emmett held up his hand to stop him. "That's an issue between the two of you. I'm not going to get involved with that or any 'me too' movement. Don't ask me to take sides. If I had to, you wouldn't like it."

Emmett's father glared at him. "You've always been ungrateful for all I've given you. When I met your mother, she was a struggling single woman with a son. Look at the life I've given her."

Unable to stand aside any longer, Crystal walked up beside Emmett, wanting him to know he had her support.

He smiled at her and drew her closer.

His father pointed a finger at her. "It's your fault. Believe me, I know all about your background. I've had it checked out. What are you doing with my son? Are you after his money?"

"Dad, stop it!" Emmett said, standing protectively in front of her.

Crystal moved to his side. "I have nothing to be ashamed of and no need for anyone else's money. I love your son, and he loves me."

Emmett beamed at her and faced his father. "It's true. Mom knows about it and is happy for us."

Emmett's father shook his head back and forth. "Yeah? Well, thanks for destroying my chances of becoming president. In these times, voters want a candidate with a close family. What can I say about mine?"

"That's up to you," said Emmett. "It's not my position to tell you what to do. Are you going to the rehab hospital for some sessions with Mom?"

His father let out a long sigh. "I suppose I have to now that word is out. Who knows, maybe it'll help." He studied the two of them standing together, turned, and headed back to his car.

Crystal watched him go, wondering what good might come out of such a twisted background. She turned to Emmett. "I'm sorry."

"Me, too. The evening is ruined." His shoulders slumped.

"I really don't like him very much. He was different when he married my mother, but ambition has made him an ass. That's one reason I had to make the break."

"Let's try to have a nice supper. We can picnic on the dock if you'd like."

He shook his head. "Let's eat in the kitchen. There are two makeshift stools there where the workmen eat."

They went into the kitchen, and Emmett poured them each a glass of pinot noir. "Here's to a better evening another time. 'Sorry about my dad."

Crystal hid her disappointment. "We've said it before and I'll say it again—we can't let anyone ruin what we share."

His turquoise gaze remained on her. He nodded and pulled her close.

CHAPTER TWENTY-EIGHT

AS SHE'D PROMISED, the next day Crystal took some time out of her day to visit GG, who was waiting to hear how her theater work had gone. It was she who'd encouraged Crystal to take part in school plays. Crystal realized now how therapeutic those activities had been, allowing her however briefly to become a person other than herself.

Walking down the hall to GG's room, Crystal filled with a sense of peace. Simply knowing she was about to talk things over with a woman she loved and trusted, she felt her mind settle.

Holding a plate of chocolate chip cookies, Crystal knocked on the door and entered the apartment.

GG got up from the couch, came over to her, and gave her a big hug. "It's good to see you. Thanks for the cookies. Would you like something to drink? Lemonade? Water?"

Crystal shook her head. "No, thanks. How are you? You look fantastic. Is this a new hairstyle?"

GG smiled and patted her silvery hair. "Something a little easier. We're letting my few curls exist. No more days of trying to tame it. I like it. It doesn't make the wrinkles go away, but I think it gives me a younger look."

Crystal chuckled. "You look fine no matter what."

"Come tell me all about your time as an actor," said GG, leading her into the living area. "And I heard Emmett's house is going to be stunning. Whitney told me all about the colors you two chose earlier for wall paint. I may be living here, but I have several informants."

They laughed together.

"Similar to the color scheme for the cottage, we chose a rich, buttery cream color for the main living area and a soft, light gray-green for the master suite. The work that Dani, Brad, and Aaron's crew did on the house has transformed it completely. It now has a clean, updated look perfect for some of the Pottery Barn furniture we ordered."

"It sounds lovely," said GG. "How was Maine? The girls had a wonderful day with you. They said you were the star of the show."

Crystal laughed. "No such thing. I was mostly in the background."

"I heard about the fall that Natalie Chamberlain had at the theater. How is she?"

"She's going to be fine, we hope. She's in a rehab hospital upstate. Emmett is very pleased, though his father is not. His father thinks it'll ruin his political chances."

Crystal's disgust brought a smile to GG's face. "I've always thought he was a bit of an ass."

"I wish my mother had dared to stick with treatment," Crystal said in a wistful tone.

GG shook her head. "Some people can't make that choice for a variety of reasons. It would've made things much easier if she'd done it. I'm sorry she didn't."

"It could've made a big difference for all of us," said Crystal, thinking of all who'd helped her and tried to help her mother.

After the Café closed, Misty helped Crystal wipe down tables and refill salt, pepper, and ketchup containers. A comfortable silence filled the air as they worked together.

"Any more thought of becoming a partner of sorts?" Crystal asked her. "I want to be able to have more time for myself in the coming months."

Misty stopped and stared at her, her lips curving. "Has Emmett asked you to take things to the next level?"

Crystal held up her left hand. "No, he hasn't. And I don't know what the next level is. Even so, it's time for me to make some changes."

"I can't afford to buy into the Café," said Misty. "But I could certainly manage it for you with the idea of someday buying into it. I loved being in charge while you were gone, though the early hours can be brutal. I understand why you might want a break from that."

"Yes, and from the constant pressure of running the Café seven days a week. I thought of closing on Mondays but we have so many regulars that I don't want to do that to them."

"Right. They're the Café's bread and butter. Let me draw up a tentative agreement for you to look at. I love living here, and I think it might work to eventually be a real partner."

Pleased, Crystal said, "That would make me very happy. Let's meet up with the gang at Jake's to celebrate."

"Okay, I'll call some people so we can make it a party of sorts."

That evening, after completing the daily financials for the Café, Crystal freshened up and went to Jake's. It had been a while since everyone had met there, and she was looking forward to seeing everyone.

She stepped inside the neighborhood bar and paused. The place held many happy memories.

"Over here," called Taylor.

Crystal turned and headed toward the back corner where two large tables had been pushed together.

The Gilford women sat with their spouses and Misty. Ross and Mike Dawson were in conversation with David Graham, while Aaron and Dirk were on their cell phones,

"Emmett promised to come as soon as he could," Misty told her. "Garth, Beth, and Brooks will be here shortly. I think that's it. Melissa will come after dinner service if everyone is still here."

Smiling at everyone, Crystal took a seat. She loved these people.

It was fun to hear what everyone was doing. David was thinking of hiring someone for the spring, Dirk was looking at a house to buy, and Aaron had decided to build at The Meadows.

"It's a perfect spot for a family," said Aaron.

"Are you telling us something we don't know?" teased Taylor.

Aaron laughed. "No. This is an investment for the future."

Crystal had always liked Aaron. Though he was quiet, there was a depth to him that she found intriguing.

A waitress showed up, and Crystal placed her order for red wine. She limited her drinking, but she enjoyed the camaraderie of socializing with friends.

The Beckman group arrived, taking all the chairs but the one Crystal was saving beside her.

Amid the talk that followed, Emmett arrived. Seeing the chair Crystal had saved for him, he walked over to her, leaned down, and kissed her.

Teasing remarks filled the air.

Emmett looked up and laughed. "What? I like her." He took a seat next to her. "What's everyone having?"

Crystal blinked in surprise. *'Liked her?'*

Whitney caught her eye and winked. She'd told Crystal she'd placed a bet with her sisters that Crystal and Emmett would be engaged within the week.

The group was congenial as various topics were discussed. Mike brought up his idea of a tennis center and all agreed it was needed.

Sometime later, Crystal checked her watch and rose. "Sorry to be a party pooper, but I have to get up early."

"I'll walk you home," said Emmett.

"I promise to stay here for at least another hour to give you time alone," teased Misty.

Everyone laughed as Emmett gave her a thumbs-up sign.

Outside the restaurant, Emmett took Crystal's hand. "Will you go out with me tomorrow night? I've got something fun and different planned."

"Yes. What is it?"

"You'll see," said Emmett. He walked her to the door to her apartment and took her in his arms. Looking down at her he said, "I love you, you know."

"I thought you just liked me," she said, giving him a teasing poke.

"That too. Maybe next week we can visit my mother together. I know she'd like to see you."

"We need to give her time, but yes, I'd like to see her too."

"You're such a sweet woman," Emmett said, lowering his lips to hers.

With his arms around her, Crystal relaxed. His kisses made her come alive. The way he made her want him felt delicious. Desire grew inside her.

When they finally pulled apart, Crystal gave him a look of regret. "I really do have to get up early tomorrow. But, Emmett, I'm talking to Misty about a partnership of sorts, sharing duties to allow me a better schedule."

"I like that idea." He kissed her again and turned to leave. "Remember. Tomorrow night is for us alone."

She waved before going inside. She needed more time with him.

CHAPTER TWENTY-NINE

ALL NEXT DAY, Crystal thought ahead to the evening with Emmett. She tried to imagine what fun event he'd created. But all that mattered to her was that they'd have some precious time alone. Misty had already promised to do the morning shift for her at the Café, and Crystal could hardly wait to have an evening, night, and morning off.

When Emmett sent a message to her telling her not to dress up, her mind spun. *'What was he planning?'*

That evening at the appropriate time, Crystal headed to Emmett's house wearing a short, denim skirt, a pink knit top with a scoop neckline, and a pair of white sneakers.

Emmett met her at the door wearing khaki shorts and a green golf shirt that brought out the unusual color of his eyes. Allowing his gaze to travel over her, he grinned. "You're wearing something comfortable."

"Just what have you planned?" Crystal asked.

Emmett laughed. "Come in. I'll show you soon. By the way, what do you think about the walls? They're painted in the colors you wanted."

Crystal studied the effects of the painted walls in the common areas and beamed her pleasure. "They're perfect. What about the master suite?"

"I plan to show you them a little later." He quirked an eyebrow at her, and she laughed.

"Come outside with me. I'll show you my new toy."

He led her out to the end of the dock. He pointed to a dark green canoe sitting in the water. "What do you think?"

"I love it. A perfect toy for the river. And look, you have paddles, life jackets and everything. Is this what you had in mind? A romantic cruise on the river?"

"Something like that. Get in the bow. I'll take the stern. I've packed something cold to drink for us."

"Well-planned, I see. Like you said, this is fun."

She settled in the bow, and he sat behind her in the stern. He handed her a paddle. "You know how to do it, right? Feathering the stroke?"

"Yes, living around the lake I'm very familiar with canoes."

With a few strokes, they took off.

The river by his house was not very big but was lovely with clear water and natural growth on the riverbanks, met by tall pines and other evergreens.

They'd paddled a distance when Emmett guided them into a tiny inlet where the water calmed.

She turned around. "Why are you stopping?"

"I'm just letting the boat drift safely while I get out the drinks. We can stop paddling for the moment. The canoe is safe left alone here."

She turned around, facing him.

When he knelt in front of her, she stared in surprise and covered her mouth.

His beautiful eyes grew shiny with emotion. "Crystal Owen, will you marry me? I fell for you the first time I saw you, purple hair and all. But it was your smile, the way you made me feel inside that drew me in. You're such a giving, loving, kind person. Everyone adores you. Me most of all. I promise to be there for you no matter what the future holds. I want you as my wife, my sidekick, my love. Marry me."

Blinded by tears, Crystal caught her breath. "Oh, Emmett,

yes! I've waited for you all my life. When I was lonely and scared, I prayed for someone like you, someone who'd love me as I am."

Still kneeling in the boat, Emmett drew her close until she'd straddled his lap and was facing him. He thumbed the tears off her cheeks and gazed at her with such love, Crystal fought fresh tears.

As they hugged and kissed, the boat rocked gently in the water.

After a while, Emmett stirred. "Hang on! I haven't given you your ring."

He wrestled a small, black velvet box out of his pants pocket. He opened it to show her.

Crystal stared at the square-cut, bluish-purple sapphire, flanked by two large cushion diamonds on a gold band. "Oh, Emmett, it's gorgeous."

He slid it on her finger. It fit perfectly. "There. Now it's official."

Crystal held up her hand. The ring was exquisite but that isn't what pleased her. Emmett's expression was one of pure joy. She clapped her hands to her chest to keep it from bursting with love. "I love you, Emmett. I really do."

"Half as much as I love you," he said. He moved away. "I've got champagne stowed aboard. Let's celebrate."

He pulled an insulated bag out from under a seat and proceeded to open the bottle of bubbly white wine.

As the cork gave out a loud "pop", ducks nearby took off with a flutter of their wings and a bird cried its surprise.

Crystal laughed, and Emmett joined in. It was such a special moment.

He poured champagne into the two crystal tulip glasses he'd packed and handed one to her. "I love you, Crystal. Here's to forever and sharing life's adventures together."

She clicked her glass against his, her sight blurring from tears of happiness as she faced him. "I'll never forget these moments. You've made me so happy."

"I'm glad we have this privacy and that we're not dressed up in some fancy place but are ourselves in such a beautiful, natural setting. That's the kind of life I want with you. Sharing what life has to offer."

"Me, too," she said. She lifted her glass in a salute to him and took a sip, then gazed at the trees on the riverbanks, the ducks paddling in the water nearby, the pinkening sky. She felt the gentle rocking of the canoe and thought of the babies they might rock one day.

Emmett beamed at her, and she knew she'd found a kindred spirit.

She lifted her face to the sky above and said a silent prayer of thanks.

After they paddled back to Emmett's house and got the canoe squared away, Emmett took Crystal's hand. "Come up to my house. Dinner should be ready for us."

"Dinner?"

He grinned. "You didn't think I'd forget to feed you, did you? I had Melissa create a special dinner for us from Fins. It should be there."

"Wait a minute. Did she know you were proposing?" asked Crystal.

"She might have guessed it, but no, I didn't tell anyone."

"Whitney placed a bet with her sisters that it would happen this week."

He laughed. "Can't hide a thing in this town, huh?"

"Nope. Living at Lilac Lake is all about family. The one you have, the friends you make, and the family you hope to create."

He gave her an impish grin. "Speaking of our family, let's start dinner with dessert. What do you say?"

"Dr. Chambers, you're the man of my dreams," she said, grinning with anticipation. His love was the cure she needed for happiness.

They kissed and walked toward his house and the life they planned to share together.

Forever.

Thank you for reading *Love's Cure*. If you enjoyed this book, please help other readers discover it by leaving a review on your favorite site. It's such a nice thing to do.

Sign up for my newsletter and get a free story. I keep my newsletters short and fun with giveaways, recipes, and the latest must-have news about me and my books. Welcome! Here's the link:

https://BookHip.com/RRGJKGN

Enjoy an excerpt from my book, *Love's Home Run:*

CHAPTER ONE

MELISSA HENDRICKSON REMOVED her chef's toque and shook her hair out from the rubber band that had held it in place. Letting out a sigh of fatigue, she unbuttoned her coat and tossed it into the laundry basket in a room behind the kitchen. She had a satisfying, creative job working as a chef at Fins, her parents' restaurant, but she was frustrated by her lack of time with friends and her lack of a meaningful relationship. A lot of people, some from her old summer gang, were moving into town, and she wanted to be part of all they were doing. And though she hesitated to tell anyone else, she was hoping to be subtle in convincing one newcomer to see her as wife material. If she only dared.

She was a popular member of her social group but was more comfortable with the guys than the women. She was a tall, trim, wiry woman who, growing up, had been a tomboy interested in sports and "guy" things. Her mother had always wanted her to be more like the charming Gilford girls and had continually pointed out all her faults. It left her feeling insecure about herself. She felt like two different people.

In the kitchen, she was strong, competent, and sure, orchestrating the work of the staff. And, after graduating from the Culinary Institute of America in Hyde Park, New York, she'd proved to have a brilliant gift when combining herbs, spices, and sauces to create spectacular entrees and desserts.

In a social setting, she tended to be quiet and a bit awkward when it came to dating. The men she knew loved having her as a friend who got their jokes and was a pal. It was both nice and annoying now that she was ready for something more in a relationship.

"Are you off to Jake's?" her mother asked, coming into the kitchen. "Better freshen up."

Melissa looked up at the wall clock. 10 PM. "I'll see if anyone is still there. If not, I'll go home. Thank goodness, it's my day off tomorrow."

She went into the bathroom and checked the mirror in the bathroom, making sure she was presentable. The face reflected there had pleasant features, brown hair that held a hint of red, and gray eyes that assessed her harshly.

Melissa grabbed her purse, anxious to leave.

She walked down Main Street passing its numerous cute shops to Jake's, the neighborhood bar her friends in town used as a gathering place.

She loved living in the beautiful New Hampshire Lakes Region, in the scenic small town of Lilac Lake, where outdoor summer and winter activities were readily available.

By anyone's standards, Melissa was financially successful, with a job that brought her recognition as well as an excellent income. She'd just built a house in The Meadows, an upscale development created by Collister Construction at the far end of Lilac Lake, and owned by two of her male friends, Aaron and Brad Collister. But she wanted the more important things in life—a husband and children, a family of her own. At thirty-three, she was beginning to wonder if that would ever happen.

As she stepped inside Jake's, she heard someone call her name and turned to see Ross Roberts wave at her. Smiling, she went to say hello to him and two of his buddies sitting at the table the locals called their own.

" 'Evening," said Melissa. "Is this all that's left of the gang?"

"We're it," said Ross. A famous former baseball player for the New York Yankees, he was a pleasant man everyone liked. Though he couldn't play ball any longer because of a knee injury, he was still featured in television ads where his sandy-haired handsome looks, blue eyes, and boyish smile captured audiences.

"Come join us," said Mike Dawson, who at one time had been a rising tennis star. Now he ran tennis clinics in Florida and was talking to Ross about opening a sports center in Lilac Lake where people could play tennis and/or participate in baseball clinics.

"Nice to see you again," said Ben Gooding who used to play on the Yankees baseball team with Ross. With his stocky, sturdy body, Ben still looked the part of a catcher.

Melissa returned his smile and sat down. She was looking forward to a glass of red wine. Working at the restaurant, she limited alcoholic drinks to having one occasionally. Working with food and wine most of the time, she was careful not to have too much of either.

Ross raised his hand, and a waitress came right over to them. "My friend will have a glass of your finest pinot noir," he said indicating Melissa.

She smiled her thanks. Ross lived next door to her at The Meadows, and any romantic thoughts were quickly stifled by her. Melissa knew Ross dated gorgeous women. She was much more comfortable keeping their relationship as friendly neighbors.

"What are you doing in town?" she asked Ben. "Here to make trouble for Ross and Mike?"

Ben laughed. "I'm thinking of investing in their sports complex. I love Lilac Lake, but I have my job in Washington, D.C. and don't plan to move."

She turned to the others. "Did Dirk show up?"

"He was here earlier with David Graham. They left a while ago," said Ross. "How'd it go at the restaurant?"

"It was busy, as usual. But that's good. A profitable summer means being able to shut down for a couple of weeks in the winter. My parents love to go to Florida then and test out new recipes."

"I imagine once you're into the food scene, it's hard to get out," said Mike. "Florida is a great place to discover new meal ideas with its diverse collection of cuisines."

"Yes. We need to add new menu items each year to keep people coming back."

"Speaking of coming back," said Ross. "I hear Sarah Miller, Bob, and Edie Bullard's daughter, is moving here next week. I only met her once, but she seemed nice. It's unfortunate her husband died, leaving her with twin girls."

"It was such a shame. Sarah is lovely. I'm sure her parents, like mine, love the idea of having their daughter close," said Melissa.

"Isn't it hard to work for your parents?" asked Mike.

Melissa thought about it. "Yes and no. Working together is easier than handling other personal interactions with them." She chuckled. "Mothers and daughters. That's the tough part at times."

"I have only brothers, so I wouldn't know," said Ross.

"How many?" Melissa asked him. It was the first time he'd mentioned them.

"Three brothers, all older, all working in the New York City area in successful careers. I was the little bro who wanted to play ball all the time. At least, that's what they tell me. They were surprised when I informed them that I intended to play professional ball when I got older."

Mike grinned at Ross. "You're a natural."

"My high school played Ross's once. I knew then that he'd make it," said Ben, nudging Ross playfully.

JoEllen Daniels came into Jake's and walked right over to them. "Hi, guys. How's it going?" she asked smiling at the men, ignoring her.

Melissa kept quiet. Everyone in her circle knew JoEllen, Brad Collister's ex-sister-in-law, had thought she could manipulate Brad into marrying her after his wife's death. Now that Brad was happily married to Dani Gilford, JoEllen had her eye on any man she could get to pay attention to her.

"We're just sitting here chatting with Melissa," Ross said pointedly.

"Oh, yes, hi, Melissa," said JoEllen, not at all perturbed by Ross's comment. "I've got tickets to see one of my favorite bands, 'Neverland', this weekend. Anyone want to go with me?"

The three men glanced at one another and shook their heads.

"Guess not," said Mike. "Thanks, anyway."

"Maybe another time," said Ben.

Ross remained quiet.

"Oh, okay. I'll just find someone else." JoEllen flounced off as the waitress headed their way.

"Anyone want another drink? They're on me," said Ross.

"Thanks, but one is fine for me," Melissa said.

"Mike and I are going to Stan's to check it out," said Ben.

Ross turned to her. "Hey, neighbor, want to give me a lift

home? Ben is borrowing my car, and I need a ride."

"Sure," said Melissa. "You're welcome to come with me."

"Thanks," said Ben. "I have a meeting in Portsmouth tomorrow morning. I'll return the car in the afternoon before I have to fly back to D.C."

The group broke up, and Melissa and Ross walked back to Fins to pick up Melissa's car.

"JoEllen has a nasty habit of ignoring the women in a group in her pursuit of men," said Melissa.

Ross grimaced. "I try to stay away from her. In the past, she's made a lot of moves to try and get my attention. She makes me uncomfortable."

"I understand," said Melissa. "But what does someone do to get a man's attention?"

"Who are you talking about? Dirk?" asked Ross, giving her a steady look.

Melissa sighed. "I like him a lot and want to get to know him better. But I can't just go up to him and blurt it out."

"No, you can't."

"Will you put in a good word for me now and then?"

"Do you mean like a Cyrano de Bergerac thing?" he asked, his eyes widening."

She laughed. "Lord, no. It's just that I can't seem to do it on my own. And the last thing I want to do is act like JoEllen."

Ross nodded. "I understand your problem. Okay, then, if that's all you want, I'll try to help."

Placing a hand on his arm, she smiled at Ross. "Thank you. You're the best, like the brother I wished I had."

While growing up, she had wanted a sibling, someone who could help counter her mother's criticism about her appearance and manner.

They got into her car and had a silent ride home.

She pulled into his driveway to let him out and turned to him. "I owe you. How about coming to dinner at my house tomorrow? It's my day off, and I'll fix you something special."

"An offer I can't refuse," he said, grinning. He unbuckled his seat belt and got out of the car. "Thanks, Melissa," he said, giving her a little salute.

She watched him go, pleased by their friendship. He was a very nice guy.

At home, Melissa went through her emails and regular mail before preparing a cup of her favorite nighttime tea. Then she took the tea and a book to the master bedroom on the first floor. She loved her house and enjoyed using this quiet time to settle down from a hectic day. Cooking for customers who expected the best wasn't for the weak. You had to be strong and in control, with split-second timing to get everything prepared and delivered to all individuals at their tables at the same time. Melissa enjoyed watching Gordon Ramsay exposing people to the rigors of the kitchen on television. The professional kitchen scene wasn't quite like that, but one had to have common sense and excellent timing to make it work.

She got ready for bed in one of her usual pajama tops and opened the book. Gazing down at the words of the romance novel she was reading, her thoughts filled with the image of Dirk McArthur, the new dentist in town. Was a relationship with him hopeless?

About the Author

A *USA Today* **Best-Selling Author**, Judith Keim is a hybrid author who both has a publisher and self-publishes, Ms. Keim writes heart-warming novels about women who face unexpected challenges, meet them with strength, and find love and happiness along the way. Her best-selling books are based, in part, on many of the places she's lived or visited, and on the interesting people she's met, creating believable characters and realistic settings her many loyal readers love. Ms. Keim loves to hear from her readers and appreciates their enthusiasm for her stories.

Ms. Keim enjoyed her childhood and young-adult years in Elmira, New York, and now makes her home in Boise, Idaho, with her husband and their lovable miniature dachshund, Wally, and other members of her family.

While growing up, she was drawn to the idea of writing stories from a young age. Books were always present, being read, ready to go back to the library, or about to be discovered. All in her family shared information from the books in general conversation, giving them a wealth of knowledge and vivid imaginations.

"I hope you've enjoyed this book. If you have, please help other readers discover it by leaving a review on the site of your choice. And please check out my other books and series:"

The Hartwell Women Series
The Beach House Hotel Series
Fat Fridays Group
The Salty Key Inn Series
The Chandler Hill Inn Series
Seashell Cottage Books
The Desert Sage Inn Series
Soul Sisters at Cedar Mountain Lodge Series
The Sanderling Cove Inn Series
The Lilac Lake Inn Series

"ALL THE BOOKS ARE NOW AVAILABLE IN AUDIO on iTunes! So fun to have these characters come alive!"

Ms. Keim can be reached at **www.judithkeim.com**

To like her author page on Facebook and keep up with the news, go to: **http://bit.ly/2pZWDgA**

To receive notices about new books, follow her on Book Bub:

https://www.bookbub.com/authors/judith-keim

And here's a link to where you can sign up for her periodic newsletter! **http://bit.ly/2OQsb7s**

She is also on Twitter @judithkeim, LinkedIn, and Goodreads. Come say hello!

Acknowledgments

And, as always, I am eternally grateful to my team of editors, Peter Keim and Lynn Mapp, my book cover designer, Lou Harper, and my narrator for Audible and iTunes, Angela Dawe. They are the people who take what I've written and help turn it into the book I proudly present to you, my readers! I also wish to thank my coffee group of writers who listen and encourage me to keep on going. Thank you, Peggy Staggs, Lynn Mapp, Cate Cobb, Nikki Jean Triska, Joanne Pence, Melanie Olsen, and Megan Bryce. And to you, my fabulous readers, I thank you for your continued support and encouragement. Without you, this book would not exist. You are the wind beneath my wings.